CORN

LADYBIR

First Printed in United Kingdom 2023

ISBN – 978-1-9996559-69

Email – davidlenderyoubooks@gmail.com

Author – Publisher

David Lenderyou

CORNISH MIST TRILOGY

Cornish Mist (1) – Pebbles & Stones
Cornish Mist (2) – Butterfly & Nettles
Cornish Mist (3) – Ladybirds & Hawks

AUTHOR

David Lenderyou's direct lineage dates back to the year 1318 of the Lynderiowe family in Mylor, near Falmouth, Cornwall. Many descendants were Yeoman, Tin Miners, Pikemen, Butchers and Paupers. David was raised in Cornwall with his good Father being from Falmouth and his dear loving Mum from Palmers Green, bless her cotton socks. Both met one another after the 2nd World War in Trafalgar Square. David laughs at the time he had to dance in the Hal an Tow on Floral day, 8th May 1971 in Helston, having to wear his Mums tights with his mate Denis Bagnall. Life has many challenges and keeping that Cornish spirit will help you on the path.

PREFACE

CORNISH MIST (3) LADYBIRDS & HAWKS

In the year 1713, of our Good Queen, five years after the doomed French revenge attack, the Spanish see a golden opportunity. They have nothing to lose and so negotiate a deal with a powerful rich syndicate in Mayfair, headed by the feared Luisa. Money and power are what they live by and the Cornish Tin industry is their next target for takeover. They are clever and discreet and live by the sword. The Cornish, with total loyalty to their Lady, are struggling to stop the piracy of their land and need help. Joshua, with the power of the Cornish Mist, will defend them.

Bodmin – Cornwall - Sunday July 1st 1713

"Mr Hosking it is not as simple as that." "Well, when can I have a drink, I need one badly." The old jailer at the Bodmin Prison did feel pity for the prisoner but could not afford to break the rules as his family depended on his meagre wages. "I will have a word to see if it can be done but I can't promise." "Thank you my kind man."

As the jailer went out Henry lay back down on the cold floor in the dank cell which he had been locked in for the last five years hoping he could, for one last time, enjoy the taste of neat brandy running down his throat before the gallows wrung his neck in the morning.

With arms behind his head and laying stretched out, Henry began to smile to himself as the memories of his past bravery and dare raced through his mind. Then after a few moments had ticked by his body shuddered with cold dread as he heard the sound of trap doors just outside his stone walled cell swing open and a cheer from the crowd go up. He closed his eyes and thought about how it would be his turn tomorrow and then started to laugh.

Chapter 1

When Antoinette and the Prince had failed to return to Morlaix after their disastrous operation to capture some crazy witch of Bodmin five years ago, the three prisoners at the Chateau were locked up in the dungeons. Then, when their dead bodies were later found washed ashore at a secluded cove of Plougasnou, north of Morlaix, the Abbot of Landerneau was called in. He was assigned to quietly sort things out and manage everything. He took the role with zest as he knew if he did well the Chateau could well pass to him for his own gain.

Initially, the Abbot had doubts as to who these prisoners were and why they were locked up. However, as he questioned each one many times through their years of confinement he began to realise that they too were loyal French people. It was only due to their bravado mistake in identifying that Jacques was the person that the Prince and Antoinette needed, they were locked up.

As the years passed he had become quite fond of them, to the point that he asked each one to take a vow to God Almighty that they would not try to escape but to work with him and his team until such time when things may change. As vowed, they had all kept their oaths so as a measure of mutual trust he ordered all three be taken out of the cold dungeons and given rooms with their own beds and washing facilities

At first, Peter the Frenchman was anxious to escape the Chateaux and get back to his work of espionage and the large amounts of money it brought him. But he had then weighed things up and if he did escape he would be a marked man for the rest of his life. So, he started to trust the Abbot and felt that this was a sign and maybe it was a time in his life he needed to rest and recuperate. He often thought about his friend the Spaniard who now had no choice in anything after that nasty Prince had killed him by a simple slit of his throat.

Jacques initially disliked Peter, but over the course of time of having been forced to live together, they had become friends and discussed many things of a personal nature. After all, Jacques had for most of his life been doing exactly what Peter had done and it was only through his love for his beautiful Jeanne that he did what he did. The only difference between them now was that Peter still had that inner ego and drive to carry on his skills of spying and covert working but Jacques was finished, he had had enough and wanted to retire somewhere out of the way to live a peaceful life. Maybe one day he would meet his lovely Jeanne again, maybe, just maybe, and if that day ever came he knew his life would be complete.

Sarah was split both ways from her fellow two prisoner's thought processes. Although she liked the idea of rest and solitude she still had the hunger for dare and treachery. Like Peter, she had also warmed to Jacques and found him to be a good man, but broken.

All three were now sitting around the table playing cards in the Chateau's library as their duties of the day had been done. Well, that's not strictly true as Sarah still had to perform tonight. "How are you feeling Sarah," Jacques asked. "I'm not really bothered Jacques, I do it as a means to an end." Peter then asked, "What time is the Abbot due back from Paris?" "I have to be in his bed by nine tonight, that's all I know." Peter and Jacques looked at each other, both knowing that Sarah's weekly sexual night time activities with the Abbot had helped them all, one way or another.

Jacques looked at the clock and said, "It's getting near seven already." "In that case, I had better get myself ready and shall hopefully see you both in the morning." "Sarah, both Jacques and I would like to say thank you." "For what," she replied. "For doing what you're doing." "Thank you but I don't have to do much, it's all rather embarrassing." With that, Sarah got up and went to get herself prepared as the Abbot liked.

"I don't know about you Jacques but I think something is up." "I agree Peter, I felt it when the Abbot said he was going to Paris to see the King, what do you think?" "Well we don't have much choice in the matter but over these many years, I think the Abbot would have warned us of any intending harm so let's see what Sarah has to say in the morning at breakfast.

It had been five days since the Abbot left the Chateau at Morlaix for the meeting in Paris. However, with that meeting now over he was now en route into the three day journey back to the Chateau. He thought the meeting had gone well and noticed that a lot of people were involved, especially the little man in charge. He then learned that although people called him the 'Little Man' he was also known in the circle as 'Le Furet,' or as the English would say, The Ferret. He also noticed a young very pretty lady called Joulie who never left his side and again was of small stature. As the meeting went on, the Ferret would every now and then point to a person and take him off to the side. Then after a brief discussion, the person left the room without word. The Abbot had not seen anything quite like it. Nothing at all was mentioned to him about the Chateau and so he sat there feeling quite useless. It was only when the little man had quietly asked the last man to exit the room that attention and words were spoken to him. After the little man told him what he wanted, the Abbot was then strictly told that his actions of loyalty were vital to their mission and if he failed to do as asked then his future running of the Chateau, and the Abbey at Landerneau, would be at risk. This direct warning shot surprised the Abbot so he needed to be on his guard.

This small man in some way gave him the creeps due to the curious way he talked and acted so after the meeting had ended the Abbot went about and asked a few quiet questions. It turned out that this little man was a sorter outer, as they say. Not up front in rank or in the heat of battle with guns and canon but behind the scenes with quiet covert thought and patience. He was also known to be very astute and not to be messed with, although you would not think so looking at him.

The Abbot had now been in the saddle for two full days and was getting tired. But, he was looking forward to getting into his bed this night with Sarah and was sure it was mutual as she had said so many times of her love for him.

Sarah lay naked waiting anxiously in the large four poster bed as she always did in readiness for the divine Abbot to enter. It was just after nine o clock when she heard him shuffling outside the bedroom door. She now had to play the game and switch off all memories of love and wishful dreams. It won't take long, this she knew, he never does. It was lying next to him afterwards and having to listen to his constant prayers of forgiveness and waiting in silence with no movement for him to fall asleep. When he did eventually nod off, it was then and only then that she could leave. And so, with her duty done and the time passing the eleventh hour, the Abbot eventually started to snore. So, Sarah ever so quietly slipped out of the bed and quickly went to her room. The first thing she always did after he had done what he had done to her was to strip off and wash herself all over to cleanse out his evil touch.

Once completely dry she got herself into her bed and lay down in total silence and stared at the ceiling. Five years she had been here and for what, to be a sex slave to a selfish prat of an Abbot who thinks he rules. But, like Peter and Jacques, she had no choice in the matter. At least she was still alive, unlike the Spaniard. Is it worth it, she thought? Her mind was trying to make sense of the situation. She then thought back about the Sniper man whom she had many a passionate time with. But then she tried to kill him on orders from Peter. What a bitch she was and started to giggle at the thought of it all. Well, it could be a lot worse she concluded and so rolled over to get her sleep. She would need to talk with Peter and Jacques first thing as the Abbot had said he wanted to talk with all of them over breakfast about a pending visit from an advisor of the Crown.

Chapter 2

With the fiasco of finding both the bodies of Antoinette and the King's son together washed ashore, the Ferret had also been called in by the French Crown. They knew the little Ferret worked slowly but the King and his advisors liked this as they were in no rush. They also did not want physical revenge as the King never really knew this begotten son who had been born to a prostitute in the port of Brest. But on hearing of the death, it did activate the King's anger, so he and his close knit people wished to discuss ways in which to equalise things. After many hours of debate, the plan was agreed that the Ferret should go away into his secret world to formulate his team and achieve their aim of increasing the wealth of the French Crown at the cost to the English Metal Industry and more over, those Cornish pigs who killed his son.

Personally, money and greed were not the Ferret's main aims in life as he was paid most handsomely. What did motivate him was the knowledge that the King liked his work and the inner ego of power that it gave him.

It had taken a long time for the Ferret to get to this stage of his plan but he had got to know a lot of things about the English and the Cornish. One of the first things he did was place many of his covert team in strategic areas on the West, South West coastal ports. Their orders were to watch and listen and be patient. Their aim was to find people who didn't quite fit. He also advised them that it didn't matter in the least if the information they sent back was of no use, he wanted to scrutinise all and tick them off one by one. Yes, it would be a slow and labour intensive process but, it was the only way to achieve the desired result. He was also aware of the three prisoners at the Chateau and knew that one day down the line they could be of use. Yes, time had passed slowly but the information he had gained from his men had come through. The Ferret knew his patience was a virtue, and so it would turn out to be. Also, one of his other first actions was to quietly re-communicate with some people in the Cornish land, especially a rich well to do person of much loyalty.

As the time went by his agents had become suspicious of many people and, as ordered, sent back the information to the Ferret. After hundreds of negative results, it was one certain man who was living on his own in a small back street cottage in the port of Le Havre that caught The Ferret's eye. It wasn't what this man did it was what he didn't do that caused the interest and also the tassel hanging from his bobble hat. This was not an unusual dress in a seaport town but what was unusual was that this man was found to live in a quiet well to do suburb away from the scrag end area where the rowdy sailors live. Also, one minute this man was in his cottage alone for many weeks at a time and then when he did venture out no one could find where he went or worked. All this just didn't stack up as the man always looked fresh and dressed smartly. They just couldn't work out where he was getting the money from to keep himself looking so well and pay the rental of the cottage too. The Ferret had the cottage checked out and was found to be owned by a French landlord who confirmed that the tenant had paid the rental deposit in full and never defaulted.
So the Ferret wisely increased the covert surveillance of this recluse Sailor type man with bobble hat and side

tassel hanging down over his right ear. He had nothing to lose except time so nothing ventured, nothing gained, as they say, but he had an inner feeling. The surveillance team were told to move closer into the neighbourhood and quietly start asking questions if anyone knew this man and, after speaking to many people, all said they did not, which again was very odd. It was then that the Ferret shrewdly organised the interception of messages this man was receiving and when this information began to filter back was when the Ferret knew he had hit on something. He then brought in a known artist friend to join the surveillance team and sketch him.

Over the course of his silent career, the Ferret had, apart from gaining much knowledge and experience, acquired hundreds of sketches on people of interest and all filed away in his out of the way office. So when the sketch came in of this sailor man in the town of Le Havre he sat down quietly and went through them all. In truth, he had already someone in the back of his mind who might fit the verbal description as he had heard rumours years ago of such a type of man from his London contacts.

Going through every sketch one by one took a long time but then he found it, a positive fit with the man known as Tassell who had been marked as an English agent of note. The Ferret didn't jump up and down with elation shouting hallelujah at the positive fit of a traitor as he was wise enough to know there were many more like him all around his beloved France. But it did bring a smile to his face as this one particular person did have known contacts in Cornwall and so could fit very nicely into the tactic of diversion. It could also at the same time rid France of some of his close accomplices in one hit. He very much liked this as even if it went right or wrong, it didn't matter, it would put the Cornish on the wrong foot which was exactly what he wanted.

The Ferret then went into many weeks of isolation going deeper into the many files on this so called sailor and the many sketches and information of people he had been seen or connected with. Even though the information he had gained was indeed good, the Ferret still carried on for months with his methodical approach of surveillance and allow more information to flow in. It was again a slow process but then a message was intercepted which gave the Ferret just what he wanted

The message received read:-

Dear Tassell,
Hosking's to be sorted as mentioned 1st July.
See friends in Helston prior week.
Bed as usual at the Blue. GK

The Ferret read the intercepted message again and again and after putting all things together concluded that the signature of the initials GK must be that of the Sailor's known assailant, George Kernow. It was now all coming together just like he had hoped. The Ferret then drew in a deep sigh of relief and took a large slug of his gin.

Then pouring another one he leaned back in the seat and with glass in hand looked up at the ceiling and then as his mind drew deeper in thought he started to chuckle. He was in the same game as this so called Sailor man and so thought, if he had become aware of one of them, were the English aware of him. After all, they are very good at deceit and clever in their tactics too. Did they know he frequented the night street Molly houses and liked tall strong men in tight trousers? Did they know he always felt feminine in his mind and drank neat gin excessively? He had tried many times to work out why he felt this way, unlike other men who prefer the female sex, but never found the reason. Maybe it had something to do with his childhood, he just didn't know. But one thing he did know was that if word ever got out of his secret sexuality and strange methods of male pleasure he would be guillotined immediately without question for being a depraved soul of the true Faith. He then quickly shook his head away from these horrible thoughts. Get a grip, he said to himself.

Meanwhile, over in the port of Le Havre, the Sailor man with bobble hat and tassel dangling over his right ear was leaving his small cottage as he had done many times. However, this time, after receiving the message from George Kernow, rather than disappear into his normal line of work, he was going to take open sail on a Dutch passenger ship set for Dover and go home to his wife and family for a week. After that, he would then ride the long journey to Helston in preparation with his colleagues to attend the hanging of Henry Hosking.

The Sailor man had quite naturally, through his many years of experience, learnt to feel an inner sense when things didn't seem quite right. And so it was this very morning while leaving his cottage. For some reason, his body felt edgy as if someone was watching. So standing still between the front door and his horse, he glanced around to see what it was that was making him feel edgy but then shrugged it off as a matter of insecurity.

The two covert operatives peering through the curtains in a cottage opposite the Sailorman's cottage saw him come out and look about. They saw he was acting rather tense and his manner was somewhat different to what they had seen before. They also saw he had loaded his horse's saddlebags with many items and were now bulging at the seams. This prompted their thoughts that he was probably going away for some time. They had been previously informed that this may happen and so smiled at each other as he was now doing exactly as they had been told. What they didn't know was where he was going and so with men placed all around the town and port, they quickly sent word ahead to find that out. It would be more than likely he was heading for the port side but they couldn't be sure.

With the French agents being notified and being put on alert around the Port, the Sailorman was seen boarding a passenger ship of Dutch origin with sail to Dover. It was then that a French agent was quickly assigned on board to watch his every movement. The voyage to Dover would take at least four to five days. This didn't bother the agent at all as when his job was done he would also disembark and report to his handler in the Pirates Inn just off from the Dover quayside. Once he had done this he would then be free to relax for a few of days for wine, women and song all around the buzzing English port.

Then seeing the Ship raise it sail and leave the Port with the Sailorman and the French agent safely aboard, they now needed to send message to the Ferret.

When the Ferret received this piece of information about the Sailor mans boarding and sail to Dover he knew it was time to act. He also knew, through his intercepting the message signed by GK, that things were to happen in Helston the week before the month of July.

So, his first plan of action was to organise a meeting in Paris to talk with his men and also with the Abbot. He wanted to meet the three prisoners held at the Chateau and once he had talked with them personally he could then decide whether to use them or not for a diversion. They would fit perfectly. In other words, if it worked then that would be very helpful but if it didn't work and they were killed it didn't matter as it wouldn't affect the overall objective of gaining wealth for the King.

And so, four days after sending word and the meeting in Paris now concluded, the Ferret asked his loyal Joulie if she could get their horses and gear ready for their off. The trip to the Chateau at Morlaix would take a good two to three days but then once matters there were done they could all move on, hopefully with two or all three of the detainees. They would then all ride to the nearby port of Brest and set sail for the Cornish Coast. Tonight though he intended to enjoy himself and meet the big strong man he had met two nights ago in the seedy bar of drink and merriment.

However, while all this was going on, what nobody knew, even the crafty little Ferret, was that a top secret meeting was taking place two hundred miles away in the port of Santander on the French-Spanish Border.

This secret meeting was of the highest order between the devious finance teams of King Louis and his Spanish kinsman, Philip V. The meeting was being taken by four high powered men, two from each Country, who had also invited one very special guest. Her name was Luisa, a rich Spanish aristocrat lady known for embezzling large amounts of goods for huge profit. This woman had a ferocious team of loyal killers across Europe and never failed to achieve her God given right of wealth and dominance. They idolised her.

The four men knew of the Little Man's meeting in Paris but were not convinced he was the right man for what they wanted. Yes, he had done some good stuff in the past and the French King liked him but he was sly and slow and that just didn't fit. He was also weird in his night time behaviour but that was another story. Both Countries were losing money due to the heavy burden of trying to win over the Americas from those damned British. They needed money and loads of it.

With this secret meeting over, both Countries agreed to let the Little Ferret man carry on with his sly, low level plan of working the rich Cornish Mineral trade. But, they had now agreed terms with the Lady Luisa who would lay in wait and watch in the background. With everything completed, they now only needed to come up with a codeword to activate their plan when the time was right. They all agreed the word would be 'Angof,' after the leader of the Cornish rebellion in 1497 and who had his head chopped off. With that, they all started to laugh. In the meantime, they would carry on and watch and monitor the Ferret in secret and pass all information to Luisa at her Mayfair address. It was a win-win.

Chapter 3

Although the ride to the Chateau took a couple of days, the Ferret and his trusted Joulie arrived safe and well. Then, as planned, the Ferret questioned the prisoners and made a decision. So now it was time for everyone, except the prisoner Jacques, to get themselves ready and prepare for the short ride to the Port of Brest first thing in the morning. While having a late night drink together before heading for bed, Joulie asked, "So where are the other two men you said were coming?" "I changed that and sent word that we would meet them tomorrow on board ship." "You didn't tell me that." "Sorry Joulie, I forgot."

With the morning soon coming, Joulie, the Ferret and two of the prisoners sat down and had breakfast. It all felt a little awkward for Sarah and Peter but when they had finished all four went out to their horses and rode away.

On their arrival at the Port, they saw that their ship was already docked. So, after the Ferret had found and talked with the Captain, they too got themselves aboard. It was then after a two hour wait that the ship finally untied its dock lines and hoisted the sails to draw the wind and drift out to sea. The two detainees, Sarah and Peter, had been assigned separate cabins but once Sarah had put her things down, she went straight back out to Peter's cabin and once outside his door, she knocked hard.

Peter was just about to lie down to have a snooze and so was a little taken aback by who would be knocking so quickly for his attention. He turned and went to the door and on opening saw Sarah. "What is it Sarah?" "Peter, let me come in I need to speak with you." No sooner had she sat on his bed, that she looked straight up at Peter and without pause, said, "There is something not quite right about him." "What do mean Sarah, who?" "Peter, I have been about this world quite a lot as you know, and I know that he is hiding something, can you not feel it?" "Sarah, I have no idea what or who you are talking of, have a gin." Sarah never used to drink but over the five years of confinement she started taking a liking to it and, it helped to do what she had to do with the Abbot.

Once she and Peter had taken a couple of swigs from the gin bottle Sarah said, "Peter, the person I am talking of is the little man from Paris." "Sarah, like you I have been in this game a long while and that man you call little is known as the Ferret." "I don't care if he's called a bloody elephant, I do not trust him, he gives me the creeps." "That I agree with but he is very clever and astute, do not under estimate him." "Well, he may be clever but my gut instinct tells me he is not quite right." "That may be so Sarah, but we have got to thank our lucky stars that we are away from that damned Chateau and have a chance to get our lives back unlike Jacques." "O yes, poor old Jacques, apart from his broken heart and silly mistake of love for a woman, I really started to like him." "Yes, me too, and just think it was us who brought him back there from Cornwall." "Well, at least he is still alive." "Well maybe not, we don't know that."

"What are we to do Peter?" "We do what we have been ordered to do and play the game. So, may I suggest you go back to your cabin and get the clothes and make up and come back here so we can practise our disguises."

The Ferret lay quietly down on his bed in his cabin and started to go over his plans. His trusted colleague was in the next cabin with an adjoining door just in case. The two tall young men he had also selected to join the team were in the cabin next to his colleague. They were good boys from the right families and Faith and were just starting out in their careers for the crown.

The Ferret then sat up and put his feet on the floor and after taking a small swig from the gin bottle thought about his time at the Chateau with the Abbot and the three detainees. He thought about Sarah and Peter and smiled to himself. It was once he had their confidence that he began to see into their minds and personalities. Sarah he thought was a bitch but she was true to the French Crown and good at what she did. Peter was also loyal and good at his job. Sarah was definitely a more front line worker whereas Peter seemed to fit better doing the background stuff. Both he thought should be given a chance to prove themselves over and above on why they were imprisoned in the first place by that stupid greedy Prince and that woman Antoinette. After all, what Sarah and Peter are to do is of no real matter to the Ferret anyway. If they get killed, they get killed; it would not affect his main objective. If they succeed then that will be good but again he looked at it with cold icy thoughts as a win-win situation. If they do succeed and survive in the diversion he could then use them later with his main plan. It would also show him that they are loyal and could be trusted.

Jacques on the other hand was totally different. His first impression was of a tall strong man with icy blue eyes, but something was amiss. He didn't have that spark of adventure as the other two had and simply came across as someone who didn't want to play anymore. In fact, as the Ferret was just about to talk with him, Jacques held up his hands and said in a sincere and apologetic voice, "Please, I do not want to be rude in any manner but I ask you not to tell me anything as I do not wish to know." The Ferret was not fazed by this and so smiled nicely and with a certain calm switched tactics to concentrate more on Jacques's interpretation of why he was being held prisoner.

Jacques had been down this road before with the Abbot and had kept his life. So, with that thought in mind, he kept the story the same explaining everything he had done before and, that he had never once betrayed the French Crown. It was only when his true love had re-entered his heart that he changed his route of work. The Ferret again kept his silence and smiled outwardly but inwardly felt what a stupid prat. The Ferret wanted to know more about this man so with experience and calm kept probing. Jacques to his credit answered all in truth as best he could and within reason but, never revealed his beautiful Jeanne as he had promised himself when he was taken from Cornwall many years ago whilst helping his friend Zoe escape.

The Ferret had taken copious amounts of notes and after twenty minutes or so had passed decided to relax things more and asked Jacques "Would he like a gin.' Jacques smiled and replied, "I would prefer a cognac." The Ferret shouted aloud at the door and when the guard came in The Ferret asked if he could fetch the cognac. Without a word, the guard nodded his head and went straight back out to do as ordered. Whilst the guard was away the Ferret turned his attention back to Jacques and asked, "Jacques, what would you like to do with your life?' Jacques looked at the Ferret strangely but then honestly replied, "I would very much like to go away and live in a forest somewhere far away from my previous life and work." The Ferret didn't reply to this but pondered in quiet thought and took more notes. Jacques watched in silence as the Ferret did more of his writing and knew he was thinking about what to do.

When the guard came back in and put the bottle and glasses down on the table, the Ferret asked him to stay in the room. The guard again did as ordered and waited in silence. The Ferret then poured both himself and Jacques a large glass and said, "Thank you Jacques for your time, here's to Love." Both gulped their drinks back in one and when empty and the glasses put down on the table the Ferret filled both again. It was as Jacques started to drink the second glass that the Ferret turned to the guard and said, "Take this man down into the dungeons and lock him up." Jacques quickly stopped drinking and looked at the Ferret in a cold stone silence but the Ferret simply responded by saying in a polite tone, "Nothing personal." Jacques did not respond in any way shape or form as the guard was well armed and so sighed with dignified disbelief.

The Ferret still sitting on his bed in his cabin and having another gin felt his decision to lock up Jacques was right. He couldn't take any chances. He was going to ask the guard to shoot him but something changed his mind, he didn't know what. Maybe he was going soft but that didn't make any sense. The guard would have done as ordered and would have simply killed Jacques without hesitation. No, he had done right not to kill him.

Sarah was still in Peter's cabin as both were busy trying to sort out their disguises. "It's alright for you Peter but I have lived around the place where we are going and it could be possible that I might get recognised." "Well, we don't want that Sarah do we now as that would then put me at risk." "Well, thank you for your sympathy, so what do you suggest." "I suggest you put some weight on to look like a fat old cow." "Hmmm, I never thought of that Peter, that sounds good. If I can do that and mix it with our old greyish looks and dowdy clothing that would be perfect, I like that." They had the rest of the day and night to prepare and get things as good as they could. And so with sheets and pillows now being cut up and anything else that could help, Sarah and Peter got on with getting their disguises correct

The Ferret suggested that all his team do what they have to do to prepare themselves and also get a good night's sleep. A meeting had been arranged in the Captain's side room at noon the following day. It would be at this meeting that the plan of diversion would be explained and, what each person was to do. It would also be the first time that all six members would meet each other.

Late the following morning, the Ferret and his trusted Joulie were now sitting in the meeting room waiting. It was nearing twelve noon and so they had a few minutes more to themselves before the rest of the team was due. Like the Ferret, Joulie also enjoyed a nice gin but not too many to hinder her actions of deception. He had chosen Joulie to work with him well over a decade ago, taking her out from a pauper's workhouse in the south of Paris and had proved a very excellent choice. Her devotion to him was one of utter loyalty and knew no bounds. She was now twenty seven years of age and very pretty. Like the Ferret she was also tiny in stature and, due to some growth disorder, looked much younger. "So Joulie my dear, here's to our Cornish operation and may it be as good and successful as we have many times done in the past." Joulie picked up her gin glass and took a nice sip of the alcohol but the Ferret drank the whole glass in one gulp. "I'm looking forward to seeing this Sarah woman again as watching her over breakfast and reading her resume you gave me she is one deceitful cold bitch." "It takes one to know one my little sugar cube." At that, they both laughed. "Let us not forget my lovely Joulie that this Sarah is good at her job and that Peter is too, so let them play their game according to the orders I give them. We can then watch and act as we see fit." "I understand." "Good, now I think I hear footsteps, are you ready?" "I am ready," she replied."

Within a few seconds, the Ferret and Joulie then heard the knocking on the door and so the Ferret raised his voice for them to enter. It was the two tall well built young men who came in and without getting up the Ferret pointed to the seats for them to sit down. Once seated the Ferret offered them both a drink and then introduced Joulie. It wasn't long after that the door was again knocked and in walked Sarah and Peter. So, when all were sitting comfortably and introductions over the meeting began.

While the Ferret was going over the plan everyone kept silent and listened intently but Sarah could not help but keep looking at the young girl called Joulie who had been introduced to her the day before at the breakfast table back at the Chateau. Sarah couldn't work it out, something didn't fit. The girl acted with maturity but looked so very young and so very pretty so why was she here? Peter didn't seem at all interested in her and was all ears to what the Ferret was saying and what he required of them. The two young men thought Joulie was lovely and smiled at her all the time with youthful bravado.

The Ferret kept things semi-brief but added extra detail when and where he thought it necessary. He didn't say anything at all about the main plan as he first wanted to see what these people, especially Sarah and Peter, could achieve on the diversion. When finished, he asked for any questions. Peter then responded, "So just to confirm, Sarah and I are to stay at a small cottage in an out of way place called Scorrier owned by two sisters called Fay and Janet?" "That is right Peter, they are very loyal to us and have so proven many times before." The Ferret knew that Peter would probably ask questions as his previous job was to manage people away back from the front line stuff. "And what of the two young men here, are they to stay there too?" "No, they will stay somewhere else." "Is everything ready like food and drink and horses." "Yes, the ladies will have all things ready, even extra pistols should you need them. Your horses will also be ready when we land at Porthtowan this evening. Peter then fell silent and so Sarah spoke, "So, when we have concluded our little mission in Helston, do we make our way back to the cottage at Scorrier?" "That is right Sarah." "And then what?" "What do you mean, then what?" "I mean, what do we do then?" "That very much depends on the outcome of your mission in Helston but either way, get back to the cottage and we will talk further." Sarah looked at Peter but both kept their mouths shut. While these questions were being asked, Joulie without being noticed was ever so carefully observing Sarah. She saw how this woman moved her body when she spoke and also watched her eyes and hands shift when she was being spoken to. Hmmm very interesting she thought.

The two young men had no questions to ask and so the Ferret said, "Right, Sarah and Peter, have you got your disguises sorted?" "Yes, they are done," Peter replied. "Fine, that's good, so could you both now go back to your cabins and put them on and we will wait here for your return." "What, you want us to redress ourselves now and come back," Sarah said. "Yes please Sarah, if you don't mind, we need to see what you both look like so these two young men and us can recognise you both, we don't want any mistakes now do we." Peter nodded his head as he knew it made sense and so nudged Sarah and both got up to do as asked.

As they were walking back to their cabins Sarah turned to Peter saying, "This is ridiculous, bloody stupid." who does he think he is." "Sarah, it makes sense and at this moment in time he has the power over our very lives so let's just get on with it and play the game." "Well, alright, I will, but." Peter quickly interrupted her saying, "Sarah, there are no buts, let's not forget that only two days ago we were stuck in that Chateau at Morlaix not knowing if we were to live another day." With that,

Sarah lowered her head in acceptance and moved on to her cabin and Peter did the same.

While they were away from the meeting room getting their disguises on, the Ferret talked with the two young men, especially the one sitting to the right called Andre. Joulie noticed this and would advise the Ferret later when they were alone to be careful as she knew his inner ways and feelings towards this type of male.

As the discussion carried on the two young men were becoming more relaxed and open. This is what the Ferret wanted as he could now get to see their strengths and weaknesses. Being this their first assignment of note and their young age, they did come across as a little naive at times, but the Ferret liked this and could work with it to his advantage. It was just over thirty minutes when the door was knocked and in walked Sarah and Peter in full disguise.

"Excellent, I would not have recognised either of you at all," said the Ferret. Sarah said nothing and felt very awkward standing there in front of these four people like some sort of cabaret show. The Ferret then looked at Joulie and asked, "What say you Joulie?" "I think they look very good, especially the old age and overweight thing, I wouldn't have recognised them either."

"So my two good young men, take a good look at your colleagues as the next time you will see them dressed like this will be in the town of Helston surrounded by drinkers and merriment." The two young men did as asked. It was then after a minute or so of silence had passed the Ferret calmly said, "Right, now has anyone got any last questions they wish to ask before I call the meeting closed?'' All remained quiet and so he added, ''Fine, now you all have your orders and I have been informed that we have had turned the Cornish headland so will be laying anchor in a few hours from now. May I suggest you get your things packed and rest up a while." As Sarah, Peter and the two young men got up and started to walk to the door the Ferret asked, by the way Sarah, you do have the poison?'' Sarah turned about and replied, "Yes I do, I never leave home without it.''

When the four people had gone from the room and the door closed, the Ferret poured himself and his trusted assistant a gin. He then looked up and said, ''So what do you think Joulie?'' ''I think they will do well, especially Sarah.'' ''Why do think that Joulie?'' ''I don't know, there is just something about her which I feel is good and will fit well but, I wouldn't trust her as far as I could throw her.'' The Ferret chuckled aloud at her responsive openness and so again asked, ''And, what do you think of Peter?'' ''I think he is past it and sooner gone the better.'' ''I feel you are right on both counts, so shall we push ahead as planned?'' The Ferret liked to bounce his inner decisions and feelings off Joulie as he trusted her and it made him feel better, even if the response was negative. ''I think we should but you will keep your distance from that young Andre, won't you?' The Ferret smiled a knowing grin and after picking up his glass of gin said, ''Of course I will Joulie.''

Chapter 4

Joshua and Rebecca were in their cottage at Gunwalloe enjoying the love of married life with their two young children. It had been a quiet time in Joshua's working life as nothing untoward had happened for many a while. In fact, apart from visiting Bull and his two teams in Mevagissey and Bedruthan his life and the Cornish land, were running rather smoothly.

Joshua smiled inwardly as he compared this calm to the difference ten years ago when he first started his new life with Rebecca and George Kernow. Then, all was up in the air and threats of many kinds were coming his way from all directions. However, his experience of life and work had taught him not to be complacent and so maintained a tight ship by always keeping that quiet vigil. He also read with in depth enthusiasm the weekly reports coming in from his teams and then acted with a sure swiftness if anything seemed out of the ordinary.

Joshua was now dressed and ready to go out as he was meeting Bull at the Halzephron Inn at Gunwalloe for a chat and a few drinks. He wanted to discuss the pending meeting with Kernow which was due next week in Helston at the Blue Anchor and also about both of them going to Bodmin.

As he got himself to the front door he turned and said to Rebecca who was sitting by the open fire, "I won't be long love." "Joshua, please don't have too many and come home early?" "Why, am I on a promise tonight?" Rebecca smiled and remarked, "You men are so stupid."

Joshua laughed and went out the door to the stables where Harry, his trusted horse was waiting.

As Joshua entered the Halzephron Inn he saw Bull was already there sitting at the table. They shook hands and Bull said, "Good to see you Joshua, I got you one in." "Thanks Bull, how are things?" "All is well, thank you Joshua, how are things with you?" As the conversation and chat progressed a fiddler started to play his tunes and the people around started to sing along. Although Joshua and Bull were very much at ease with each other and had things to discuss the music made things very relaxed and so every now and then both men joined in. Bull then asked, "So are we meeting at The Blue Anchor or are we going straight to Bodmin?" "George said he would like us all to meet the evening before at the Blue and leave very early in the morning." "It's a long old run to Bodmin Joshua, what time is Henry being hung?" "I have been told it is two in the afternoon so if we leave by seven, we should get there." "Well, we had better not have too many." "I agree Bull, by the way, that reminds me, Rebecca said the same to me just before I left the cottage this evening." Bull smiled a knowing smile and said, "Shall we have one more for the road."

The following week passed slowly and again with no major turmoil to speak of. And so, as planned, Joshua and Bull were now sitting with George Kernow in the Blue Anchor in Helston drinking and talking about Henry Hosking's execution the next day. They were all to attend and so George Kernow made the point of saying it was to be early to bed, early to rise. All three were drinking the local brew and knew it was strong so had to take things steady. Kernow asked Joshua about his wife Rebecca and their two children. "They are all well thank you George, in fact, we all rode in together today as Rebecca is taking the children to see their Granny Jeanne over the road in Lady Street." "That's nice Joshua, I bet Jeanne is loving every minute of being with them." "Yes, she loves them very much especially little Richard whom we named after her late husband. His little sister Vivienne doesn't hold back though as when Jeanne gives Richard her attention she wants double." "And you Bull, how are you and the Missus getting on, any children yet?" "We are fine thank you George and no we have no children yet but we keep trying, like the missus keeps saying to me, I am very trying." All three laughed aloud and then Joshua asked, "And how are you George, keeping well?" "Yes, I am well Joshua, thank you for asking." With that George Kernow looked over and saw his Sailor friend wearing bobble hat and tassel enter the bar area from the upper room's doorway. George stood up and waved his hands and when his friend saw him he started to make his way across.

Joshua and Bull were sitting facing George Kernow so when they saw him get up and wave at the bar area they turned their heads to look at who or what he was waving at. They noticed a man wearing a bobble hat walking towards them and when the Sailorman got to the table, George Kernow shook his hand firmly and said, "Good to see you my old friend, please take a seat." Once Tassell was seated, George introduced him to Joshua and Bull and both extended their hands in friendship. George then went on to explain who the Sailorman was and the work he did abroad. He also went over who Joshua and Bull were and their roles. It was important to all seated that George explained things truthfully as best he could as they were all part of one team. George then motioned the nearby waitress over and ordered four ales.

Once all the niceties were over, all four men started to get comfortable and chat away. Tassell quickly felt at ease and likened to Bull and Joshua very quickly. After about ten minutes of chatting Bull said, "She's taking her time with those drinks." As soon as he said these words the young waitress appeared behind him with the full tray and apologised for the delay blaming it on the Inn being very busy tonight. "Thank you my young lady, we fully understand," George said. She then carefully laid each full tankard on the table.

Although the four men were making light conversations they all knew why they were there and the dreadful fate that awaited Henry Hosking on the Moro. So with all four tankards filled, George Kernow raised his tankard and said, "To Henry, a once good fellow and comrade." Joshua, Bull and Tassell raised their tankards and clicked them with Georges and then all drank a big gulp. After wiping his mouth with his sleeve, Bull said, "Where did Henry go wrong George?" "I have no idea Bull, some say he had just gone insane whereas others say it had something to do with a thing called mental stress or trauma from his days fighting in the Army abroad, but I am not sure of either. What we do know is that he betrayed our good Queen and our new United Kingdom so whatever made him do it, is a sorry state."

Kernow wanted to say more but it was he himself who had authorised the periodic torture of Henry to try and get to the very reasons why he had done what he had done. Whilst Henry was being tortured, he did not say much but what he did say over and over again was that Jeanne should be his and that Jacques should be killed. After nearly five years in the dungeons and never changing his story no matter what was thrown at him, George and his bosses concluded that he had simply gone mad. However, it was also the fact that Henry, while still alive knew too much, and they were very concerned about who he had talked with and what he had said. George wanted to explain this deep concern to Joshua, Bull and Tassell but knew he could not.

While all four men were busily chatting away about past and ongoing events the barmaid had once again been called over to refill the tankards of ale, so now all we're waiting with dry throats for her to come back. Kernow was looking forward to having a few more as he needed it. He had a lot on his mind and wanted to open up a bit more to the three men around him whom he trusted. But again, he knew he had to be careful and, they all had to be up early with the dawn.

"Is Tassell your real name," Bull asked. Tassell smiled with ease and said, "No my friend, my real name is Michael but as I have worn this type of bobble hat from a child, everyone has called me Tassell since I can remember." "And you live in Dover?" Joshua asked. "No, I live in a small village with my good wife and two children in West Kent" Then Kernow interrupted by saying in jest, "Leave the poor man alone you two, your acting like the Spanish inquisition." With smiles on their faces Bull then said, "Just one more question Tassell, I promise." Tassell chuckled and said, "Go on then if you must." Allowing a few seconds of silence to creep in before he spoke, Bull leaned over and said, "Do you put the cream on top?" Both Kernow and Joshua laughed aloud but Tassell didn't get it and looked baffled.

Sitting quietly close to the left side of the bar area was an old looking overweight couple with long scraggly hair. Both were wearing worn tatty clothing with low torn hats and sipping the cheapest ale. They looked bent and tired as though they had been potato picking all day and had just come in from the fields. This wasn't unusual and fitted in well with the majority of the low working class people in the area.

This old looking couple had visited the Blue Anchor the last few nights leaving at about eight o clock each time. As they were strangers in the area a couple of locals had come up to them asking where they were from. The old lady had answered in a simple quiet voice saying they were living in the old workhouse in Redruth but were trying to get into the new more modern workhouse in Helston at the top end of Meneage Street. Although the people felt sorry for them it always did the trick as once she had said this they were more or less left alone. Sarah and Peter had prepared themselves well for this type of intrusion as they knew the Cornish to be nosey parkers.

Sarah, looking the very part as the scraggy haired fat old lady of low status then sipped the last of her ale as an old lady would. After putting her glass down, she leant over and whispered to her old fat husband by her side, "Peter, she is coming back to the bar now." They had been watching everything and everyone since they first entered the Inn and had always acted with guile and reservation of calm like an old poor couple would do in a strange town, appearing to others that they just liked a drink. But it hadn't been easy getting to this stage.

After taking ship off the Port of Brest and landing at the inlet of Porthtowan they were met by a woman called Fay, one of the sisters at the Scorrier cottage where they were to stay. After saying their hello's, Fay then showed them both to their horses and led the way back to her cottage over five miles away. Then meeting her sister Janet and being shown their quarters was when both Sarah and Peter realised that these two women could talk the hind leg off a donkey. My God, they thought, could they gossip, they wanted to know everything that was going on, who they were, what they did and then talk and talk about the slightest thing. Peter and Sarah did their best to chat back but they had to get themselves sorted and get up early to prepare for the day ahead. So with all the politeness, he could muster, Peter stopped the chatting and suggested they go to bed. Fay and Janet looked at each other with bewilderment as to why they wouldn't chinwag as they like to. Although Peter and Sarah knew they had upset them it was a good decision made.

When that first morning came, Peter and Sarah prepared themselves for their ride into Helston. Fay had prepared some food for their breakfast, as she had kindly done every day since. They wanted to acquaint themselves with the town of Helston as quickly as they could and start the scouting process, then get out and back to the safety of the cottage. Although the cottage was in a good out of the way location it meant the ride to Helston was taking well over an hour to get to. However, they stuck to their routine and after a few good days of watching and learning, decided to enter the Blue Anchor and wait for their prey to arrive. The Ferret had said to them that there was no guarantee these men would appear, only a certain confidence they would, based on the information he had received.

They had specifically kept an eye on the young waitress and her ways and movements of serving. When they understood this they had to move tables to fit in with their plan. All they wanted now was for their intended victim or victims to show. It had been a slow process of watching but now their patience and experience of work had been rewarded. After two days of nothing and both starting to feel unsure that the information the Ferret had supplied was correct, the Sailorman had appeared in the bar area. That was yesterday evening but he had stayed and drank on his own so they just watched and didn't do anything except remain calm and alert. The Ferret had given them facial sketches of the Sailor man called Tassell and one other man called George Kernow. Their mission was to kill both.

So tonight was their lucky night as not only had Kernow and the Sailor arrived but two others were with them. Sarah had quietly said to Peter that she had seen these other two men before when she was lying low in the safe house in Falmouth. These were the men who had taken her away for questioning before she escaped back to France. It was these two men whom she was most afraid of as she could be recognised by them, hence her relief in wearing their heavy disguises. So Peter, putting two and two together, surmised that these four men must be all close knit and therefore they had an opportunity to take all four men out in one action. The Ferret will be well pleased.

Sarah was now getting tense with inner excitement as the time to act was only minutes away. Keeping her eyes alert on the people around the Inn she was now waiting for Peter to do the signal as they had practised. It had to be spot on as there was no turning back once he had done it. Peter drank the last of his small ale and said in a low serious tone, "Are you ready Sarah?" Sarah opened her bag to check the poison and when she had loosened the cap slightly, looked up and said, "I am ready when you are."

Peter looked across to the two young men sitting in the corner who were also watching him. The young waitress girl was now standing at the bar in the usual place and the barman was filling the four empty tankards, placing each one on the tray as they were filled. Seeing the third tankard being put on the tray was when Peter took off his scraggy hat and rubbed his hair with both hands.

With the signal done both Sarah and Peter got up and went to each side of the young waitress at the bar. Andre then also got up and went and stood by the side of Peter. Just as the last tankard was placed on the tray, and before the young lady could pick the tray up, the other young man went up behind her and kissed her passionately on the side of the neck while sharply pinching her bottom. She quickly turned around to shout at whoever had done this but as she did, saw it was one of the tall handsome young men that she had noticed earlier sitting in the corner. So, as women do, she smiled back and fluttered her eyelids. It was then that

Andre stepped away from Peter and punched the young man hard in the side of the head. The young waitress screamed as the two men crashed together and started fighting and while doing so moved themselves away to the right side of the bar, as they had been told. As the two men bashed wildly around the Inn crashing into other drinkers and furniture causing as much mayhem as they could, all eyes were focused on them. Then, as predicted, the barman moved away from the bar shouting and waving loudly for them to stop.

With all eyes and attention now on the fight was when Sarah, with Peter standing by her side as cover, pulled out the small bottle from her bag and poured the lethal Belladonna into all four tankards. Once done, Sarah and Peter then held hands and with their heads and shoulders down as old people do, shuffled away from the bar and out the front door. No one in the Inn noticed them leave except Andre who then quickly stopped fighting and ran out the back door, like a coward would. His fellow comrade ran out after him showing all the onlookers that he was the stronger fighter and would finish him off outside. As they ran out the entire pub cheered.

When everything had calmed down, Kernow and the other three men sat back down in their seats. They had all been standing and straining their heads to see what all the fuss was about. "Well that livened the place up a bit," Joshua said. "It certainly did that," George replied. "Is Helston always like this," Tassell asked. "Yes, it's a bloody rough old place, not like where I come from," Bull said. "And where do you come from?" "St Just," he said proudly. George, Joshua and Bull himself started to laugh but poor old Tassell again didn't get it.

When a few minutes of peace and calm had passed the young waitress appeared and after again apologising for the delay put the drinks on the table, Kernow said, "Thank you, my good woman, here is a penny for your service." Then, after taking a hold of his full tankard of ale said, "Well, my good men, here's to us, Henry, and good old Cornwall." "And to our good Queen," Tassell said aloud." All four men then raised their tankards in good cheer but not before Joshua, for some reason, quietly murmured under his breath, "And to Zelahnor."

Then without any warning, as they lifted their tankards to their mouths the tankards started to uncontrollably tremble. The shaking was so severe that the contents of all four tankards started to spill out over the table. Then the oil lantern above them started to flicker. All four men with tankards still in their hands raised halfway to their mouths stared wide eyed in utter amazement. No matter how hard they tried to hold still their tankards they could not stop them from shaking. As natural as one would, they put their other hand on their tankards to strengthen their grip to try and control the spilling but to no avail. Whatever it was it would not let them put their tankards to their lips. With no other choice, all four men put their tankards back on the table and as they did all went still and silent. All four men looked at each other in total bewilderment. Then from out of nowhere four yellow and black coloured butterflies flew over the table and out through the open window. "What was that?" Kernow said aloud. "I tell you what that was George, that was someone telling us something," Joshua replied. Bull then said, "Try and pick your tankard up again George." Kernow looked down at the tankard but as soon as his hand touched it, the tankard started to shake again. "There is something not right here," Bull said. "You're telling me Bull," Tassell replied. Joshua reached for his pipe and flinted it alight saying, "I need a smoke."

The four men didn't know what to say to each other and so all went quiet giving time for them to think. It was then that Joshua said, "I have seen this mysterious type of action before when I was in the cave at Gunwalloe a few years back." "Yes, and what did you do," George asked. "I did nothing as I was dumbstruck like I am now." Tassell, in total confusion, said, "What do mean Joshua you have seen the thing before." "It's a Cornish thing of long ago, that's all I know." Then Bull, who was still scratching his chin in total awe said, "Whatever it is, it doesn't like our tankards of ale." "Let's have a look at this," Joshua said, then leaned over and put his nose over his tankard to smell the small content of ale still inside. "What are you doing Joshua?" Kernow asked. Joshua didn't reply but kept his nose fixed firmly over the tankard taking his time to draw in the smell over and over. Once he was done, Joshua sat back and said, "I have drank this ale many times and if I am not mistaken this smells nothing like simple ale, more like an acidic berry drink." Bull then leaned over and did the same as Joshua and then on his sitting back said, "I agree, there is something not right." Kernow and Tassell repeated the action on their tankards and said, what is going on here, I ordered four simple large ales of good crop and yeast, not fruity berries." Joshua, after taking a large puff on his pipe and blowing the smoke upwards said,

''I say someone has spiked our drinks and lucky for us someone somewhere has intervened on our behalf.''

Hearing what Joshua had just said, Kernow and Bull didn't think in the least that he was mad as they know strange things like this happen around here in Cornwall. Tassell too didn't say anything as he had heard many stories about this place too. Although the table was well away from the bar area, Kernow got up and looked over to try and find the young barmaid who served them. On spotting her he put his right hand up and when she noticed him, he waved her over. When George sat back down Joshua asked, ''By the way George where are your personal guards tonight.'' ''Would you believe it Joshua; I gave them the night off and are both in the Red Lion having a well deserved drink.

When the young waitress got to the table she politely asked, ''Yes gentlemen, is it the same again?'' Kernow asked the lady to take a seat. ''I'm sorry, I'm very busy and I don't take offers, if you want that sort of thing then go up to the Bell in Meneage Street.'' ''It has nothing to do with that, we would like to talk with you only for a few seconds, now please just a take seat.'' The barmaid looked over towards the bar area and saw the barman who was also the owner pulling the beer. On getting his attention she gestured that she was going to take a seat with these men. The barman knew George Kernow as a good reliable customer of drink and stay and someone of considerable note and so nodded his head in approval.

Once she was seated, Kernow introduced the other three men and said, ''Thank you, my good lady, now please can you tell us if you were in full attendance when we ordered the last round of drinks." She looked at him in a rather confused manner saying, "Yes, of course I was." "So you never took your eyes away from the tankards from the moment you took them from this table, had them filled at the bar, to the moment you delivered them back to us on the tray?" "Sorry, I don't know what you mean, I am a simple woman." The young waitress didn't know what he was getting at and started to get a little anxious so Joshua stepped in and politely asked what her name was. "My name is Verna Lugg and I am from Porthleven." "Well Verna, we have a slight issue and need to know exactly what happened when you last left our table to refill our drinks order and then delivered them back to us. Please take your time and speak your thoughts of exact movements aloud and do not leave anything out." Verna sat quietly for a while and then went through stage by stage what happened. While she was talking, she remembered the unknown handsome man pinching her bottom when she was just about to pick up the tray. She then thought about her turning around and then the other young man punching him and starting the fight but, she didn't know whether she should say anything about that. It was Kernow who felt she was being a little too vague in her answers and so stopped her and asked her to talk in more detail like who was at the bar and did she ever take her eyes away from the drinks. Verna looked at all four men and knew she had to be careful and explain things as they wished. So she took a deep breath and went over things once again but this time as Kernow wished. She mentioned the old lady and man standing on each side of her at the bar. She also said about what the handsome stranger did and then admitted that her attention on the drinks had been drawn away to watch the two young men fighting.

When she had finished, George replied, "Yes, we heard the chaos, so when you turned around to pick up the tray, you say the man and woman leaning at the bar to your left and right side had gone." "That is right Sir, I thought it a little odd as they normally wait at their table for me to serve them. So seeing them at the bar standing close next to me felt a little odd. When I turned back around to the bar after the fight had ended they were gone." "And you have never seen them or the young man who pinched your bottom before?" Helen went red faced but said, "I have never seen the young man until this evening but the old lady and man had appeared about three or four days ago and have been in the pub every night since." "Thank you Verna you have been most helpful, you can now go back to your duties." "Am I in trouble?" "No, you are not my kind woman, please accept our apologies for taking up your time." As the young waitress got up and left the table, Kernow turned to his three colleagues and said, "So what do you all make of it?'

"Sounds like we've been set up," said Bull. "And you Tassell, what do you think?" "I agree with Bull, something is not right." "And you Joshua?" "I think we should take what's left of our drink and get it analysed and get out of here quickly." "Not so fast Joshua, if they, whoever they are, intended to inflict harm upon us then they may still be watching somewhere, we have to be smart." Kernow's alert brain on covert planning and action had started to kick in. Joshua, Bull and Tassell all kept quiet while watching and waiting for Kernow to make up his mind on what they were to do. "Bull, please could you go over to the bar and ask the owner to send a messenger boy over." "What are you thinking George,"

Joshua asked. "I am thinking that if we don't play out their game of being hurt or dead then it is just possible they could have planned something else. If we play their game, that will give us time to regroup and sort things out on our terms." When Bull and the young messenger boy returned to the table, Kernow gave the boy orders. He was to go at speed via the back door to the Red Lion. Then describing the two men who would be in there drinking, he was to inform them that their master needs them urgently and to say the word, 'Gunpowder.' He was then to run to the constable of the town in Wendron Street and say there are problems at the Blue Anchor and that he must come immediately. He then put a penny in the boy's hand and with that, the young lad dipped his head and with gusto ran out the back door as ordered.

"What do we do now?" Tassell asked. "We wait for my men who will be armed to come. Then when I have talked with the owner and constable of this town we get all the drinkers to leave and close the pub. We stay inside. Do you men have your pistols on you?" They all nodded that they have. "Good, then I suggest you make them ready." While all three men were quietly checking their pistols, Joshua turned to Bull saying, "You have your protective vest on I presume." " Yes, I do Joshua, I have learnt."

Sarah and Peter were still dressed as the old overweight couple but were now out of the way in a narrow alley across the street from the Blue Anchor. After a few tense minutes of wait, they were then joined by the two young handsome men. Peter then said, "Well done lads, you were excellent." Andre, replied, "Thank you Sir, did you do it?" "Yes, Sarah here done her job well." Sarah didn't respond to what Peter had just said as her mind was on getting out of the town as planned and quickly. Peter then added, ''Well boys you have both done a good job tonight so I suggest you get to your horses and report back to the Ferret. By the way, where exactly are you both staying?'' Both young men looked at each other but stayed silent as they had been advised by the Ferret that Peter or Sarah may question them on this and they must not reveal it. So Andre vaguely replied, ''O somewhere near a place called Truro, I don't know what it's called only the route to it.'' He then quickly added, ''Well good luck to you both and we hope to see you again soon.'' With that Andre then grabbed his friend Pierre and both ran away down the alley as fast as they could.

When the young men were out of sight Peter turned to Sarah and said, ''That Ferret is hiding something,'' ''I agree with you Peter but what can we do.'' ''Nothing for the moment but I got a bad feeling inside.'' So, keeping quiet and tucked away unseen in the alley they waited. It was after a long thirty minutes had passed, that they started to hear all the fuss coming from the Blue Anchor. They saw the drinkers being forced out of the pub's front door all moaning and groaning at being told to leave and some even shouting at being treated like scum. It wasn't long after the last drinker was out that they saw the Land Lord then come out and turn the two outside oil lamps off and take them down. Then with the lamps in his hands, he went back into the pub and slammed the door shut behind him. After a few minutes of silence, they then saw the curtains inside being pulled together. The only people they did not see come out of the pub were the four men whose drinks Sarah had laced with the deadly Belladonna.

Chapter 5

It was still dark in the early morning when Andre gently crept out of the Ferret's bedroom and tiptoed away with candle in hand, back to the bedroom he shared with his friend, Pierre. As he undressed and got into his bed he blew the candle out and then heard, "Andre, you are a bloody fool." "That may be so Pierre but he has power and pays good money." "You're still a bloody fool." "Well, you like that Joulie woman, you told me." "Yes, that's right Andre, but she is a female." "I don't care, as long as he pays me in cash, I don't care." Pierre was going to reply to Andre's last comment but it was just too early and they both needed sleep, so in a friendly voice said, "Good night Andre, what's left of it." "Good night Pierre."

It had been well over a week since the two young men had their diversion fight in the Blue Anchor in Helston. Then, after they had met Sarah and Peter outside in the alleyway and got details of how things had gone, they rode with haste back to the Manor at Mingoose to report.

When the dark of the early morning had turned to light the Ferret opened his eyes and smiled with satisfaction at last night's action with his adorable Andre. Then once he had stretched and yawned aloud he got up to prepare himself. He needed to be on his toes for the important breakfast meeting with the Lord of the Manor and his lovely Joulie.

On entering the vast dining room the Ferret saw Joulie sitting on her own at the very large table with cutlery and china all ready prepared. "Good morning my lovely

Joulie, how are you this fine morning." "I am fine thank you and how are you." "I am excellent my dear." Joulie knew what he had been up to and was going to have a go at him about his goings on with Andre but decided the timing was wrong and to leave it for now.

As soon as he sat down opposite Joulie the door opened and in walked the maid who started to pour them both their morning tea. As she did so the butler then walked in and apologised to the Ferret that his Lordship had sent message saying he has been delayed in Launceston and asked that he see them both tomorrow. "Thank you," the Ferret replied. "My pleasure Sir, if there is anything I can do, just ring the bell." "Would it be possible to make this breakfast for four people?" Yes of course, I will get things organised, is there anything else." "Could you go up to the bedroom of the two young men and ask that they join us." ''I will get the maid to do it right away."

As they waited, Joulie couldn't hold back any longer and said, "I thought we agreed that you would keep away from Andre." "O Joulie, do not fret yourself my girl, I'm not doing anything wrong, I think he loves me." Joulie looked at him in stunned silence not knowing what to say. Then before she had time to reply the Ferret said, "Anyway Joulie, I've seen the way you look at Pierre."

It wasn't long before the two young men came in and after saying their good mornings to both Joulie and the Ferret, sat down and quietly waited to see why they had been called. It was then that the Ferret spoke, "Good morning Andre, good morning Pierre, there has been a slight delay in our plans. I know it's been rather boring hanging around but his Lordship has sent a message that he has been held up and will see me and Joulie early tomorrow to discuss. Therefore, I suggest we all have a big hearty breakfast and then get our horses and go riding around the estate and get some fresh air."

The ride out around the estate was a good idea and would do done them all the well of good as they had been cooped up now for well over a week. And so it proved as all became more relaxed which allowed each to chat away about their homeland and things personal. It also gave Joulie time to get to know Pierre a little more and vice versa. Andre noticed this and would point this out to Pierre that evening before he walked out of their bedroom to be with the Little Ferret.

The next morning as requested by His Lordship, Joulie and the Ferret were once again in the large breakfast room. Then dead on eight thirty the door drew open and in walked his Lordship. Both Joulie and The Ferret stood up and as they did so, were politely asked to sit back down.

This man was very wealthy and owned much land. He was also a member of the Cornish Gentlemen's Club and knew many people of influence. What they didn't know was that although he made out he was loyal to the Cornish and the Crown he's loyalty was to only one person and, that was himself. Wealth mattered and it brought a great many things and he loved it. He had passed information many ways and many times in the past, no matter to who or what Country that be, it just depended on the profit.

Ten years ago while living in Devon he got wind of a wealthy man and wife who had died from a freak accident and who owned a large Manor in a lovely area of Mingoose, Cornwall. This was an opportunity he had been looking for and so secretly, through friends of stealth, gained more information and also found that the estate included a small Mine called Wheal Coates. There was no direct inheritor of the estate which made things easier but there was a small cottage that irritatingly encroached on the land and was owned by a young couple. This young couple also had a small child but that didn't bother him one bit. Through simple deed and title forgery compiled by his lawyer friends, the small family were deemed illegal squatters and made bankrupt. They were then, through the rights of law, marched off the property and living in poverty somewhere he didn't care where. Once all was done in his favour, he then sold his property in Plymouth, and moved across the Tamar to the Mingoose Manor near the town of St Agnes. The man now called himself Cuthbert Troon but his real name before all the deed changes was Richard Gingell, a shady businessman, originally from Devon

Cuthbert knew this man called the Ferret as he had passed information his way a few times in the past for much reward. When he received the message that the Ferret wished to visit him he knew this could be a very rich encounter and so accepted and made plans for his stay. Mingoose Manor was a large house with much land in the wild countryside and therefore was a safe place to meet away from any unwanted prying eyes.

When Cuthbert had sat down and got comfortable, the maid came to his side and served him his tea and breakfast. Then after she left the room the discussion on what both parties wanted, began.

The Ferret wanted to start the conversation but knew it was rude, so waited for Troon to begin. Troon knew this and out of curiosity prolonged his silence. This was a good tactic as it confirmed to all that Troon was in charge and also would put pressure on the little man opposite. The Ferret was familiar with this type of person as he dealt with them many times. After a few minutes of this silent inner egotistic pleasure had passed, Troon began. "So how are you both and please let me apologise for my delay, certain things needed my attention. Has my estate welcomed you?" "Yes, very much so, your staff have been most kind," the Ferret said. "That is good to hear, I would expect nothing less."

He then looked at both the Ferret and Joulie and said, "Before we get into things please tell me what are your real names as I only know you both as the Ferret and his right hand person?" Joulie turned her head to look at the Ferret not knowing what to do. The Ferret on the other hand was not fazed and knew he had to be truthful as this Troon man would probably know anyway, and the question his asking was a teaser of trust. "My real name is Francois DuPont and this lady here is Louise Blanch."

Joulie had not heard her old name spoken aloud for many years and didn't know what to say. She then started to blush with sadness of her past as a common gutter girl put into the Paris workhouse as a person of nothing. It was then that she felt something touch her ankle and as she looked down noticed it was the Ferret's foot. She looked up and saw he was looking at her in a knowing way of comforting sincerity and for her not to worry. This tiny piece of love gave her the strength to smile and do as advised. Sometimes she thought to herself she could kill him for the things he does but then he does something like this and she could love him forever, no matter what.

Troon was closely watching both after he had asked the question and wanted to see and hear their reactions. He was no fool and had done his homework. He already knew their real names and also knew that this Ferret man worked in the shadows for King Louis and at the very least had the ear of some person high up in the French nobility. This didn't bother Troon at all as if you play ball with me, I will play ball with you. It is that simple. Even loyalty to his own Queen was an outward veil unless of course there was profit to be made. "Thank you Francois and thank you Louise, please call me Cuthbert. Right then, now we have the formalities out of the way, what exactly can I do for you?"

Chapter 6

As the butterflies flew across the still of the night sky of Bodmin Moor they entered the shack and went straight to the one they love. As soon as they landed on her body, Zelahnor opened her eyes. Laying still she listened to what they had learnt and when they had finished she kissed each one tenderly and thanked them. They then flew up to the rafters to be with their family and friends and then fell asleep.

Zelahnor remained in her lying position but kept silent, waiting for the answers to come. After ten minutes of quiet thought, she started to move. Zoar, who was by her side, got his muscles ready in preparation.

Zelahnor raised herself off her bed and with Zoar at her side quietly walked out of the shack into the midnight air of the vast moor. Zareb, Zoar's brother, was already outside lying in the nearby shrub area out of sight to protect all that was inside the shack. Zelahnor went straight up to him and caressed his neck and kissed him on the nose. After He purred with love and comfort she then walked away. Zoar then came up to him and after rubbing his neck on his neck, he too then went away with Zelahnor. Zareb laid back down in silence.

After two hours of being away on the Moor, Zelahnor and Zoar then returned to the shack only to find the fire was now aglow and young Christine and Deborah up and about. From their very birth, two of Zoar's cubs had attached themselves to each girl and would not leave their sides. Everywhere they went, they went too but they weren't cubs anymore as they were both touching six years of age and were as big as their Father and Zareb, their Uncle. This connection was exactly what Zelahnor had wished from the moment the cubs were born. But it wasn't just the cubs who followed the girls around but the squirrels and butterflies would also not let them out of their sight.

It had been over eight years since Deborah had arrived and nearly six years for Christine. Both girls were of the same age and were now touching their eighteenth year on this earth. Zelahnor smiled at this tender thought and then again smiled with the inner delight for their next two hundred years of being in the light of love. As Zelahnor sat by the glowing fire with Zoar lying over her feet, Christine took the boiling pan off the fire and then poured the hot nettle tea into a cup and handed it to Zelahnor. "Thank you my Christine, did you have a beautiful sleep." "Yes, it was wonderful." "And did anything come to you in the dream of life that you wish to confide." "Yes, I have talked with Deborah and she too had the feelings." "Well, let us all get together and talk while the fire is glowing with warmth like the sun and our nettle tea is hot." As Zelahnor said this, the butterflies who were supposedly fast asleep up in the rafters flew down closer as did the squirrels and of course the two cubs.

As both Deborah and Christine quietly opened up their inner thoughts, Zelahnor listened with devoted love. They were only young and the signs they were being given were testing their advancement in the true way that Zelahnor and her cousins lived. Christine told her of the fear her Father was feeling and that a certain curtain was being pulled over the area of Redruth. She also said about the love pouring out of her Mothers heart. When Christine fell silent, Deborah added that she too had seen this curtain fly over the Redruth area but also this same curtain had moved to the area of St Agnes.

Once the girls had finished, Zelahnor sipped her nettle tea and then spoke. "My dear girls how you are both growing and, it is true as you say that a certain darkness will fall in the areas you name. It is also true Christine what your Father and Mother are feeling. But let me reassure you that your Father will be well and when the time is right will summon the strength to do what he knows he must do. As you both know the union of our nation joined some five years ago is proving difficult and many threats are coming from many different ways. We may not be able to repel all but we must always love and protect our good Cornish people." When she said this all the butterflies flapped their wings in unison.

It was then that Deborah spoke, "I also have felt that our Queen is upset as I saw rain drops fall over her palace." "That is true, the Queen is poor in health and is going through some difficult times." Zelahnor looked at both girls and felt both were wishing that they could better understand their visions in a more precise manner. So, with tender love she said, "All the feelings you are having will one day be clearer in your minds and bodies as they are to me now, and then with that experience deep inside, you can talk with the powers that can help. Do not feel down as you are both still young in age and are doing wonderful and how so pleased we all are to have you here with us. Now let us all hug one another with love and happiness and sing a song together and then we will all go out onto the Moor and sing a ballad to the morning stars above.

When they had finished their singing and were walking back to the shack, Zelahnor knew that the time had come for both girls to leave the Moor in continuation of their learning, as she had done at the age of eighteen, many moons ago. They would go and stay with her cousins all around this land for many years. So, as her guardians did before, she would ask them how they would feel about this.

When all were safely back inside the shack and with that last thought in Zelahnors mind, she asked them over to the fire place. Then when all were holding hands and feeling the love, young Christine spoke. "Deborah and I have talked and we have only two things to ask before we give you the answer to your question." Zelahnor smiled with love and joy that they knew what she was going to ask. So with a similar inner mind response replied, "Then before you ask me these two things, the answer to your first question is yes, you can both come back when you have fulfilled your stay throughout our good lands in fifty years when you reach the age of sixty eight of this earths time. And the answer to your second question is also a loving yes as my cousins, with who you will stay, have all agreed that due to you both being brought up here together; it would be most wise for the Cornish people that you stay together. Although it is unusual for two ladies to be in one land it has happened before many centuries ago in the land of Wales with two young ladies of the valleys and was seen as good for all." Christine looked at Deborah and with glowing smiles coming from each, Christine turned to Zelahnor and said, "Our answer is yes but we will miss you all so very much." "We will all miss you too but, we can all meet up every ten years in the land you are in during your stay away and look forward to the time you return."

Whilst they had been talking, all the animals were in total silence, listening to every word, especially the two large cubs. Then when the two cubs heard that Christine and Deborah had agreed to go away they put their massive paws over their big golden coloured eyes and started to cry. On hearing their weeping of sadness Deborah spoke, "Can we take the two cubs with us?" "Of course you can my sweet hearts, how else are you to travel and be protected." When the two massive cubs heard this they lifted their heads and stopped their tears and wagged their tails with pure joy.

So with the knowledge that the girls are willing to leave the Moors and the Cornish land to pursue their learning of the true way, Zelahnor now had to send messages to her cousins in readiness for their leave. As her cousins were hundreds of miles away in Scotland, Wales and England meant she couldn't use her butterflies as she needed friends with stronger wings to carry her words.

With this thought in mind, Zelahnor and Zoar again went outside onto the moor and after a few minutes of walking away from the shack, they stopped. Zelahnor looked up at the moon in silence and when the feeling of connection came to her she started to sing a melodic song letting the sound drift peacefully across the silent dark sky. Then waiting with her arms outstretched three male tawny owls appeared.

Zelahnor smiled a loving smile and sat herself down on the heather. When she was settled and the owls had landed they toddled forward towards her and stopped at her feet. She leaned forward and kissed each one in turn and then talked with them about her wishes. When she had finished she thanked them all for their love and kindness and wished them a safe journey. With those last words said the three owls then flew off into the night. Zelahnor waved them goodbye and as she did a loving teardrop fell from her eye.

Walking slowly back to the shack Zelahnor knew she needed to ask both girls one last question. Their answer would then confirm that they indeed are absorbing and learning the true inner way of life and both are ready for their journey. As she got closer to the door she realised she had been crying and so stopped and wiped her eyes dry. Zoar felt her inner love and knew she was saddened and so went up close and gently rubbed his massive head on the side of her body. Zelahnor looked into his bright golden eyes and said, "Thank you my darling."

On entering the warmth of the shack she saw the girls still by the fire with the squirrels and cubs all wanting their attention of love. They were both stroking all the animals as best they could and while doing so singing a beautiful song in harmony.

Zelahnor sat gently down beside them and looked at both remembering the first time that each had come to her and how very young they were. When their song had been sung and both girls were relaxed in smile, Zelahnor asked the question.

"My sweet girls, when you said you had seen the dark clouds over Redruth and St Agnes did you see anything over the lands of Helston?" Christine looked at Deborah and smiled for her to answer as they had both agreed beforehand, should Zelahnor ask. So Deborah replied, "It is true that we did but unlike Redruth and St Agnes which was a week ago, the Helston vision happened yesterday. I saw a heavy dark cloud with rain gushing out and then felt the earth tremble. Christine also felt this but she also saw the cloud go away and the sun shine bright." Zelahnor completely understood on what Deborah had said and replied, "What you felt and saw is true and my heart now is in full knowing that you are both truly ready for your next journey of faith and love."

It was then that Christine spoke in a gentle voice saying, "Zelahnor, we know we have agreed to go to the lands of your cousins and you have sent messages but, we feel we must ask if we could stay with you and our family here for a while longer. We feel the Cornish people are asking us to help them through a coming darkness."

Chapter 7

Time had passed very slowly at the sister's cottage in Scorrier and both Sarah and Peter were now bored stiff just waiting around for further orders. Eight days had passed since their task at the Blue Anchor in Helston but still had not heard anything from the Ferret. Sarah was getting agitated at not knowing what was happening but Peter reassured her that all will be well and they must wait patiently.

It was then around nine in the morning that they heard the loud knock on the old wooden front door. Sarah was in Peter's new ground floor bedroom talking about what if anything was to come and their uncertainty about the Ferret's motives and desires. Peter then raised his finger to his mouth for her to keep hush and crept quietly over to the window by the curtains. Sarah remained sitting in the chair. He saw two horses and knew straight away it was the two young men who had helped them in the Blue Anchor.

Peter then crept back and sat down very close to Sarah and whispered what he had seen. Sarah looked puzzled as she assumed they were relaying a message but that normally meant one horse, one rider and one message. Peter agreed but countered by saying, "I agree Sarah but it could be that they are on a joint mission and this was on their way so why waste resources when you can hit two birds with one stone." "Well, then maybe I am just being paranoid," Sarah replied. "Maybe we both are but hanging around here and doing nothing has got me feeling jittery too, especially with our inner feelings on that bloody Ferret." "What shall we do Peter?"

Fay and Janet were sitting by the fire chatting away like they always do and then on hearing the knocking on the front door immediately went quiet and looked at each other in bewilderment. The cottage was in the middle of nowhere and isolated so getting an unknown visitor was a rarity. Fay got up and brushed her frock down with her hands as whoever it was, she wanted to look her best. As Fay walked to the door Janet also started to stroke her hair through. Fay then unlocked the door and pulled it open.

Andre, as a young gentleman, quickly apologised for the interruption and explained very politely who he and his friend Pierre were and that the Ferret had ordered them to come. Fay and Janet knew the Ferret and so relaxed a little but knew something was going on. Andre then said that they needed to talk with Peter before the Ferret arrived later in the day from the Manor at Mingoose. Fay without hesitation, accepted his story as true and asked both to come in out of the cold and she will put some tea on. Then as Fay turned about and before either man put one foot in the cottage, Andre asked where Peter was. She stopped and turned her head about and said, ''He is in the ground bedroom which we made up especially for him.'' She then turned and pointed to the bedroom door. ''And where may I ask is Sarah.'' ''I think she is in there too, hold on a minute I will ask my sister.'' Janet had been listening to all that had been said and so when Fay turned to her she simply said, ''Yes, Sarah is in there with Peter.''

Fay then walked away from the door heading for the fire place to put the water on for boil. The two young men, who had still not crossed the doorway, then put their right hands into their pockets. Then taking a firm grip of their loaded pistols and using strong thumbs they slowly pulled the flint levers back ready for firing."

Then, keeping their grip on their pistols hidden in their pockets both young men walked in. Fay introduced her sister Janet and then knelt by the fire to get on with making the tea. Janet suggested they come on in and take a seat but the two young didn't move and stood together, close to the still slightly open front door. It was then that Andre asked Janet if she could ask Sarah to come out. "Yes, of course, just hold there a minute."

Sarah was bent forward with her ear firmly against the inside of the bedroom door listening intently to what was being said. When she heard that Janet was to ask her to come out she turned her head to Peter with a very worried look. Within a few seconds, she heard the quiet knocking on the bedroom door and Janet say, "Sarah, can you come out." "What for," she replied." "There are two gentlemen here who wish to speak with you."

Sarah looked at Peter who raised his hand showing three fingers and mimed the words three minutes. "Tell them I will be out in a few minutes I just need to get my shoes on." Janet turned about and told the young men she will be out in a few minutes. The bedroom door was only ten to twelve feet away from where the two young men were standing and so had heard Sarah's response but out of respect didn't say anything.

"What do I do," Sarah whispered. Peter thought that maybe they were both overreacting but his experience had taught him to take no chances when things don't feel right. So, he fetched his two pistols and started to load them in readiness for whatever may happen. It was better to be prepared than not. He even thought about jumping out the window and running away. "Do as they ask Sarah, you will be alright. It's not you they want as I have this horrible inner feeling it's me." Sarah, although always coming across as loving and caring, didn't give two hoops about what he thought; it was her life that mattered. What was she to do? She had no choice and so with a feeling of dread she walked to the door. Peter looked up from loading his pistols and said, "If they ask, tell them I am in bed not feeling well." Sarah nodded, opened the door and walked out.

After closing the door behind her she saw the two young men standing just inside the front door and Fay and Janet by the fire. Andre smiled and gestured that she come over to them which she did without question.

Once she was standing close in front of the two men, Pierre then quickly grabbed her arm. Andre then said in a very clear manner, "Sarah, you will be alright, please keep calm, where is Peter?" He's in the bedroom." "Yes, we know that but where exactly in the bedroom?" "He is in bed, he is not feeling very well."

With that, Andre turned and smiled at Pierre and with a youthful confidence, pulled out his pistol and walked to the bedroom door. Fay, being dumbstruck, looked at her sister Janet who just shrugged her shoulders. So turning her head back to Pierre asked, "What is going on here?" Pierre, still holding a tight grip on Sarah said, "All will be well ladies, this won't take long."

Andre took hold of the bedroom door knob with his left hand and with the pistol in his right hand kept down by his side opened the door and boldly walked in.

He saw the bed straight in front of him but Peter wasn't in it. Then he glimpsed a movement to his right and saw Peter with pistol in hand aimed straight at him. Without any thought of care or cowardice, Andre dived to the floor and whilst doing so raised his pistol at Peter and pulled the trigger. Peter moved his aim accordingly and also pulled his trigger. On hearing the two loud shots being fired in quick succession Pierre pushed Sarah to the side, drew his pistol and rushed to the bedroom.

He saw his friend Andre on the floor and Peter by the window bent over as if he was going to fall down. Pierre raised his pistol and without hesitation shot him. Peter fell to the ground but as he was falling he raised his left hand and with one last gasp of air, shot Pierre.

Over at Mingoose Manor the meeting between Cuthbert Troon, the Ferret and Joulie was going well when all of a sudden the grandfather clock on the wall struck aloud nine o'clock. The Ferret moved his foot under the table and touched Joulie's ankle. As she looked at him, he winked in the knowledge that it was the time that the two young men, as ordered, would have killed Peter. Joulie smiled back but ever so gently shook her head from side to side as if to say to him, 'Don't say anything.'

The Ferret had told her this would happen when they met each other the night before. He had also told her about the message he had sent the Abbot to kill Jacques at the Chateau in Morlaix. Joulie felt edgy with these decisions and didn't agree he should do either and so tried to argue. But, he simply dismissed her with a wave of his hand as being naive. He then, without a second thought or word ended the meeting and walked away to his bedroom where his adorable Andre was waiting.

Cuthbert Troon saw both the wink and smile coming from them and asked if he had missed something. Joulie kicked the Ferret's ankle under the table as if again to say, keep quiet. But the Ferret didn't take any notice and said, "I do apologise Sir, it was the chiming of the clock that made me realise that our team now consist of the people we said a little earlier." You mean it's still the five of you, you two both, the two young men and a woman called Sarah." "That is right, we had to eliminate someone and it happened at this very moment."

Cuthbert did not like to be involved in any way with the dirty side of his profit making and so quickly replied, "I understand, now shall we move on and get into more detail on how we are going to achieve what we want."

What Cuthbert Troon didn't mention is that when he heard the name Sarah being one part of the Ferret's team added by her description and coming from Plymouth, he immediately drew a quiet breath. He had worked with this woman many years before and also bedded her too. Yes, it was a very long time ago when they were in their early twenties but he had never forgotten her and the devious ways she got things done. It just had to be her and so smiled at the thought of meeting her again.

The Ferret continued, "So to confirm, Joulie and Sarah are to infiltrate as Bal Maidens the Wheal Peevor Mine and are to find, by any means they see fit, how they are producing so much Ore but very little is being shown. They are also, if they can, to find who exactly is running the Mine and the money." "That is exactly right but don't rush this as it could backfire, we need to know who is behind this Mine of wealth as something is not adding up. Their employment starts in three weeks at five o clock on the Monday morning prompt, all has been arranged. We have also found a worker's cottage for them to stay which will shortly become vacant so they can live together as Mother and Daughter. Once we know where all the money is going and the people involved, we can then twist them by any means we see fit to get what we want." Cuthbert knew the Aubyn family owned the land but had nothing to do with the Mine production.

The Ferret had fully understood what Troon wanted but then asked, "And how may I ask is our King going to get his rewards?" Troon thought for a brief moment about whether he should release his thoughts or keep them to himself. After taking a sip of his tea he thought why not and decided to tell. "We have a couple of options as I see it, we can blow the Mine shafts and kill production and let my friend at another Mine close by take the gain of which your King will take royalties of fifty per cent. The other option is to ambush their secret supply route with the same royalty split. These options may change subject to the information gained, hence the utmost need for Joulie and Sarah to do a good job. Whatever way we choose your King will be well paid, especially now the price of Tin has ballooned out of all proportion due to its new chemical element Arsenic and its huge demand in the Americas." The Ferret listened intently to this part of the meeting as he needed to know what size of money his good King was to receive and so asked, "And what is fifty per cent?" "Well let's put it this way, if all goes well, your King could probably build another Palace at Versailles and still have coins after." "That is excellent, my King will be pleased." Cuthbert smiled at the Ferrets response as he knew this little man with his team, which thankfully were in no way connected to him, could bring the results he wanted. He had of course over estimated on the monies side of things but that was of little matter. However, with that aside, he was starting to feel a little anxious being seen too close to these people and also of them living in his Manor especially after just hearing of the killing of one of their Team. He liked to be in the background well away from any dirt of the working people that could hinder his lavish rich lifestyle.

The atmosphere then went a little quiet while each took a sip of their tea but once Cuthbert had put his cup down he nonchalantly asked, "Could you please just remind me of what happened in Helston last week as there seems to be some gossip of fuss going around?" The Ferret didn't blink an eye and explained that before he took this operation he was working on an English Agent called Tassel. Through some form of fate it then all just steered itself to Cornwall which fitted very well with the King's orders. It was also a rare opportunity to devise a simple plan to finish this enemy off and anyone else who was with him. It was a zero-risk strategy and either win or lose it would achieve a good diversion tactic for this new mission to gain wealth for his king. If someone tried to assassinate a known spy, especially on his home soil, it would look like an inside job or some kind of a serious leak had occurred. If this being the case they would need to put all their resources and effort into who has done it, which gives us better movement and time." "Hmmm," said Cuthbert, scratching his chin.

Joulie looked and listened to the Ferret brag about his work and knew that something had changed as this was not his usual style. He was normally the secretive type but now seemed to be full of himself without a care in the world on what he said. Something is wrong. She looked at him again to study this new manner and then it dawned on her, it's that bloody Andre she thought. He was in bloody love with him. She could feel it oozing out of him.

Troon then asked, "And what of your plans of stay here in Cornwall?" The Ferret looked at Joulie who he had noticed had kept very quiet throughout the meeting but she didn't respond. So, with confidence, he replied, "I was going to mention that as we both wanted to thank you for your hospitality in this fine house but we are leaving your lovely Manor this very afternoon. We are to stay with two old sisters in their cottage in Scorrier who are very loyal and whom I mentioned earlier." "O, I see, yes I do know of them, I will send message there on where we can all meet again safely away from the Manor." Troon had a few more questions to ask before he would wrap things up but was really pleased to hear that they were moving out this very day. But, he kept a straight face and just picked up his cup and sipped his tea once more.

He then looked at Joulie and asked, by the way, my good lady, how old are you?" "I am twenty seven." He looked puzzled as she appeared like a young teenager.

He was just about to say aloud what he thought but the Ferret quickly intervened by saying, "Yes, she does look much younger but that's the beauty of her." "Yes, of course, I meant nothing by it, I was just curious that's all. He again looked at Joulie and said, "I have also noticed in your speech that a certain soft French twang is coming through which could cause concern whilst working in Cornwall." Troon did not want to sound rude but it was something he had picked up upon when she spoke for the first time. He did not want anything which could associate him with foreigners, especially French ones. She was just about to respond but again the Ferret spoke on her behalf, "We have tried many times to rid her of that but to no avail and so when Joulie enters the Mine with Sarah, she will act as her simple daughter being mute." Troon got it and thought, yes, that would work and knowing Sarah as he did, would play the Mother well.

With the meeting coming to a close, Troon got himself up and went over by the wall and pulled the cord for the servants to come back to clear the table. As he did this he turned about and said, "I would like to meet this Sarah woman before she and Joulie are put in the Mine, I will send word where and when." "Yes, that can be done, we will be seeing Sarah later today at the cottage." Troon nodded and suggested they stay and finish their tea. Then wishing them both well, he walked out of the room smiling at the thought of meeting Sarah once again.

As soon as Troon had closed the door behind him, Joulie turned to the Ferret and said in a most scorning manner, "What is your problem?" "What do mean Joulie." "I mean what I say, what is your problem, you told Troon everything, what did you do that for?" "Joulie, I have no idea what you are talking about." "You know exactly what I am talking about, you have changed, your mind is elsewhere, I can feel it. Where is the Ferret I know who is calculated and calm." "Joulie, calm down my girl, I know what I'm doing." But Joulie knew differently and said, "I will not calm down, this is also my life we are talking and if things go wrong I am a dead woman. This is serious and you just gobbling off with an ego of bloody self righteousness is not right. It's that bloody Andre, that's what it is, you are besotted with him, he has taken over your very brain." It was then that the Ferret raised his chin and said in a most defiant arrogant way, "I don't care what you say Joulie, you don't know what it's like to love someone the way I do. I love him with all my heart and soul as I have never loved another." Joulie didn't respond but just closed her eyes and lowered her head in total disbelief.

Chapter 8

Rebecca was in her Mothers cottage in Lady Street upstairs in the second bedroom with her two children fast asleep. While still dark in the early morning she was awoken by the knocking on the back door. Jeanne, fast asleep in the other bedroom, also heard the noise.

Rebecca got up to investigate and with a candle in hand, went out of the bedroom only to meet her Mother, Jeanne, on the small landing. ''Who can it be at this time of the morning,'' whispered Rebecca. ''It must be Joshua drunk after too much beer.'' ''I don't think so Mother, Joshua had said that he and the others were to stay at the Anchor this night as they were all riding to Bodmin jail very early.''

Jeanne like her daughter Rebecca had lived and worked in this tight covert working arena with Joshua and the others for many years and, had the scars to prove it. When things don't add up no matter how trivial, you must be on your guard. ''Rebecca, have you the pistol?'' ''Mother, let's not over do this, it's probably something very innocent.'' Jeanne knew that may be the case but again through the experience of hurt wasn't taking any chances. And so, before both going down the stairs, Rebecca went back and got the pistol from the bedroom and made it ready for firing. Rebecca then came back out and after putting the candle out carefully led the way down the stairs with Jeanne close behind.

Then, as both stood either side of the back door, Jeanne spoke aloud but not too loud, just enough for whoever it was to hear, ''Who is it, what do want?'' ''Jeanne, it's me,

John Richards, of the Blue Anchor, let me in." Jeanne recognised the voice straight away and said, "Is anyone else with you?" "No, it's just me, please Jeanne, let me in." Jeanne then looked at Rebecca in a way to lower her pistol. Rebecca did as asked but kept a sharp wit about her, just in case, while Jeanne unbolted the door.

As soon as John entered he quickly turned around and bolted the door behind him. When Jeanne saw that he was indeed alone, she relit the candle and asked, "What is it John, is Joshua drunk?" "Please Jeanne, can we sit down there has been an incident."

When all were sat down at the table, Rebecca and Jeanne listened intently to what John Richards had to say. He explained all that had happened and then, after many hours of wait, was asked by George Kernow to sneak here without sight to ask if you could take four men in need of silent refuge for a short while. "Are they alright, are any of them hurt?' "Not that I have seen no, they all looked fine except for coming across a little edgy and concerned." John knew that the man Kernow worked in quiet ways of some importance, so it was best and right to say nothing, keep quiet, and do as asked.

While John was in the cottage with Jeanne and Rebecca, the four men were sitting in the Blue Anchor around the table discussing things with the Constable of Helston. Kernow's personal guards were also there but standing in the shadows out of sight keeping an ever keen eye on the entry points of the Inn. Joshua, Bull and Tassell sat with their pistols on their laps, loaded and ready to fire. It had been a long night, but they were alive.

When all the drinkers had been kicked out of the Inn and the place secured, the Constable's men were then ordered to scour the streets for any unlikely characters. If any were to be found they were to be brought back to the Blue Anchor for questioning. So, keeping in pairs they set off but apart from seeing a few drunks and paupers, they found no one of any real significance. So, reporting back this information they were then told to stand guard outside. After three hours of doing this with again nothing to report, they were then all told to stand down and go home to their wives. That was around one thirty in the morning. It was now nearing the hour of five giving them another hour of darkness before the start of the new dawn.

Although the Constable of the town was a respected and good fellow, Kernow kept things simple and to the point without ever going into much detail on the why's and where's. The Constable understood the position this Kernow man and his fellow colleagues were in and so helped and cooperated as best he could. He had a certain respect for these four men as although his job was to openly protect and enforce the laws of the Parish their job was in the background, covert, with no rewards of open grandeur.

The Inn had now become spookily quiet but as the time ticked past the five thirty hour all ears pricked up as they heard the back door being unlocked.

As John Richards the Landlord walked into the bar area, George Kernow got up to meet him half way so he could he what he had to say out of earshot of the others. Richards explained to Kernow what had happened and that Jeanne and Rebecca had both agreed for them to come. George thanked him for his good work and said he would reward him at a later date. "Is there anything else you wish of me or can I now rest my body in bed?" "No, you have done well my good man, please go up and retire and tomorrow, sorry I mean later today, open the Inn as usual and please act as if nothing was amiss or untoward." As the Landlord turned away, George looked back at the table and saw all eyes were on him waiting for what was to come. George stood where he was and waved the Constable over to join him.

"It is time for us to part but I just wanted to say thank you to you and your men for getting here so quickly and doing a fine job." "Thank you Mr Kernow, is there anything else you wish? "No, all that needed to be done is done but I would ask one thing." "Please ask." "Everything you have seen and heard this night is not to pass your lips." "I understand and feel assured that this will be so." Then shaking hands and the Constable walking away to the back exit door, George walked back to the table and when sat down waved over his two loyal guards to join them.

"Well, it is time to move out, I suggest we leave all our things in our rooms and get away fast. Joshua and I will go first followed by Bull and Tassell. My two guards will watch as we cross the street just in case. Jeanne has left the back door unlocked so we can enter quickly without fault." George's loyal guards were told that they would be staying here in the Blue Anchor. But, once they had slept they would need to be over at the cottage in Lady Street, which was only a few minutes walk, as soon as darkness fell this very evening.

George then looked at Joshua who he had noticed had kept rather quiet since the time the Landlord had left the Inn just before five o clock. He knew Joshua was feeling a little edgy after agreeing in principle to Kernow's plan of them hiding at Jeanne's place, especially with his wife and two children being there. And so, with this in mind, Kernow asked, "Joshua, I know we may be putting your relatives under undue risk so please answer the truth, are you alright with us staying at Lady Street?" Bull and Tassell had also felt for Joshua as they too would feel unsure if it were their families.

"Thank you George, yes, I have thought it through and you are right, as at first, I was unsure but now feel it to be the right thing. Whoever did this to us last night is still out there somewhere so at the very least I will be with my family to protect them."

George thanked Joshua for his honesty and then turned his attention to Bull and Tassell. "Joshua has spoken the truth so let me assure you both that once darkness comes we will send messages to your wives of your safety and if needs be put guards on them for their security." Bull and Tassell were also feeling uneasy about their wife's safety and so replied, "Thank you George." "Right, now we have all that sorted, please check your pistols and let's move."

While Bull and Tassell remained in their seats, Joshua and Kernow went out the back door and crept along the side path to the front of the Inn. Then looking up and down the street many times and assured that no one was around they darted across. Once safely over they went through into the alley and then turned left down into

Lady Street. Then getting to the small horse walk at the back of the cottage they stopped and listened. They saw the candles inside the cottage were lit but decided to wait in silence and watch for a few more minutes. Once feeling all is well they ran quickly to the back door. As promised it was unlocked and so went straight in.

It wasn't long after, that Bull and Tassell did the same. The only difference being was when they got to the side of the Inn to look up and down the street, Bull pointed down to the two foot wide water gully flowing down each side of the street and whispered that he be careful when running across. Again, like Joshua and Kernow, they stopped at the back of the cottage to wait and watch and when feeling all was well went in.

Before either of the men had got to the cottage, Jeanne had stoked the fire to boil some water to make them tea. While doing this, Rebecca was busy finding things like pillows and blankets and anything else she could find for their rest.

Kernow had not seen Jeanne for many years as she was now early retired and out of his service but it felt good to see her looking well. "How are things Jeanne, how are you keeping?" "I am well thank you George, how are you." "Well, I was doing fine thank you Jeanne, until last night." "Yes, you mentioned what happened but I still can't understand why none of you didn't drink the ale." Kernow was just about to reply but stopped out of courtesy as Rebecca was just sitting down to join them. She heard her Mother's simple question and so looked at Kernow waiting for the answer. George looked at the other men and all nodded in approval to say things openly. ''Well Jeanne, as we lifted our tankards of ale to drink they all started to shake uncontrollably.'' Jeanne and Rebecca looked puzzled and so Rebecca said, ''What do you mean they shook?'' ''Exactly that Rebecca, we tried many times to drink them down but not one of us had the strength, and the beer was spilling out all over. Then each time we put the tankards down the shaking stopped. It was only after Joshua had smelt the contents that he noticed an unusual fruity aroma coming from the contents which simply didn't add up. Ale is ale, not a fruit, therefore could only mean that someone had put some substance in them. But then something or someone stopped us from drinking it, which sounds bizarre''

Rebecca and Jeanne didn't seem in the least bit fazed at what Kernow had just said and, without hesitation, looked at each other and held hands knowing with love that it was Zelahnor's doing. Then with the most lady like manner, Jeanne asked, ''More tea anyone.'' The men were waiting for some sort of rebuke or dismissal of what George had just explained so sat silent, looking bemused at Jeanne's simple calm acceptance. Joshua smiled at his loving wife Rebecca as he knew that she and her Mother believed.

Whilst the four men were drinking their tea, Jeanne got up and suggested that she and Rebecca leave them in peace to discuss things while they go upstairs to sleep and be with Richard and Vivienne. All four men put their cups down and stood up in courtesy of the women leaving the room. Kernow then spoke up, ''Jeanne, we would all like to thank you and Rebecca for doing this. And just so you know we should be gone from here, all going well, this very night." "That's fine George, we will see you all a little later when the day brightens."

With the women gone, Kernow turned his attention to the three men and said, "Right my good men I suggest we get the pillows and lie where we can but before we do this, we need to sort an hourly guard rota." The men knew this was wise but still didn't know what Kernow had in mind to do. So Joshua spoke up saying, "George before we rest, could you let us know your thoughts and intentions."

"I intend for us all to lay low, out of the way and wait until we have a clearer path on what best to do. I have already sent messages and tonight we all ride to Truro and stay, out of sight, at the Red Lion in Lemon Street. My men have their orders and will bring our gear and horses over from the Blue Anchor an hour after dark." "What, we are to do nothing but wait." "That is right Joshua, we wait in physical person but not in activity, that is for others in our defence of the realm to do, who will be directed by me, on our behalf." Kernow then looked at all three men and said, "We cannot rush this and it may take some time but we are alive and I intend for us to stay that way.

Chapter 9

The Abbot of Landerneau was sitting quietly alone in the library at the Chateau Morlaix reading the message once again. He had received this message marked urgent over a week ago but had done nothing. It read:-

My Dear Abbot,
In Loyalty to our Good King, terminate the life and dispose the Prisoner Jacques.
The Ferret

He closed his eyes and started to slowly rub the writing with his fingertips as if the words would speak to him. Who was he to take a person's life? What right had he to simply take the breath out of God's children? He had made mistakes before, that is true and plenty of them, but God had chosen to be merciful. He had even bedded women claiming it was his right as being some powerful member of the clergy. He started to laugh at his over inflated ego but then stopped, looked down and read the message again.

If he simply did what the message says then all will be well. He need only reach behind and pull the cord and then order the guard to do what he wanted, it was that simple. His loyalty would then be shown to be true and so would keep the running of the Chateau and the knowledge that its ownership could well pass to him if the Ferret's mission is a success. He would then be rich beyond all means. And so, he reached over his shoulder and pulled the cord.

Within a few minutes, one of the servants entered and the Abbot asked, "Please inform the guards to bring the prisoner Jacques to me." "Yes, your worship," Then, with a bow of the head, turned about and went out.

The Abbot waited in quiet thought and as he did he looked around the walls of the opulent library. He noted the many portraits of people of grandeur known of high status and all connected to the Chateau. One particular portrait caught his eye among all the others and that was of one Philip de Albret, Count of Morlaix. As he stared at this painting he could not help but feel a sense of self importance coming from it. As the silence ticked away the Abbot again closed his eyes to think. It was then that he heard a scratching sound coming from behind.

He turned his head and saw a small young sparrow inside the library trying, without success, to get out of the closed window. He watched it carefully and saw how again and again it tried to fly out and away. He smiled with inner warmth for the little creature and its determination not to give up. The Abbot went over to help and as he opened the window to give the young bird its freedom, he spoke to the little creature with a softness he hadn't felt for a long time. "There you go my little child." The sparrow quickly took the opportunity and flew out and away into the world with a newness of life. As the Abbot watched him fly, he felt a warm flow of goodness inside that he hadn't felt for many years. How wonderful.

It wasn't long after he sat back down that the knock on the door was heard and the door handle started to turn. Then one of the guards entered and said, "The prisoner is here." "Is he chained?" "Yes, he is, both ankles and wrists." "Then please bring him in and sit him in that chair opposite me." With that, the guard turned and motioned to his colleague, who was holding Jacques by the elbow, to come in.

Jacques had not seen daylight for over a month and looked ashen and weak. This was not the man the Abbot knew when he had first arrived at the Chateau many years ago. He remembered Jacques as a lean quick witted man who stood six feet tall, active in mind and body with piercing blue eyes. Now he saw an unshaven thin man with a look of despair that any hope of life was gone. For his protection, the Abbot asked the guards to chain Jacques to the chair and then when done please wait outside for further orders. So without further ado, the guards completed the task and after two or three minutes they were gone. Now the Abbot and Jacques were alone together in complete silence.

The Abbot was looking at Jacques waiting for some kind of acknowledgement but Jacques was just gazing out through the window as if spellbound. The Abbot picked up the written message from his lap and leaned over and placed it face up on the edge of the table close to where Jacques was sitting. Jacques didn't respond in any way to the Abbot's movements or the piece of paper put in front of him. So, the Abbot broke the silence by saying, "Jacques, Jacques, this message is for you." As Jacques bent his body forward to read the message the Abbot got up and pulled the cord. Jacques read the message in silence and then when done just looked up and stared again out of the window at the open fields and beyond.

The Abbot walked over and waited by the door and when the servant came in the Abbot stopped him and whispered in his ear. The servant looked a little bewildered but nodded and went back out to do as was told. The Abbot looked up to the ceiling in praise then went back to his seat.

The Abbot then, looking at Jacque's pitiful state, knew now that he had to be strong for Jacque's sake and so said in a snappy voice, "Jacques, wake up, wake up man." Jacques shook his head as if coming out of some kind of a trance and said, "I'm sorry your worship, what do you want of me?" "I want nothing of you but your attention, but first, did you read the message?" "Yes, I read it." "And what do you make of it." "As I said to the little man before, I want nothing to do with things anymore, you must do what you will." "Or what the Lords will?" Jacques didn't know what he meant by this and so looked puzzle eyed by what the Abbot had just said about the Lord's will. Then the door opened and in walked the servant with Cognac and a glass. Following behind him was one of the guards and, while the servant was putting things on the table, the guard got his keys and unchained Jacques. When both had finished they looked at the Abbot who simply said, "Thank you my good men, that is all, you may go."

After being in the lower dungeon, chained up with no natural light for the last month, Jacque's wrists, legs and body felt eerily free. He bent his head down and rubbed the palms of his grimy hands up and down his face as if washing away the deadness of his brain. The Abbot sat quietly and watched.

Jacques then looked up and with his eyes opened wide watched the Abbot fill the glass with cognac and when filled pushed the glass towards Jacques.

"Jacques, let me ask you if you were released, what would you do?" Jacques looked at the glass filled with cognac and after licking his lips said, "May I." "Yes, please do." Jacques picked up the glass, closed his eyes and drank the whole thing in one long delicious gulp. His then body burst into a heavy fit of coughing and spluttering. After the last splutter had come out of his lungs he managed to put the empty glass back down. The Abbot then calmly refilled it and while doing so repeated, "So what would you do Jacques?"

Jacques was feeling the cognac run through his whole body like a warming fire. Then with a calm thought replied, "I am not sure what I would do but I know what I would not do." "And what would you not do?" "I would not ever go back into the life of threat or fight for other people's gain." "And where would you go Jacques?" "Far away from here as I could." "You said you were not sure what you would do, so tell me in truth, what would you wish to do, and please Jacques, be honest to me." Jacques knew what he wished out of his life. He wanted peace and love and if that love was with Jeanne, he would be content forever. So, taking a large deep breath, he spoke the truth, "After five years apart, I would, if I could, find my true love and ask her to forgive me for what I have done and that we live together once again, forever."

The Abbot did not want to dwell on who his true love was, or the ins and outs of the romance, so simply asked,

"If I did give you your freedom of life, would you swear to me now, on Gods oath, that you will not hurt or harm any person from this moment on and live a good life of love and self control." Jacques looked at the Abbot with his icy blue eyes and said, "Before I do this, why are you asking me these questions of my freedom when the message from the Ferret states the complete opposite? Also, if you were to free me, that would put you in an extremely difficult position" "That you are most very probably right Jacques, so it would be good if we both say nothing of what we have discussed or agreed. Let's not also forget Jacques that you too will be in a difficult position so I would suggest you keep your head down and get well away." "May I ask why you are letting me go now, after so long of being a prisoner here." "It's a good question Jacques and I believe that having been in charge for so long we get complacent about our own divine power. It was when I received the message of your death to be done by my own hands that I felt the evil of unjust. So, I must do what is right through God's love." He didn't mention the little young sparrow he had just released which brought him much warmth.

Jacques now knew that the Abbot was being true and so said with genuine feeling, "Then I swear to you on God's love, that I will live as you ask of me." The Abbot smiled and raised his head saying, "Thank you Jacques, thank you Lord." The Abbot then continued, "I have worked things out and tonight at midnight I will come down to your dungeon and set you free without eyes or ears around. You will then be free to do as you see. A horse and saddle are being prepared as we talk and here are five guineas to help you on your way."

With that, the guard was asked to come in and put the chains back on Jacques and when done escort him back down into the dungeon. While the guard was on his knees shackling Jacques's ankles, Jacques looked at the Abbot and silently moved his lips saying, "Thank you." The Abbot smiled and replied in the same manner, "No, thank you."

Chapter 10

The Ferret and Joulie said their goodbyes to the maids and servants at Mingoose who had prepared the small gig and horse for their short ride to Scorrier. Troon was not there to see them off as he had other business to attend.

The Ferret, with Joulie by his side, then flicked the reins on the horse's back and they were off. The Ferret was in a buoyant mood but Joulie was not and sat stony faced as the small gig moved away at a gallop. It was five o'clock in the evening and the light was fading but they should reach the sister's cottage before darkness falls.

As Joulie sat quietly without word the Ferret began to sing a merry song of love. As both were looking around at the wide open countryside the Ferret stopped singing and turned to Joulie saying, "What a lovely country this Cornwall is, not as nice as France I know but never the less it is quite beautiful." Joulie didn't respond but simply moved her head aside away from the Ferret's sight. "Joulie, what is wrong, why don't you talk?" "I told you before, I don't like this new way of yours, it's irritating and dangerous." "O, you are just being silly now, come on let's enjoy the ride." With no response, the Ferret started to sing again seemingly without a care in the world but Joulie just took a deep breath and crossed her arms in front of her.

At the cottage, Sarah didn't know what to do. Fay and Janet had screamed on hearing the gun shots and quickly ran to each other in tears and comfort. Sarah did not do upfront confrontations so rarely, if ever, carried a normal pistol. But she did always keep a small lady pistol hidden in her belongings for emergency purposes and so ran up upstairs to fetch it.

Hastily rummaging through her things she found the small flintlock and whilst ramming the small ball and cartridge down its spout she was thinking quickly about what to do. 'Get away now was rushing through her mind, yes get away and do it now it kept telling her. But where was she to go? It doesn't matter, just get away. So she opened the window and looked down at the ground and grass area beyond. It was about a fifteen foot drop, which was doable, but she could break something if landed awkwardly. Her heart was racing so she quickly went over and got a blanket off the bed and tied it by the window frame. 'That's it,' she said to herself, 'scale down and get away, regroup and move on. But where should she go, she was in the middle of nowhere. It doesn't matter, get the horse and get away.'

While holding the blanket and looking down out of the bedroom window was when she heard the loud pleading voices of the two old ladies from downstairs. "Sarah, Sarah, where are you, please come quickly, Sarah, please come quickly." Sarah didn't care about others, this was her life, and her life was in danger so she kept quiet and carried on with her escape. She threw her bags out of the window and was just about to follow when the bedroom door banged open and the two old ladies stood there watching. They were shocked to see what Sarah was doing and pleaded for her to stop and help them. "Please Sarah, don't leave us on our own, one of the men in Peter's bedroom is groaning with pain and we don't know what to do."

Sarah came down off the window ledge and put her feet back on the bedroom floor. "Please Sarah, don't leave, all will be alright." "Well, that's all right for you to say isn't it, you're not in danger. Peter was my friend and colleague and he has been shot and killed by the Ferret's two men, it could be me next." "The Ferret is coming over here later, he will explain everything, we are sure." "Yes, I know he is, I heard them say so when they arrived, why do you think I am leaving now." Both sisters looked puzzled about how Sarah knew the Ferret was coming as they hadn't said anything. However, ignoring this, Fay said, "Sarah, we promise no harm will come to you, we will support you and say so to the Ferret, please help us."

Sarah stood still looking at the two sisters thinking about what to do. "You say one of the men is groaning, which one is it?" "We don't know Sarah, we are too scared to go in, it could well be Peter." Sarah shook her head in disbelief and knew she had to go back down the stairs. She would then have to face what is coming that is for sure but whatever that is, she would need to be ready as best she could. So with reluctance, she agreed to help but for reassurance, she moved her right hand and felt the small loaded pistol in the pocket of her dress.

The door to the ground bedroom was still slightly ajar being held open by the boot of the young Pierre. Sarah moved the boot aside and after pushing the door wide open went in. Fay and Janet stood behind at the door's entrance watching her. Sarah first noted the large blood stains splashed all over the bedroom walls and floor. She then went over to Peter and knelt down to check him but knew instantly that he was dead having two big gaping holes, one in his upper chest and one through his neck. His eyes were wide open and he lay still like a grave. She next went over to Andre and found that he was the same except having one large blooded hole through the right centre of his head. It was while being knelt down tending to Andre that she then heard a groan behind her coming from Pierre.

He was seriously injured with blood oozing out from a shot wound in his upper chest. He was unconscious, eyes shut and breathing badly. "Quickly Janet, go and get some bandages," Sarah said aloud, and then added, "And hot water too, and Fay, help me get Pierre into bed."

Sarah tended to Pierre as best she knew and through her efforts, he was still alive and breathing. However, even with her best efforts, it wasn't long after, that Pierre breathed his last. So with heavy hearts, all three women helped drag the dead bodies of Peter, Andre and Pierre over into the far corner of the bedroom floor and placed a clean bed sheet over each.

Throughout the sullen day, tea was made for all with Fay and Janet appreciating Sarah's actions of help and thanking her for it. Then around just after six that evening while Sarah and Janet were in the bedroom clearing things up, Fay heard the familiar sound of horse and gig coming up close to the cottage front.

As the sister's cottage got closer the Ferret saw the two young men's horses tied up outside and so smiled and said, "Well, Andre and Pierre are still here, that's good." Joulie was still in a non talking mood and so just pursed her lips with false smile. He stopped the gig next to the young men's horses and as they were both about to jump down, Fay ran out to them with a handkerchief in hand. "Good evening Fay, how are you and how is your sister Janet," the Ferret said jovially. "There's been an accident, O it's terrible," she replied sobbingly. "Calm down Fay," he replied, "What has happened?" As Fay began to recount what had happened the Ferret became much alarmed, jumped down and rushed by her.

Without thought or care, he ran into the cottage but noticed it was empty of people and so turned about and said to Fay, who had followed behind in tears, "Where is everyone?" "They are in the ground bedroom just there but please be careful." As Joulie then entered the cottage she saw the emotional trauma Fay was in and so went up and cuddled her in the reassurance of affection. The Ferret didn't care and again without thought rushed into the bedroom.

Just under a mile away up in the forest overlooking the cottage, Zareb watched. He had been there dug in for the last two days and had seen all that he needed including the two butterflies leaving the front door. So now he would silently wait without movement for the dark of the night to fall. Then, when the moon had risen and his inner feelings said it was time, he would move his huge body out of the forest and get back to the moor.

Chapter 11

Cuthbert Troon was no fool and would use the Ferret to achieve what he wanted. It had taken a couple of weeks but the small miner's cottage, for Sarah and Joulie to live in, was now vacant at Pennycomequick in an area called the Honeycombs, on the outskirts of St Allen. The once hard working husband of the small family that had lived there had died in a mining accident. But without his income, the wife and children could not afford the rent and so were simply turfed out and evicted as paupers.

For Troon, the position of the cottage was excellent as it was not too close to his Mingoose Estate and not too far away from the Mine at Wheal Peevor. It was the best of both worlds. Troon then sent word to the Ferret at the cottage in Scorrier. It read: -

Dear Ferret,
Cottage available, meet women this Friday to move in - 7 pm the Half Moon Inn, Zelah.
Cuthbert

Troon arrived at the quiet Half Moon Inn in Zelah at five that Friday afternoon. He had got there early as he had also arranged to meet his loyal steward called Stephen Bagnall. Stephen was the one doing all the running around and so Troon needed to get an update on how things are going. Both sitting relaxed, drinking Sherry, Troon asked if he had spoken to John Hughes, known quietly as Hughesy, a tough man and rebel bandit leader from Truro, whom you just didn't mess. "Yes, we talked for a short while and he left just over an hour ago. He said he is ready when you give the word." You didn't say too much?" "No, I did as you asked and kept it vague and simple telling him nothing more than you may wish to use his services shortly." "That's good." Stephen Bagnall then asked, "What time are the women to be here." "In about two hours which gives us good time to discuss things. Have you the keys to their cottage?" "Yes, I have them here." "How much does the owner want?" "He wanted more but we agreed on two guineas deposit paid in advance and a guinea every week thereafter, again paid in advance." Troon nodded his approval and delved into his purse.

Troon also asked if all was ready at the Wheal Peevor Mine and that the Pennycomequick owner knew the two women were not going to be working at the near St Allen Mine. Stephen replied, "Yes, all is ready at Peevor for the women to work and Yes, the owner has no problem as long as the weekly rent is paid. He has also left a small two person cart for one horse to pull in the cottage backyard. He suggested, that if the two are to work at Wheel Peevor and start at 5am then they should leave very early before sunrise as it would take them an hour at a steady trot." Troon was happy with this but then it wasn't him getting up.

Joulie and Sarah, had, at last, left the cottage at Scorrier earlier that afternoon riding freely on their own horses to the Half Moon at Zelah. It had been a long difficult two weeks since the shooting and the arrival of Joulie and the Ferret after leaving the Manor at Mingoose.

Although it had been exhausting and very trying for all, Sarah and Julie, with the help of Fay and Janet, had prepared for the task ahead by acting many times as Bal

Maidens. They had to fit in immediately it was as simple as that. So over the last week, they had practised the art of breaking up rocks and stones in the back garden with hammers supplied by the sisters. Their hands were now looking dirty and worn, unlike before being all clean and fresh. Their outfits too had been changed and both were wearing long dresses with tightly wrapped aprons made of hessian over the top called a 'towser.' On their heads, they wore a curious large hat which the low working class called a 'gook.' Sarah asked the sisters why, O why do we have to wear these outfits and why do people call them silly names like that? The sisters had no answer and just raised their eyebrows. But then Fay explained that it was to help them fit in and also protect their faces and shoulders from the rays of the sun and provide protection from flying debris. When Sarah and Joulie were fully clothed in their new work gear they then turned and faced each other and started to laugh.

It was after they had ridden a few miles away from the cottage that Sarah and Joulie decided to pull up and rest. Finding a nice spot under some trees they tethered the horses and sat down. Sarah untied her tight apron and pulled out a gin bottle. Taking a swig she then offered it to Joulie who took it willingly and did the same.

''Thank God we're away from that bloody cottage,'' Sarah said. ''Yes, I agree, it's been awful.'' ''I couldn't believe the Ferret's reaction, he always seemed to come across so calm and calculated.'' ''He was Sarah until he met that Andre.'' ''Well, whatever it was, I have never seen a man so broken. In fact, I thought we were going to have to bury him with the other three.'' Joulie was listening to Sarah but had her eyes closed and shaking her head from side to side in dismay, thinking about the Ferret and how he had nearly died from the grief of it all and his heartfelt loss. ''Sarah, can I ask why did you not run away after the shooting.'' ''I was going to, in fact, I was halfway out the bedroom window.'' ''So, what stopped you?'' ''It was Fay and Janet, they ran up the stairs to find me and pleaded with me to help them.'' ''But that would have not stopped you in the past of what I've been told.'' Sarah thoughtfully looked at Joulie before saying, ''You are right Joulie but it was the way Fay spoke, it sought of touched me inside.'' ''Sarah, are you alright, your sounding like a loving Mother.'' They both giggled at the thought as Sarah again passed Joulie the gin bottle. ''Well, I will be your Mother from tonight so behave yourself my girl.'' Again, both laughed at the thought.

After taking another little nip of the gin, Sarah asked, ''Tell me Joulie, what is this Troon man like?'' ''To me, he is just another wealthy man, full of ego and want.'' ''No, I mean is he handsome or ugly, married or what'' ''Well, I suppose you could call him attractive but I'm only twenty seven, I think he is about fifty or close to it. As for a wife, I saw no other woman about the place only maids in service.'' Sarah was in her late forties now and thought, hmmm. But then thought why on earth she was thinking like this? The two women carried on chatting for another twenty minutes as though they had caught the Fay and Janet bug. As the time pushed on, they both realised that they had better get a move on and get going. As they mounted, Sarah for some reason, thought back to the two butterflies that had passed close to her face by the front door just after the shooting.

It was as the light of day was starting to fade that the two women saw the Half Moon Inn at Zelah. With about a hundred yards to go, Sarah put her hand up and when Joulie saw this, both pulled the horses to a halt. Closing themselves together Sarah asked, ''Joulie, are you ready for this?'' ''Yes, I am, are you?'' ''Yes, I think so but I am a bit concerned if he starts asking questions about the Ferret.'' ''Well, let's stick to our plan and say nothing other than all is fine apart from him not feeling too well. After all, it is not us that is running the show, we are just two stupid females.'' With those last words spoken, both women flicked the reins of their horses and pushed on.

After getting to the Inn and tying up their horses in the stable yard, Sarah took the lead and walked boldly up to the rear door and entered. The Half Moon was a quiet Inn many miles away from the hustle and bustle of any town. It was mainly used for the miners when they had finished a long and hard shift, if they could afford to.

Both Troon and Bagnall, still sitting talking in a relaxed manner, like the other few drinkers in the Inn, looked up when they heard the back door open and saw the two women enter. Bagnall looked at Troon who nodded, and so got himself up and went over to meet them. After politely introducing himself he then asked them both if they would join him. Troon watched his man talk to the two women but when his eyes saw the one standing next to Joulie, he couldn't believe it and knew straight away it was bloody Sarah. 'All those years gone by and he meets her again in a shabby Miners Inn in the middle of bloody nowhere, and in Cornwall of all places.'

As the women got close to the table, Troon got up and said, "Good evening Joulie, hope all is well, please take a seat." He then turned his attention to Sarah. "And good evening to you, you must be Sarah?" Sarah looked at Troon in a polite manner and replied, "Yes, I am Sarah." "My name is Cuthbert Troon, please take a seat." Once they all were sitting comfortably, Troon asked what they would like to drink. In unison, both replied, "Gin." On hearing what they wanted, he glanced at his Steward. Bagnall understood and so got up and went to the bar. As he walked away, Troon asked Joulie if she didn't mind helping him. "Yes, of course, won't be long."

Now being alone together, Troon and Sarah looked at each other in silence before he said, "Sarah, you don't remember me, do you?" Sarah flicked her eyelids in confusion and then before she said anything she looked at him further in depth and then it dawned on her. "Ginge, is that you?" "Shhhh, Sarah, yes it's me." His real surname was Gingell but she had always called him Ginge. Troon looked across at the bar and seeing that Bagnall and Joulie were still there turned back to Sarah and said with a grin, "I thought you were lovely."

Sarah smiled and said, "What are you doing in Cornwall Ginge, you were always so loyal to your Devon roots?" "I could say the same to you Sarah with your Devon and jam on top roots" They both smiled with inner laughter before Troon said, "Seriously Sarah, how have you got mixed up with these Frenchies?" "It's a long story Ginge but let's just say I had no choice." Troon knew the game she played and so sort of understood. He again turned to look at the bar to see where Bagnall and Joulie were and noticed that both were now getting ready to walk back with drinks in hand. Sarah also saw them coming back so quickly said, "Ginge, I need to talk with you privately." "And I you Sarah." Troon knew the area where she and Joulie were to stay so quickly thought and said, "There are some woods at the top of your row of cottages where you will live, I will meet you there on Sunday night at nine" "Where is the cottage we are staying?" "It's called Pennycomequick in the area of the Honeycombs, two miles from here." With those last words said, Bagnall and Joulie arrived at the table and laid the drinks on the table before sitting themselves down to talk.

With drinks in hand, Troon quickly changed tact and said, "Right, now let's get down to business." He then went on to talk about the hows and when's of what he expected of the two women. As he talked, Sarah couldn't help but look at him and think back to the last five years of being held captive at the Chateau Morlaix in France. And then, against her wishes, being forced back into a mission in Cornwall and out of the blue meets her long ago lover on a simple Friday evening. How life turns in mysterious ways.

Back at the cottage, the sisters, Fay and Janet, were very worried for the Ferret. Now that Sarah and Joulie had gone it was down to them to sort things. Every morning since the deaths of the three men and just as the sun is about to rise, the Ferret goes outside and sits on top of the buried body of Andre. He sits there for hours and only comes in when Fay or Janet beg him to. He won't talk and barely eats anything. The only thing he does is drink a lot of gin.

He had forbidden them both to get him any outside help as being a stranger in the area, especially a French one, could trigger problems. Fay and Janet were thankful for this and so were doing their best to help him. They had asked him many times what is going on but his response is always the same, that he must keep a low profile until had news from Troon. The Ferret had also ordered both Sarah and Joulie to keep hush about the deaths of Andre and Pierre. Although a tragedy, if anyone asks anything about them they are to say that all is well and the Ferret is sorting things. The two young men were meant to be covertly guarding both women on their new venture at the Mine and at the cottage where they were to live. That would have been their job. The Ferret was very much in a dilemma and couldn't think quite right. His mind was in turmoil. He needed to replace both men, but if he sent message back to France asking for more manpower then suspicion and doubt could seep into his world. At the present time, and as agreed, Troon has the two women, albeit unguarded. He needed to think things through, so sat on the bed and sank a large one and thought about Andre.

When Troon finished the meeting at the Inn, Sarah and Joulie got on their horses and were then escorted to the miner's cottage at Pennycomequick by Stephen Bagnall. Troon had said his goodbyes at the Inn and gone back to his estate at Mingoose. The ride to the cottage didn't take long at all as it was only a couple of miles away. Once they arrived and dismounted, all three then walked to the front of the cottage. Bagnall had the key and so with Sarah and Joulie close behind, he unlocked the door and all went in.

It was a simple terrace cottage built of granite with two bedrooms upstairs and a basic open room downstairs to include an open fire with chimney. The water, toilet and scrub area were outside in the backyard. Stephen helped the women in with their bags and as it was getting late asked both if they were alright as he needed to get on. Both women said that all was well and so he said his farewells and would see them again soon. ''What a very nice man,'' Joulie said. ''He gets paid for being nice Joulie and anyway, he's married with kids.'' ''Sarah, you're so hard.'' ''Tell you what Joulie, I will sort out our things, why don't you get the fire going and we can then sit down and talk.''

It wasn't long after that a knocking on the front door was heard. As Sarah was upstairs still busy unpacking, it was left to Joulie to answer. As she unlocked and opened the door she saw a pretty woman standing there with an enclosed glass lighted candle in hand. Although it was late in the evening the woman asked politely, ''Would they like any help.'' Joulie thought how very kind and was just about to say something when her role as a mute kicked in. So for the first time in her life, she started to play the mute game with her hands and whilst doing so opened and closed her mouth with only groans coming out.

The woman looked at Joulie in a startled manner as she was not expecting to see a small young girl answer the door, especially one that couldn't talk. The woman didn't say anything only looking on in sympathy and kindness. Joulie put her hands together in prayer and mumbled while pointing upstairs. The woman nodded her understanding and so Joulie turned herself about and went to fetch Sarah.

After quietly explaining what had gone on at the front door, Sarah quickly went down to see the woman caller, leaving Joulie to finish off the unpacking.

"Yes, can I help you?" Sarah said with sincerity. "O no, it is I who have come to see if you would like any help, we live next door, number five." The Honeycombs was a terrace row of ten small cottages and Sarah and Joulie's cottage was number four. "That's very kind of you but I think we are alright at the minute." "Alright, well good luck and if you do need anything just ask, my name is Celia." "That's very kind of you Celia, and thank you." "Is your husband working at the St Allen Mine?" "No, I don't have a husband, I am a widow and we are simple Bal Maidens." "O, I'm sorry, so what Mine are you working.?" Sarah had to be careful here in not saying too much. "I'm not sure, we haven't been told yet, we just work the tin." "Hmmm, that's strange cos St Allen is a Lead mine." "As I said, I am not sure what or where we are going, is there anything else?" "Well, before I go, was that your daughter I spoke to before?" "Yes, but she is mute and cannot talk" "O, I didn't know that, God bless her." "Thank you, but if you don't mind we really do need to get on." "Yes, of course, but don't forget, just knock if you need anything." With the conversation finished and the woman gone, Sarah closed the door and went upstairs. "Who was it," asked Joulie. "It was the woman from next door being nosey and asking if we need any help. I said we are alright, and then she asked if you were my daughter." "What did you say?" "I said yes, you are my daughter but you are mute, so whatever you did, it convinced her which is a good start for Monday" "Right then Mum, you carry on up here and I will get on and get the fire going." Sarah chuckled at Joulie's childish act of response but then thought why was she feeling so at ease when she should be tense and alert? 'Smarten yourself up girl, don't get cocky.'

Chapter 12

After the hard work of both Miners and Bal Maidens, the cart at Wheel Peevor, hidden out sight, was now heavily laden with the smuggled Tin, It was now ready to leave the Mine and head directly for the Mine at Wheal Tye just south of the cliffs at Porthtowan. Although Tye was only a few miles away it would be a two hour slog. The driver of the two men up front with four horses to steer then whipped the reins for them to move on. Alongside the cart rode four men all fully armed. It was six o'clock Saturday evening and the sun was starting to set.

Over at Wheal Tye, the three men were getting things ready for the delivery. The Mine had many oil lanterns lit all around and so looked as if it was active albeit in some small way but in reality, it was disused and had been for many years. It had bored nothing and was ignored by the locals as a complete waste of space. But the man these three men reported to, called Jose, didn't see it that way and had gained the rights to work the Mine, under an alias two years ago in preparation for his Cousin Luisa. It was in the ideal location for what they wanted, should all go to plan.

As the clock passed the hour of eight the heavy cart loaded with the tin, arrived at the gate to the Tye mine. The four armed riders guarding the cart stayed on their horses but kept their distance, as ordered. The moon was now up and darkness was all about. Then, when all were ready one of the men inside the Mine opened the gate to allow the cart through but not the arm guards, they were to stay outside. Once the cart was in and stationary with the brake on, two of the inside men, with their lamps a glow, jumped onto the cart and threw back the cover to check the cargo. The two upfront cart riders didn't move and stayed on the seat without word. Although this felt like a strange practice, it was just the way it was and the two cart men accepted it due to the rich cargo that was aboard. The three men had an important job to do, this they understood, and if anything went wrong in them taking over the cargo, their heads could be chopped off. So silence it would be. When the two men were happy with what they had seen, they threw the cover back over and jumped down. Putting their thumbs up, the two cart riders jumped down and went straight over to a similar cart, without load, again pulled by four horses. They quickly jumped aboard and with reins in hand released the brake and rolled out the way they had come in. The four armed guards on their horses who were waiting outside then followed.

Once the empty cart and their guards were away out of sight the three men inside the Mine shook hands with each other and laughed aloud with a sense of victory. Then with a faint Spanish lilt, one of the men laughingly said aloud, "Bloody stupid Cornish."

The four riders and the empty cart eased themselves up by a small dense copse two miles away from Wheal Tye. When all were hustled together and quiet, two men jumped down off their horses and with shovels in hands, walked quickly into the woods. After a few minutes of waiting, they came back out full of smiles and laughter each with a heavy sack on their shoulders. "What do you think lads," said Fin, the leader of the team. "I think we should all get back to the Plume at Redruth as fast as we can and get drunk," said one of the men. They all laughed aloud with careless joy. "How much do we get," said another man. Fin stopped his chuckling and replied, "Well, with forty pounds weight of fine ground tin in each sack, I would say Hughesy would give us a good twenty guineas cash which, after taking the costs out and my cut, would a leave a good two guineas for each man." With a happy roar of approval from all, they galloped off to the Inn with the two men on the empty cart trying to keep up with them

The Wheal Tye Mine lay extremely close to the cliff edge with full view out to sea. Its position was directly above a small rugged cove, exactly what the owner wanted. And so, it was now the job of the three men to get the cart with the loaded Tin into position. There was no rush as they weren't expecting the signal until the midnight hour.

The two Cornish Luggers with drop down frontal ramps and two sails apiece were anchored and waiting quietly a few miles south of Wheal Tye. They were in a small cove known as Sally's Bottom which always made the sailors giggle. They had set sail from the coastal town of Portishead some twenty four hours ago while the stars were up and darkness was all about. Each lugger carried four men and two strong mules. They were a gang of pirates which was not unusual in Cornwall, but these men were not Cornish. They all lived in the bustling port of Portishead and their paymaster was a foreigner but this didn't bother them in the least. Money was money and they will be paid extremely well this night. They had now done this mission many times over the last two and half years and each time, apart from the first few, had been a success. At first, they couldn't quite work it out but after many tweaks and turns using different boats and gear, they got it.

It was now nearing the hour before midnight and both Luggers and crew were, like the three men at Wheal Tye, ready and waiting for the Galleon to send signal. Once seen and replied they will weigh anchor and sail to the cove at Wheal Tye. So, they now all waited and watched for the ship to appear which, as planned, would be sailing from the South West up the Celtic Sea

Chapter 13

For ten days now Kernow and the three others had been in lockdown at the Red Lion in Truro. Joshua and Bull had remained in their twin room bored stiff but alert and pistols always at the ready. Tassell and George Kernow shared the adjoining room next door. Armed guards had been placed all around with information from his scouts coming backwards and forward every day.

Ten days and Kernow had found nothing to link anyone to the poisoning back at the Blue Anchor. Since that very day, all his people had been on red alert with messages sent to every port and town but again nothing. The only positive thing he did have was the report back from the alchemists in London. They had found that the ale in the tankards had indeed contained the Belladonna poison called locally as Deadly Nightshade.

All four men had discussed things every day trying to pinpoint who and what could be responsible. Kernow had even asked all three to think back out of the box for anything they felt untoward or suspicious. Joshua and Bull always came up with a negative as everything had been calm these last years. It was only Tassell who said that he had a feeling of unease leaving his covert cottage in Brest and on his sail to England but that's all it was, a feeling of being watched.

Kernow had made a decision when they had first moved into Truro that if after ten days nothing was found then they must get on with their lives. As naive or dangerous as it may seem, he couldn't do anything else, what else could he do? They had their work to do in protecting the

Cornish people and couldn't be just shut out. And so, in keeping with this decision, tonight they will get merry for the first time in nearly two weeks and enjoy song and laughter.

At seven that evening Kernow knocked on the adjoining door to Joshua and Bull's bedroom. Knowing it was time, Joshua opened the door and said, "Ready when you are George." "Good, then let's all go downstairs." With guards placed all around all four men strode down the stairs with a sense of freedom. Entering the bar area, they all smiled with relief as they felt the familiarity of men drinking and laughing. So, after finding a table in the corner and with full ale tankards in their hands they drank merrily.

"So we are all to get back to normal tomorrow," Bull asked. "That's right Bull, all has been arranged. The guards at all your homes have been informed, and are expecting your presence tomorrow and in Tassel's case, the day after. Two armed guards will escort each of you home from here and leave once arrived." "What about Jeanne," Joshua asked. "Guards will stay at her cottage in Helston until such time as we reduce the alert status." The three men didn't ask how long that would be as they knew it was a silly question. Kernow then waived his empty tankard at the roving barmaid who then came across to refill all. As she did the musicians started to play their instruments and everyone in the Inn cheered.

It was going to be a long night and so before they all got too drunk, Tassel asked George about Henry Hosking's situation. "As you all know I am going back to London tomorrow and aim to stop off on the way at Bodmin to visit him. I can't really say any more than that until I have spoken with him but I don't think things have changed other than his lucky stay of execution due to our problems at the Blue Anchor." Although Henry Hosking had betrayed them and Country, all four men fell silent.

The night carried on in good spirit and banter between all four men but time went all too quick. Even Kernow, who had to be seen as the intelligent and logical one, mixed in and let his hair down. Then before they knew it the landlord called time. So, after singing in with the last song and sinking back their ale, they all twaddled off to bed. The guards shook their heads with a quiet smile knowing they would have probably done the same.

After a good night's sleep, the men woke with heavy heads. However, as ordered by Kernow they were up on time and getting their things ready. They had to be ready to ride with rooms vacant and be in the bar area for breakfast and tea on the stroke of eight thirty.

Then, just before Kernow was about to go down to the breakfast meeting a guard knocked on the door. It was a rider with message from the Bedruthan and Mevagissey teams. Normally, riders of message would report direct to Joshua but since Kernow was now involved, he would take charge. After handing the message into Kernow's hands, George thanked him and suggested he go and get something to eat and rest up a while.

The message read: -

GK,
Nothing seen or heard – all quiet both North & South.
Signed by – LB & LM

On reading the message George smiled and would now ask the rider to send message back to both teams saying their alert status be reduced to amber. The message from the rider was just what George was waiting for as it eased his mind on giving the all clear for all to go home. Now that he had it, things could move on, but the thought of who carried out the poisoning at the Blue Anchor would not leave his mind.

During a somewhat delicate breakfast due to all four men having heavy heads, Kernow informed them of the message received and confirmed the alert status stand down. Joshua, Bull and Tassel raised their tea in salute.

With the breakfast meeting over, Joshua went outside to have a last minute puff of his pipe. It wasn't long before Bull joined him and both were now standing by their horses in readiness to ride away back to their homes. A few minutes later George and Tassel came out and got themselves into the small gig pulled by two horses. All four men were ready for the off but were now just waiting for their armed escorts who were by the side of the Inn having a last minute discussion.

"Thanks for your company Joshua, it's been, shall we say, interesting." "And you Bull, say hello to the missus for me." "Will do, and say hello to Rebecca from me too." Joshua then saw the armed escorts start to ride over and so shook Bull's hand and said with firm emotion, "Were still alive Bull so let's make the most of it and give my thanks to your good men at St Just." With that, both men saddled up and rode off at pace to their wives and warm homes at Zennen and Gunwalloe with their armed guards close behind.

It was late that afternoon when Joshua arrived at his cottage in Gunwalloe. On hearing the gallop of horse's hooves, Rebecca took the pot off the fire and looked out of the window. Seeing it was Joshua, she quickly ran out to greet him followed by little Richard and Vivienne. The armed guards didn't know what to do at seeing this softness of love so just smiled and looked at each other with embarrassment. The two guards inside the cottage then came out and talked with the ones on the horses. Once Joshua, Rebecca and the children had finished their cuddles, Joshua asked the two armed escorts to come in and have some tea and rest a while before they go back to Truro.

While Joshua walked into the cottage holding Rebecca's arm, she leaned over and whispered into his ear, "You need a bath Joshua."

Chapter 14

Sarah was in two minds whether to tell Joulie or not. The time was nearing eight thirty Sunday evening and so she had to make her mind up now or never. They were both sitting in the front room by the warmth of the fire in the cottage at Pennycomequick. Sarah was fully dressed except for her hat and coat but Joulie just had her scruffy indoor rags on.

"Are you alright Sarah, you're very quiet." "O I'm fine Joulie, just thinking about tomorrow, that's all. Both had to be up before the dawn and ride to the Wheal Peevor Mine to start their operation. "What are you thinking about?" Sarah never thought about others when she was in her covert frame of mind. It was her life and if things went wrong she was the one who would be killed. But, whether it was the Peter thing back at the two sister's cottage or the past problems with the likes of the Sniper or Zoe, her thought pattern was softening. But then maybe, it could just be her getting older and wiser. This she inwardly giggled at. Sarah then got up and said, "I think I need to go for a walk," and headed to the front door. "Would you like me to come with you Sarah?" "No thank you Joulie, I just need to clear my head with some fresh air. "Don't be long Sarah, we are up very early tomorrow." "I know, I won't be long." Sarah had decided not to tell her.

Sarah walked out of the front garden and carried on to the end of the terrace where she saw the forest up to her right. She thought about taking the horse but it was only a ten to fifteen minute walk so with a deep breath she got on with it. Richard Gingell, now known locally as Cuthbert Troon was already in the forest waiting for her. He was tucked up just inside the forest out of view but was watching the cottages below. When he saw Sarah come round the end of the terrace below, he smiled.

As she neared the forest edge Cuthbert gently shouted, "Sarah." She quickly stopped and after looking about saw him just off to her left. She was feeling edgy and had tried to work out what things she should or could say, or not say. Should she reveal all or should she just remain impassive as she had always done? She decided to play it by ear and see how things go.

Cuthbert also felt the same. He had got to his position of wealth through devious ways and dishonesty. Yes, he was rich but at what cost? Ducking and diving and mischievous dealings had been his way for nearly two decades but, was he happy? Outside he looked happy and most people were envious of his position and status of wealth but was he really happy inside? He thought he was until he heard of Sarah being in the Ferrets team and then seeing her in the flesh back at the Inn was like a belated kick in his heart.

As they stood facing each other it was Cuthbert who put out his hands. Sarah put her hands around his hands and she did so, Cuthbert pulled her close and kissed her cheek.

With the ice broken they both relaxed and sat down and talked. Sarah's mind went back to the last time she had met a man in the woods in Falmouth. That was over five years ago with the Snipe and the energy and mood were so different then. She chuckled at the thought. However, she now felt a sense of warmth and ease, something that had been so unnatural for her to feel most of her life.

They talked about the old times together so many, many years ago and chuckled at some of the things they had got up to. They were very young then and full of vigour and youth. How time flies. Now they were in their fifties with carefree zest replaced with more careful practices. How drab that sounded. But one thing they did have was a smile on their faces towards each other.

As they chatted and laughed for over an hour the point came as to why Sarah had got into the position of being part of the Ferrets team. Sarah went a little quiet and thought about what she should say or not say. It was then Cuthbert who said, "Sarah, by some strange fate of coincidence we have been brought together, let us not keep things hid away." Sarah thought on these words and replied, "Cuthbert, it is not easy for me to do this as opening one's heart and thoughts brings pain." "That may be so Sarah, I too know these feelings but I feel we must be truthful with each other."

Sarah looked at Cuthbert more closely and said, "Before I say anything about how and why I am here, please give me some time to let me think on things and I promise when we next meet I will tell you all. It is also getting very late and I must get back." "Why can't you tell me now, is there something I should know? "The answer to that is yes and no but I feel I must first talk with Joulie before I reveal anything."

The atmosphere then went a little quiet before Cuthbert said, "Sarah if I would have known it was you being one of the Bal Maidens to get the information from the Mine I would not have approved things.." "O Cuthbert don't go all soppy on me now." Cuthbert laughed at her quick defence mechanism of wit but replied, "Sarah, I'm not being soppy, I am being truthful, it could be dangerous." "Well, I have been in a lot more dangerous places than this so I am sure all will be well, anyway, its only inside information you want."

Cuthbert felt he should stop the operation or at the very least replace Sarah and Joulie with two other women to do the job. So he asked, "Sarah, would you like me to get some other people to replace you and Joulie." "Not at this moment Cuthbert, Joulie and I have worked hard to get this far and are all ready for tomorrow." "Then you promise me you will be careful and if you feel anything untoward you will both leave the Mine immediately and come to me at my home in Mingoose" "Yes I promise Cuthbert and thank you."

They then both got up and once again held each other's hands and then kissed cheeks but this time with more inner warmth. "By the way Sarah, a Knocker man has been ordered to awaken your number four cottage at three o clock in the morning." "A Knocker man at our cottage?" "Yes, all the mining families around here use them for their early wakening." "I didn't know that, we have been trying to use those stupid nail candles." "I understand that but you don't have to now." "I will tell Joulie as she was getting a little over worried, now I had better be off." "Sarah, can we meet again here next

Saturday but a little earlier say seven thirty." "Yes, of course, it would give me and Joulie time to talk."

As Sarah walked slowly back down to the cottage with the clear night sky above, she went into deep thought. All her life she had gone from man to man and lived a life of dare from one day to the next. She thought about what Cuthbert had said about her not needing to do this thing at the Mine. All her money had been taken from her and now she had a chance to get away and lead a life with safety and security. But is this what she wanted? She had worked Falmouth and the surrounding area many times over the years and could be recognised as a traitor at any time. With Ginge's help she could go back to her beloved Devon and be free. But could she trust Ginge, or in fact, could she trust herself?

"Sarah, where have you been I was getting worried." "Sorry Joulie, I got caught up in my own thoughts and sat silently at the edge of the forest." "Well, that's just great Sarah, thanks for telling me." Sarah liked Joulie a lot and had warm feelings for her and so smiled at her sharp response of telling her off. Sarah also decided not to tell Joulie about who she had met in the forest. It was too late in the evening and both were tired. She would sleep on it and probably do it tomorrow as they rode to the Mine. "By the way Joulie, I bumped into Celia next door and she asked are we up early tomorrow. I said we were and so she has organised a knocker man to wake us up at three o clock." "Whatever," Joulie replied in a strop and then went up the stairs with heavy feet. After hanging up her hat and coat and taking the candle in hand, Sarah too went up to her bed.

As the tired women went off to sleep it was all too quick when Sarah heard the noise of the window being hit by something or other. It was The Knocker man from No 1 outside her cottage with his pea shooter blowing peas at the window. He would keep on going until such time as someone inside showed themselves. It was his job and the Mines depended on his ability to get the people up on time and ready for work. Sarah wearily got out of bed and went over to the window. Seeing the man with the pea shooter in his mouth and oil lamp in hand she opened the window and waved. The man then simply raised his hand and walked off.

Sitting back down on the bed, Sarah held her head in her hands and just wanted to fall asleep again. But that just wasn't possible as she had to get up and get moving. The first thing she needed to do was wake Joulie.

This first early morning proved most chaotic as all had to be done in haste. The horse and cart needed to be prepared, the fire needed sorting and their clothes had to be right. They also needed to make some tea and have something to eat. It just seemed to take ages with both women passing each other many times going backwards and forwards and passing each other up and down the stairs. But, after all was done, they both stood together facing each other at the back door.

After checking each other's clothing and making sure all was right, Sarah said, "Are you ready Joulie." "Yes, I am ready, do you have the food bag." "Yes, I have and some water too." With that, both women went out and got into the cart. Once settled, Sarah flicked the reins and jerked the horse forward. It was just passed the fourth hour of the morning and they were off.

Once they got out of the darkened lane up onto the main drag, Sarah then steadied the horse into a slow trot. The early morning was peaceful and quiet and both women let the dawn of the day drift in. Sarah had thought about this moment and knew inside that it was the right time. And so for the first time in her life, she truthfully told Joulie all that had gone on with Cuthbert Troon. Joulie listened and was just dumbstruck at what Sarah had revealed. "So why are we doing this Sarah when Troon has said we don't have to." "I don't know Joulie, I don't know, but something inside me just said get on with it. I have to be careful Joulie. In all my life I have never trusted anyone and you are really the first person to who I have opened up. I think being locked up at the Morlaix Chateau for five years has affected me." "Did you tell him what happened at the old sister's cottage and the Ferrets state of mind." "No, I didn't."

Joulie understood Sarah's way of inner thinking as she herself, who had been plucked out of the gutter and worked this covert way since she was twelve, knew you just kept things to yourself. You just got on with it and if a mistake was made you would be killed. Inner silence and showing no emotion of truth was the way. "And you say you are to meet him again next Saturday." "Yes, that's what he asked, not me, and I agreed."

It was now Joulie's time to stop and think. If they didn't go to the Mine as expected then people of unknown would get suspicious. That means they would be hunted to find out what is going on. If they did go, then they would have time to talk and consider their options. With the Ferret in a state of hopeless confusion, her options were limited. She had no one back in France and although pretty she wasn't exactly a normal looking woman being only four feet and a few inches tall. But she had a brain and would use it as best she could. Sarah is right, they needed to do the work at the Mine to keep things running and talk together on what best to do.

.

Chapter 15

Just past the midnight hour, the middle weight ship of two masts was sailing with good wind northeast up the Celtic Sea. The wind and the darkened night had been kind and they had made good progress. This would be their second covert pick up of the night and so were already laden with a good amount of smuggled tin. The first pick up had been three hours ago from a cove south of St Just. All had gone smoothly and so the captain was happy and would be paid handsomely.

As they approached their agreed position, the Captain gave orders to slow the ship down and for the coded signal to be sent. Standing close by with lamp in hand the midshipman did as ordered. Although two miles out at sea the directional lighted lantern would be seen from the shore, if you were alert and watching. The lantern code was to be three long bursts of light followed by two short ones. Once the code was given the lantern was put out and put away.

The observer for the two luggers lying in the cove at Sally's Bottom saw it and replied as agreed by mirroring the code. The leader of the two lugger crews then looked about and with his thumb raised, they set sail. The three men lying low at the top of the cliff edge at the Tye Mine also saw the coded sign and replied as ordered. It was time to get up and get moving.

The Captain of the ship saw both replies as correct and so ordered sails to be lowered. When done, ropes with weights were then thrown overboard to steady the ship without anchor. The Captain then went into his cabin for a rest. He had at least two hours to wait before he raised the sails again to move to the position due east of Wheal Tye.

The two luggers drew out of the cove and sailed around the eastern cliff edge of Wheal Tye. When they were in line with the small shingle cove they steered starboard. Then letting the tide and surf help their movement they moved closer into the dark cove. As the lugger's bottoms scraped the shingle the boats started to shudder to a natural halt. As soon as both boats were still the front ramps were released down with force. Then quick as a flash two men with ropes and weights jumped forward onto the shale to steady the luggers into position as best they could.

When both luggers were steady, two men on each lugger with a mule in hand walked off the boats and up the shingles to bottom of the cliff where the rocks protruded.

While all this was going on, two of the three men above the cliff at the Mine were now getting the loaded cart of Tin into position under the winch. The other man stayed by the cliff edge. When he saw both the lugger teams below and his two men were ready and in position, he waved his hands above his head. The leader of the luggers teams below saw this and so waved back.

Then one of the two men above at Wheal Tye heaved back the cover to the secret shaft. Once fully opened, he then unlocked the rear flap of the cart and attached the front to the winch above. He then got hold of the gear handle and started winding. As the uplift started, the force of gravity came into being and the tin ore poured out down the shaft.

The secret shaft was excellent. It had been dug two years ago and was direct without bend or fault and near vertical to the cove below. The two lugger men down on the beach below heard the crushing of the ore streaming down from inside the cliff face and waited for the sound to be still.

When all was silent, the two men, with the mules by their side, then removed the large rocks covering the exit hole of the shaft. As they did, they saw the tin gush out. It was now time to get to work. So with large shovels and sacks at the ready, they spat on their hands and started. There was a lot of tin and without stop would take a good two to three hours to complete. They were strong men and their method was good as every time each of the two mules was loaded with four forty pound sacks, the two men stopped their shovelling and took them down onto the luggers. As they did so the two men and mules from the other lugger took their place. And so the hard graft went on and on until every ounce of tin had been taken from the shaft. When all the loading was done and everything cleaned up, the heavy rocks were put back in place to seal and hide the shaft.

With the lugger's front ramps now back up and secured, it was time to head out to sea. So with the ropes untied and the help of the sea tide the luggers ever so slowly drifted away from the shingle and moved out from the shore. It was time to send the signal to the waiting ship. Their signal was acknowledged correctly and so direct sail to unload the Tin was on.

All the men of the two Luggers were exhausted but with large flagons of cider in each of their hands were happy and cheering at their success. Their onshore job was complete and they were in fine spirits. They could now sit back and relax and once the cargo had been winched aboard the waiting Ship they would turn sail and head back to their home port of Portishead. The time was just past three thirty and darkness was still all around.

After seeing the Luggers signal, the Captain aboard the ship ordered his crew to get the winches in position in readiness for their arrival. Once the cargo was safe on board he would raise full sail and without stop head East by North East without stop to the port of Bristol.

Chapter 16

It was now early Saturday evening and the week at the Mine had been hard graft for both women but Joulie had played her part well as the mute daughter. When both arrived at the Mine at the said time early last Monday morning they were stopped at the gate and asked what their names are and who their governor was. Sarah had been warned this will happen and so politely said, ''Mr Stephen Bagnall.'' The guard checked his roster and when he saw their names matching the Bagnall name he ticked them off with his pencil. He then looked up and pointing his finger said without any emotion, ''That is correct, go straight to the hammer and silt section over there by the large building and report to Mrs Brooks.''

And so all week they had toiled like every other woman and child they were with. Sarah had never worked liked this in her life and found the whole thing brutal. Joulie, even though she had lived and worked on the streets in Paris in her youth was also shaken by the harshness of it all. Even acting the mute and being small in size didn't stop the reality of having to work hard like everyone else. Mrs Brooks seemed a nice person but she too had a job to do and so kept everyone going all through the day. When they first reported to Mrs Brooks the first thing she asked was if Sarah and her mute daughter had done this work before. Sarah confirmed that they had but as soon as she said this Mrs Brooks asked, ''And at what Mine was that?'' Sarah quickly realised she had to be careful here and so went straight into her sheepish act of being a simple scrag end woman with no money and replied, ''I'm sorry Mrs Brooks, I don't know the names, we were just sent to places we were told. Mrs Brooks was not at all surprised by this meek answer and so accepted Sarah's response. It had been a tough week.

So, as it was nearing seven fifteen, Sarah, once again, left Joulie on her own in the cottage as she went out to the forest, as planned. As expected, Troon was there waiting and so both were now lying together on the blanket looking up at the stars. "Ginge, I'm scared, I've always done things on my own and trusted no man." "Sarah, I too have done the same all my life but this is different." As the still of time ticked away, Troon turned his face to Sarah's and kissed her gently on the lips. She responded by saying, "Let's do it again Ginge." Troon smiled and said, "I don't know if I can do it twice in one night." "Yes you can silly, here, I will help you." Both started to giggle at their silly light heartedness of what they were doing. Sarah then moved her body closer into Ginge.

It was now nearing eleven thirty and Sarah had told Troon everything. She and Joulie had discussed things all week and decided they had nothing to lose. Both knew they couldn't carry on doing the painful work of undercover Bal Maidens anymore, it was just too hard. Also, the low position they were working in had not produced any real useful information. Yes, the hard working Maidens talked and chin wagged all day but it was all social stuff with no one daring to mention the Mine or its workings. They were all low life women and children on the poverty ladder and needed every penny they could get to stay alive. So Joulie agreed that Sarah should open up and tell all to Cuthbert Troon and see where things go.

After separating their bodies again, Sarah said, "See, you can do it Ginge." "Sarah, I have missed you so much." "You say that to all the girls Ginge," she replied jovially. However, in reality, she was enjoying this moment of fun with her long ago partner. She somehow felt young again with that innocence of what youthful love brings. Troon also felt a happiness inside that he hadn't felt for years. All his life he had worked for money and power, and for what. They cuddled up closer and without word let the beautiful world go by.

Troon couldn't quite believe that he was lying next to his young love in a dense wood in the middle of Cornwall. How life turns. Sarah, quietly looking up at the night sky and considering her own life of fight and captivity also felt something wonderful inside.

After a few more minutes of quiet thought, Troon sat up and with his arms around his knees said, "I've put my Mine up for sale." "You done what?" "I've put my Tin Mine at St Agnes up for sale. When we met in these woods last week, I thought and thought about what exactly am I doing with my life and decided to change things. Also, when I met that weird Ferret man nearly a month ago I have felt nothing but unease." "What are you thinking Ginge?" "I don't quite know exactly but now you have told me about what happened at the two sister's place in Scorrier it's all starting to fit. "So what are you going to do?" "Sarah, would you like to come away with me and start a new life?" "What about Joulie, and what about the operation you agreed with the Ferret and all the money you are to get for the Frenchies?" "There is something not right Sarah, I can feel it. It's all getting too close and very unhealthy. I'm no angel but am used to working the paperwork side of things and underhand finance not get involved with stealth and murder." "So why did you agree to see the Ferret and get involved in the first place." Shaking his head slowly from side to side he said, "I don't know, maybe I was bored, maybe it was ego, I just don't know. But what I do know now is that I would like to share my life with you in safety and without fear, somewhere away from here." "And what will you do with the Manor?" "I will sell all."

Sarah, who was still lying down and looking up at the stars, thought quietly about what Troon had asked and about all the men she had had and how strong and forthright they were. She even thought about the Abbot back at the Chateau in Morlaix and how she had been used for so many years. Now she was with a middle aged paperwork man of ill repute but gentle in thought and manner next to her. Then with her mind made up, she too sat up next to Ginge and put her arms around her knees. She then said, "Ginge, I also would like to share my life with you but my life has been so erratic and isolated I may need time to get used to things." "And me Sarah, and me."

The air between them was gentle and nice but Sarah realised he hadn't answered her questions so once again asked, "So what of Joulie and our work at the Mine, and what are you going to do about the Ferret." "Sarah, what do you think I should do?" "Well, knowing what these people are like after working and living with them, I would ask Joulie to come with us and you get us both away. As for the Ferret, that one is dangerous so will leave that in your hands, but be careful Ginge." Troon considered in silence what Sarah had just advised and while keeping his head still and forward moved his hand across and clutched Sarah's hand tightly.

"Ginge, would you like a drink?" "Have you got any left?" With that, Sarah pulled out the gin bottle and both took a guzzle and started to laugh. "Right Sarah, I think it's time I escorted you back to your cottage." "Ginge, I do know my way home." "I know you do but I would like to see Joulie before I leave for Mingoose." "It's very late, I don't know if she will be up." "Well, shall we take the chance as I would like to ask her some questions on what she wants and about the Ferret, do you mind?" Sarah felt that Ginge just needed some reassurance on these issues and so accepted his offer to take her home. So with both in agreement, they got up and with blanket and their other things in their hands walked towards Ginge's horse. The time was now way past midnight.

On reaching the side of the terrace row Sarah and Troon dismounted and tied the horse. Keeping things very quiet they then walked together to number four. Sarah opened the door and walked in first quickly followed by Troon. Joulie was asleep on the couch but came awake on hearing the door open. The single candle was still alight as was the fire.

When Joulie saw Cuthbert Troon standing next to Sarah, she looked bemused and so quickly looked at Sarah for guidance. "It's alright Joulie, Mr Troon has brought me back and just wants to ask you a few of questions. Why don't you go and freshen up and I will put the water on for some tea." Joulie, without word, got up and did as asked.

Sarah then put the water pot over the fire and suggested to Ginge that he take a seat. She then walked up to him and after quickly touching his hand said, "I won't be a minute," and went out to the wash area to see Joulie.

"Sarah, what are you doing bringing that man bloody back here?" Sarah quickly went over all that was said between her and Troon, as they had agreed before she left. "So, does that mean we don't have to work the Mine anymore?" "That is right Joulie, it's up to us now what we do." As I said before Sarah, I am an orphan from the streets of Paris, with nothing." "I too have nothing Joulie but we can't stay here, it's just too dangerous." "Will he treat us well?" "I am sure he will Joulie."

When all three were back by the fire and with tea in hand, Troon asked Joulie what she wanted to do. Joulie explained her past life and situation and affirmed that she would like to stay with Sarah wherever she goes. Troon looked at Joulie whilst she was talking and still couldn't quite believe she was twenty seven years of age as she was so small and young looking. With her last words spoken, Troon turned and looked at Sarah and said, "And where would you like to go." "Sarah smiled and said, "How about we go back to Devon our County of birth, somewhere like Exeter would be nice or even by the sea." Troon smiled back and said, "Why not."

Troon then turned his attention back to Joulie and asked, "I now also understand that you have certain feelings towards the Ferret, could you explain as I am a little lost on what to do." Joulie, without hesitation, explained all and how the Ferret had got her off the streets. She also explained how she and the Ferret had worked together for more than ten years. Troon listened carefully to what Joulie was saying as he had to sort this Ferret man out somehow, or did he? It was then that Sarah interrupted and said, "Joulie, what Mr Troon is trying to say is, what should be done with the Ferret?" "I say you get him out of Cornwall and put him on a ship back to France, where he will be safe." Joulie knew the Ferret had contacts and money all over France and so if this could be done he would stand a good chance. It's the least she could do for someone who picked her up off the streets all those years ago. What goes around?

Troon sipped his tea and considered quietly what Joulie had suggested. Going back to Devon felt good, far away from the strife and the dark feeling of oncoming trouble. He really didn't have to do anything about the Ferret but it was all too close and with the shootings and killings just too much could be linked to him. Yes, if he could get the Ferret away out of Cornwall to France that would be good for all.

"Right Joulie, I will get things sorted and do as you asked, are there any other questions you have of me?" "What do we do now?" Again, glancing at Sarah said, "I will ask my steward Bagnall to come here tomorrow and escort you both to my manor at Mingoose. You can then both relax and we can talk more." Sarah's ears pricked up to this, as although it sounded reasonable it felt like coming out of the fire into the fireplace. "Ginge, are you sure that is a good idea." "What do you mean Sarah?" "I mean, if we are going to change our lives and get out of this mess wouldn't it be better to get us away into a new safer place where no one will know us." "What do you suggest?" "Do you have anywhere we can go further out of Cornwall? Joulie and I can then fully relax and await your being." Troon realised that what Sarah had just said made complete sense so said, "I do have a contact in Bodmin How about we stick to plan A and get you both out of this place tomorrow and back to mine and I will send message?"

Sarah looked at Joulie and after a couple of seconds nodded to each other. "So we are all agreed said Troon." "Yes, we are all agreed Ginge." "Thank you Mr Troon," Joulie added. Well. I better get myself off as I have a lot to do. I will see you both at my Manor tomorrow.

.

Chapter 17

The message to the Mayfair address read as follows:-

Our Dear Lady Luisa,
Please Proceed.
Angof

Luisa received this coded 'Angof' message five days ago and with a smile on her face, activated the go ahead. So, two of her men were now in the port of Bristol, sitting in the far corner of a grubby Inn called the Hatchet. One of the men was called Shanks, also known as the London Man, who had come especially from the Capital city. The other was a Bristolian man who worked in the port of customs and was responsible for the efficient and quiet unloading of the smuggled tin from Cornwall. This man had no loyalties to the Cornish and was only interested in the lovely royalties he receives on each shipment that he passes through. So with the Inn in full swing with heavy drinkers and women of song, they got down to business.

"So what are we to do?" said the customs man. "We don't pay you good money to ask those sort of questions, we pay you to sort things out. But whatever it is, it has got to stop from immediate effect as again the shipment was light and we are losing vast profit." "Yes I know, that is why I have agreed to come here in your presence, this is serious and seems well organised." "Well, at least you are honest about it, that's good. Why don't you start from the beginning and see where it goes but, before you do, order me some more wine."

Their discussion went on for quite a while and Shanks, being all ears, let the customs man tell all that he knew. The main problem was that all the cargos of Tin being smuggled out from Cornwall were each at least ten to twenty per cent light of their initial mined weight. The Captain of the two mast ship had wisely weighed and labelled all the loads from the varying places where each had been put aboard. People in London had been aware of this and tried to find out what was happening but never got anywhere. But that was before Luisa was involved and things were about to change,

Luisa was ruthless and doesn't take prisoners, especially simple Cornish ones. She is of Spanish high blood and lives alone, when it suits her, in a very expensive town house in Mayfair London. Being close to the London stock exchange and her team of villains and thieves she could control and coordinate everything. Now she had been given the go ahead and their money deposited, she quickly dispatched her London man and his small team to the South West. Their task was to eliminate anyone who gets in the way and get answers, no matter what, as someone somewhere was smuggling the smugglers.

The Bristolian man had many contacts and told Shanks all he knew so it was time for reflection and thought. Shanks supped his wine and could not stop thinking about the one name the customs man mentioned. Was it coincidence or fate but the name Cuthbert Troon startled him as he was having a meeting with this very man in a week's time at his Manor in Mingoose. It was not to say that Troon was in on anything but the very mention of his name from a customs man, albeit a smuggling one, was alarming. The reason he was to visit him is that

Troon had put word about that his small non producing Tin Mine at St Agnes was for sale. This Mine and its location would fit extremely well with Luisa's Cornish mission. Another name that was mentioned was a man known as Hughes of Truro.

However, this was all well and good but Shanks had his orders. So after gaining all the information he could, he ended the meeting and thanked the customs man for his loyalty. As both men got up and shook hands Shanks put his left hand into his side pocket and passed over an envelope of money. "Thank you," the customs man said. "No, thank you, you have been very helpful. Now, why don't you stay here and enjoy your drink but I must be on my way."

As Shanks walked away to the front door he winked at two men sitting off to the left. They saw the wink but acted as if they had seen nothing and just carried on drinking and laughing.

It was about fifteen minutes later when the two men saw the self satisfied customs man get up. They watched him like two beaded hawks but you wouldn't have noticed it. The stronger of the two men was especially eyeful looking at the man's weight and size. As the customs man got to the aisle by the bar area he turned away and walked to the outer latrine. The two men quickly sank their wine back in one and got up to follow. As the place was packed no one noticed anything untoward which was just as they had planned. All were too busy enjoying themselves.

As they got outside the doorway of the stinky latrine they stopped and waited. Then as trained, one of the men went in while the other waited outside. He saw the customs man was alone facing the wall with his hands by his front weeing in the bucket. This was just what he wanted to see. The man was carrying a sharp blade and pistol but knew he would not use them, not this time. So quietly, he crept up behind his prey. The custom man with his eyes closed feeling a sense of relief of urinating, heard the footsteps so quickly looked about but it was too late. The man grabbed him forcefully with both his hands around the neck and forehead and squeezed tight. Then with one violent twist ripped the man's head away from the shoulders and snapped his neck.

The customs man had no chance and died on the spot. On hearing the man breathe his last the killer readjusted his grip but still held him firm in his arms. He now had to make it appear that a fatal accident had happened. So with brute force he threw the dead man's head forward against the latrine wall. Then quickly releasing his grip watched him drop to the floor amongst the stink of the urine. The killer then quickly searched the dead man's pockets and pulled out the large envelope of money.

With the job done the killer simply turned around and walked out. Showing the thumbs up sign to his mate both quickly went to the stables and once on their horses rode away to the nearby trees. Shanks was there waiting and on seeing their smiles and the waving of the large envelope knew that all had gone well. This is the way the new owner works, obedience, efficiency and pain of death. No one messes with Luisa, no one.

The three men then quickly galloped away from the area of the Inn to a large out of the way forest where they could rest and talk. Shanks then explained the next phase of the operation. He was now to get to Plymouth via an overnight stop at Bath and asked if the two men were ready for their next mission in Portishead. Both smiled and said they were. "That's good, then let us all be on our way and I will see you both in Exeter in four days. Shanks had to go to Bath to meet his contact and also send message of progress to Luisa in Mayfair. He would then ride to Plymouth the next morning to meet their new customs man. So, with everything discussed and in place the three galloped out of the forest with Shanks heading due East and the two assassins West.

Mayfair was a truly opulent area and only the very rich could afford to live there. London was also at the top of capital cities in the world and Queen Anne and her royal elegance only added to that style.

Luisa was now fifty years old and had been in London for the last twenty years. When she was twenty nine years of age she married a very well respected financier who worked in the new London Stock Exchange at Jonathan's Coffee House. After their beautiful wedding, he bought the mansion at Mayfair for them to live in. It all sounded and looked lovely and everyone was happy for their love of each other. Although her husband was totally besotted with his new beautiful bride, for Luisa it was all a ruse. He had been earmarked as a target for his money and Luisa had played the game well, but then she had learnt well from her Spanish family. Then one dark night after just two years into their so called loving marriage he died. Luisa was seen as totally heartbroken and all the people around gave her the love and support to get through. He had drunk a lot of brandy that night and slipped over the top floor bannister railings and fell to his death. It was just tragic.

With the post mortem, confirming her affidavit of death accepted, the burial and all relevant paperwork signed and completed, her job was done. What she forgot to mention was that it was she who got her husband blind drunk that night and enticed him out of their top floor bedroom. Then after luring him close to the balcony, she pointed to the chandelier behind him. As he turned his head and full body to look he started to sway from the excess drink, which was when she pushed him over.

With all assets now being passed to her, including the mansion, she now had a central London base and wealth in which to work. Then slowly as the years passed her rich aristocratic family in Spain and their loyal villains came to her which is exactly what she wanted. Twenty years had gained her incredible wealth and power. She wanted for nothing. Even when she wanted sex, which was often, she got it. She had built up a loyal network all over Europe. Anything she wanted she got.

Luisa was now sat down in her drawing room sipping her morning tea when she heard the gentle knock on the door. "Enter", she said aloud. On hearing her words the butler walked in with a message. "For you my Lady." "Thank you, please wait while I read."

The message read: -

My Lady,
Bristol – God Bless
LM

When she had finished reading the message she smiled and looked up saying, "That's fine thank you, you can go." As the butler turned to walk away she then added, "I am expecting two well dressed men to arrive in about twenty minutes, please escort them straight in." "Yes, Madame."

When the butler left the room, Luisa read the message again which had been sent from Shanks, her London man. So, Bristol is completed, she thought, good, and the words 'God Bless,' meant that they had killed. With that, she smiled broadly and after laying the message on the table picked up her teacup with elegance and style.

Nearby, over at Pimlico, the horse and carriage stopped and the Spanish gentleman got in. "Good to meet you again my friend, how are you," said the Frenchman. "I am very well, thank you, how are you." "I too am well." With that, the Frenchman leaned his head out of the window and shouted to the driver, "Let's away my good man."

These two gentlemen are always given high guest status and privilege no matter what embassy or Country they visit. The last time these two men had met in person was at the secret meeting in the border town of Santander, North Spain. That was quite a while ago but they had always kept in regular contact through messages and other means. It was now time to meet Lady Luisa again and so both needed to go over their plans and agree on things beforehand. So as the driver whipped the horse ahead and the carriage started to gently ride the cobbled streets the two men inside got down to business.

Just prior to the hour of ten, the carriage pulled up outside the Mayfair house. Then after paying the driver, the two men proceeded quickly up the front steps to the front door and gently rapped the brass knock.

Luisa was still sitting contemplating her plans when the drawing room door knocked and in walked the butler with the two gentlemen. Both men had taken their hats off in accordance with etiquette and bowed their heads. Luisa didn't get up as she knew this would demean her power so said, "Good morning my two good gentlemen please come in and take a seat." When both men had sat down and seated comfortably, Luisa asked, "Tea?" With both saying yes, she looked at her butler who had heard their agreement and went out to fetch.

Both men kept silent as it was polite to let the Lady talk first. Luisa knowing this, also kept quiet but then after a short period of silent woman power said, "Well, have you heard anything?" The Frenchman looked at the Spanish man who nodded his head and so replied, "We have heard nothing Luisa, all has gone ghostly quiet." "And what of the Ferret?" "Again, we have heard nothing which is very concerning. As you know we have received information on a regular basis since he left for Cornwall but there has been nothing for over a month now." "So, what do you make of it all." "We have no idea, we can only presume he has been caught or killed or something. We know he left France with five other people in his team but again haven't heard from any of them. As you know we cannot be seen to know anything but what we do know is that no monies whatsoever have been forwarded" "So what are your plans?" "As far as we are concerned the Ferret and his team are history and have now wiped our hands of them. It has also been agreed between our two great Countries that should the Ferret or any of his team raise their heads in the future they are to be silenced without trace. We want you to have a clear path to do what you have to do without obstruction. So our aim is as we discussed and agreed at Santander".

As the Frenchman was talking, Luisa was listening with a keen interest but was being somewhat distracted by some moths fluttering away by the window off to her left of eye. It was then that the butler reappeared with the tea so all three went quiet.

Once he had laid the tray down and poured the tea for the two gentlemen, his job was done and so started to turn to walk out. It was then that Luisa said, "Before you go, please get rid of those bloody moths." The butler looked at where she was pointing and went straight over to them. When he got to the window frame, he noted they were not moths but small butterflies. So he said, "Excuse me my lady they are not moths their little butterflies." "I don't care what they are, get rid of them they are distracting me, bloody pests."

The butler did as ordered but was careful not to hurt them and gently gathered them in his hands and carried them out. Luisa would have just swatted them without care or thought.

As the butler got out of the drawing room he asked one of the maids to help him. Both went to the front door of the mansion and as she opened the door he opened the palms of his hands and released them. The butterflies then flew up and around the heads of both butler and maid as if to say thank you and then flew out into the open air. "That was just beautiful." said the maid.

Back in the drawing room, Luisa took another sip of her tea and listened to what the Frenchman had to say. When he finished she turned her head slightly to face the Spanish man saying, "Are you in agreement on what has been said." "Yes Senora, our two Countries are one.

"Right, then let me inform you of our plans which from the message I received this morning has already begun." Luisa then went on to tell them of her plans to switch the smuggling customs route from Bristol to Plymouth. She also mentioned her intention to buy a disused Mine at St Agnes. All that had gone on in the past including old routes, landings and people were to go. Nothing will be left to chance, nothing. She and her team are going to wipe the slate clean and within a period of nine months, control of Cornish smuggling will be theirs, as it should. Also, should they choose, the Ore can also be sent direct from Cornwall to any Country of their choice without going through the London exchange. "Excellent," said the Spanish gentleman and the Frenchman agreed.

Chapter 18

Joshua was sitting on the rocks watching the sea and the surf. He was in his favourite position on the right hand side of Gunwalloe beach. The sea was up, the air was fresh and the sun was out, what a beautiful day. Sitting quietly alone he started to take deep slow breaths in and out making the most of the lovely sea freshness. With his eyes closed he thought how wonderful his life now was.

He then looked over to his left across the barren sand at the cave under the cliff. He smiled and thought back as it was there that it all began. It was also where he first caught sight of Rebecca, his now wife and mother of his two children. How life twists and turns, from his fidgety lonely life in Bristol to the love and warmth of his family now. Yes, his job was sometimes hard and dangerous but he would not change a thing. Even the near fatal poisoning at the Blue Anchor he wouldn't change things. He then looked up at the sky and said ever so quietly, "Thank you Zelahnor."

He then reflected on the sad message he had received a week ago from George Kernow confirming the execution of Henry Hosking by the rope at Bodmin Jail. Joshua did feel an inner sadness for Henry as he had worked with him and knew that before he became mentally ill he was a good man.

Joshua looked back out at the deep rough sea and shrugged his shoulders back and forth and said with the energy of life, we all need a jolly good knees up. He would send messages to his three teams in Cornwall to meet up at the Bolventor Inn. Bolventor was on Bodmin moor but it was central to all and, he always felt safe there. He started to laugh at the thought of all his so called hard men dancing and singing but then his mind, for some reason, thought of Jacques.

Jacques was still living in Southern France as a pauper in a nowhere village. Gone were his bravado and strength. Five years of being imprisoned at the Chateau Morlaix had deeply affected him. Yes, the money and horse the Abbot kindly gave him a month ago on his release had helped but it didn't last long. Also, the sentence of death given by the Ferret meant he couldn't just go into a town and work, as he could be recognised. So quietly he went from woods to woods and from village to village. But by scrimping and scrapping and saving every penny he got he now knew he had to do what his heart had told him. Win or lose he had to do it.

Jacques had made his way to the small coastal village of Mimizan where his wit and patience had achieved sail to Plymouth. Due to the small size of the ship meant he couldn't take his horse which the Abbot had given him. So, he sold it at the small port for the best price he could, which wasn't much. Jacques also knew that the port of Plymouth was a long way from his main destination of Marazion but beggars couldn't be choosers. He would have to make do and sort something.

The voyage had taken a long four days but he had got there. It was on the midnight hour when he stepped off the foot plank and couldn't believe he was back on English soil, albeit Devon. He looked up to the stars and thanked them. So with rucksack packed with simple food on his back, he ventured into the city. His job was to find a horse somewhere anywhere which he could grab and get away. So, the outskirts and back alleys he went. He searched for hours but then found what he was looking for. The horse was tied to the side of a well to do house and was bareback with no saddle or bags. This didn't bother Jacques at all and so quietly went up and after gently calming her, untied the rein and walked her on. He was expecting someone to hear or see what he was doing but being very early in the morning only an hour past midnight all was quiet.

It had then taken over a week of night riding and laying up in the day to get outside the old cottage in Marazion. But he was there and would now wait up in the woods for daylight to come. He noted that some candle lights inside the cottage were aglow so someone was definitely in there. The time was nearing five thirty in the morning and darkness was still about

At around eight thirty with the sun up Jacques breathed in deeply many times to try and calm his nerves. When he had finished and dusted himself down he then went to his horse. He had named the horse Mary, he knew not why but after saying many names aloud it was the name Mary that she flicked her ears and nodded her head. So with that, Jacques jumped on her back and with rein in hand said, "Come on Mary." Jacque's heart was now beating fast as he couldn't wait to see Jeanne again.

As Jacques got to the front gate of the cottage he yielded his horse and dismounted. He knew he looked like a bag of bones and was filthy but with Mary's rein in his hand, he walked to the front door. Keeping hold of Mary's rein in one hand he knocked on the door with his other.

Jacques waited and on taking one last deep breath the door opened. "Yes, can I help you," said the old lady. Jacques was somewhat surprised to see an old lady and said, "I'm sorry to disturb you madam but is Jeanne in." "I'm sorry, no one called Jeanne lives here, who are you?" "I use to live here many years ago and thought I would drop by." "I'm very sorry Sir, but we bought this place four years ago and have lived here ever since." When she finished her last spoken word a grumpy old voice shouted from inside, "Who is it?" The old lady turned her head and said, "O it's just some poor man, that's all." "Well tell him to get lost I am trying to sleep." With that, the she turned back to Jacques and apologised but said, "She had better get back inside." Jacques dipped his head in understanding and walked away with the horse in hand. Once outside the garden gate, Jacques jumped on Mary and galloped back to the woods to regroup. What was he to do?

Once back into the safety of the wood, Jacques sat down and started to think while eating a raw carrot he had stolen from a nearby field. He had no choice. There was only one person who could help him now. So with his mind made up, he threw away the carrot stub, got up and went to Mary. Yes, he would do it and although it was daylight, which in all fairness was probably a good thing, he galloped off out of the woods heading east to Gunwalloe.

Joshua, after sitting for many hours on the beach getting his fresh air and energy of the sea, decided it was time to head back to his cottage. So putting his pipe and flexi flint back in his pocket, he got up. As he neared the front garden he saw the fullness of the cottage and thought, what a lovely place to live, especially with Rebecca and children. Then just as he opened the gate he heard a man's voice come from the bushes on the left, "Joshua."

Being completely startled by the voice, Joshua went for his pocket pistol. He had learned his lesson well. "Don't shoot Joshua, it's me, Jacques." Joshua was now on one knee by the gate post with pistol aimed at the bush where the voice was coming from. "If you say who you say you are then show yourself." Jacques, being on his hands and knees pushed his head through the leaves.

On seeing Jacque's face appear, looking gaunt and full of scraggy hair, Joshua was stunned and said, "Jacques, My God man, what are you doing here, we thought you were dead." "Joshua, I need your help." Joshua, quickly looked about to see if anyone was watching and then said, "Are you alone Jacques, is anyone with you." "No Joshua, it's just me and my horse back yonder." Joshua's mind was racing on what best to do.

"Jacques, listen to me. Stay where you are, I will walk back away from the cottage and down the footpath to the beach. Pull yourself out without being seen and I will meet you a hundred yards down the path by the trees." "I understand Joshua, thank you."

Joshua walked off and after standing very close to the trunk of an old oak tree, checked his pistol was ready for firing. Then keeping his pistol steady in his right hand, he waited for Jacques. It wasn't long before he heard the rustling of the bushes and then, Jacques appeared.

Both men stood on either side of the footpath and said nothing. Joshua just could not believe the state of the man. Jacques knew what Joshua was thinking and so stood there with his head lowered in shame.

"Jacques, what are you doing here?" "I have come back Joshua to see the woman I love and ask if she will take me back." "Jacques, it has been over five years, where have you been." "It's a long story Joshua, and one I did out of loyalty to a special person." "You mean Zoe." "Yes Joshua, that is her. "Jacques, are you armed." "No Joshua, I have no weapon and I pose no threat."

Joshua stared at Jacques for a few quiet seconds and then looked down at his own pistol and pushed the flint catch into the safe position. Jacques saw this and felt an inner calm come over him. Joshua then said, why don't we sit here and talk a while."

They talked for well over an hour as Jacques explained everything that had happened. They could have talked for a lot longer but time was moving on and Joshua needed to sort this out. Yes, they had to talk more but they couldn't do it where they were.

Joshua decided that he would fetch his own horse and take Jacques down to the Halzephron Inn where he could stay out of sight and get washed and fed. Mary could also be stabled and looked after. On agreeing with Jacques that this was the best course of action, Joshua went to the cottage to fetch his trusted stead.

The Halzephron Inn was a good drinking place but had a reputation for smuggling as being very close to the sea and the coves, especially Dollar Cove. But that aside the Landlord was a good man and friend of Joshua.

As the two men rode down to the Halzephron, Joshua looked out to the sea and saw a couple of medium sized galleons anchored. This was not unusual but it did mean that the crewmen were more than likely ashore or would be ashore later for drink and merriment.

Joshua led on and when they got to the side of the Inn both dismounted. Joshua suggested to Jacques that he stay outside while he goes into the Inn to discuss things with the Landlord.

As he thought the crewmen of the anchored Galleons were indeed already ashore enjoying themselves. Joshua walked through the busy bar area and saw the Landlord pulling the cider. As their eyes met, Joshua nodded his head to the side as a sign that he wanted to talk. The Landlord got it and after quickly talking with one of his bar staff to take over his duties walked over to where Joshua was standing.

"Hello Joshua." "Hello Peter, have you a minute to talk?" "Yes, sure Joshua" Peter Williams, the Landlord, knew the area in which Joshua worked but always kept things quiet and more importantly, Joshua trusted him.

Peter took Joshua out of the busy bar to a quiet back area where they could talk in peace. Joshua explained about Jacques as best he could while keeping things which needed to be kept secret out of the discussion. What he wanted most was for Jacques to have room and bed and be quietly left alone. He was to be given what he needed and Joshua would pay all. Also, Mary, his horse needed to be looked after and fed. "How long do you expect him to stay Joshua." "I am not sure Peter, it's all up in the air at the moment, can we take it a week at a time, if that is alright." "That is fine Joshua, anything else?" Well, you saying that, if you could organise him a hot bath and shave that would be good." "Consider it done, I will get the maid onto it. "Thanks for your help Peter." "Your welcome Joshua." Peter then suggested that it would be best if Jacques enters the Inn from the side door by the stables. He will then be taken to his room by a young woman called Leanne. With all things agreed Joshua went out to find Jacques.

After explaining to Jacques what had been agreed with the Landlord, Joshua needed to get back to Rebecca and figure out whether he should tell or not tell her. Also, should he inform George Kernow? Just as Joshua was about to get on his horse, Jacques put his hand out and with a sincere voice said, "Thank you Joshua." Joshua shook Jacque's hand and said, "Jacques, get some rest and I will see you tomorrow evening."

On entering his cottage he saw his lovely wife Rebecca who immediately said, "Joshua, where have you been, you said you will be only a couple of hours. You know I need to get to the market in Cury to get our meat and groceries." "I'm sorry Rebecca, I forgot." "Joshua, are you on this planet and what do you mean you forgot, I told you just as you left the front door that the children needed looking after." "I know you did Rebecca but I need to talk with you and think you better sit down." "Joshua, the children need feeding and we have run out of stores, I don't have the time to sit down." "Rebecca, give me the list and I will ride to Cury, but please sit down, I need to talk with you, something's happened."

Rebecca quickly felt an inner concern as she noticed that Joshua's tone had changed. So, taking Joshua's advice she sat down by the fireplace and waited. Joshua also took a seat opposite and said, "Where are the children Rebecca?" "They are out playing in the garden." Joshua went quiet as he was a little hesitant about what and how to say things. Rebecca knew him well and felt his strain and so delicately took the lead. "Joshua, what is it, what has happened." "Rebecca, Jacques was here." With a startled face, she responded, "Jacques here, when?" "I met him outside the cottage this very morning, on my return from the rocks." "O my dear Lord, I thought he was dead." "I'm sorry Rebecca, I didn't know if I should have told you or not." "Joshua, you have done right, I know you want to protect me and Mother, but you have done right. Now tell me all." "I think I need a brandy first." Rebecca replied, "I think I also need one."

After telling all that had happened, Rebecca went silent in thought. She was thinking about her Mother, Jeanne, and how she would feel. "Well Rebecca, what are we to do, shall I inform Kernow or what." "I think we should stay quiet for now and tell no one, not even Mother. You said you were going to meet him tomorrow." "That's right Rebecca." "Then, if you don't mind Joshua, I will join you and we can both make a decision together." "Well, let's hope he has cleaned himself up as he looked like a bag of bones." "Yes, you said." Rebecca then got up and took both their empty brandy glasses to the wash area but then remembered and stopped and went over to the cabinet.

She picked up the sealed message knowing it was from George Kernow and passed it to Joshua saying, "It came for you this morning by the known courier."

Joshua took the message and broke the seal. It read:-

Joshua,
Customs Man found dead in latrine in Bristol tavern.
Strange – Be Alert
GK

Chapter 19

Sarah was lying still in the four poster bed next to Troon in the master bedroom at Mingoose Manor. It was very early and the morning light was trying to appear. Her eyes were open and she was staring up at the tapestry above. She thought about how only a few days ago her life was so very different being in the scraggy old cottage over at Pennycomequick in St Allen.

She was once again safe or at least as safe as she could be under the circumstances. Little Joulie was also safe in the bedroom a few doors down. She put her hands up close to her eyes and looked at how dirty and rough they were due to the hard work at the Mine. What a way to live she thought. But that was then and this is now. Sarah put her arms down by her side and lay in silent thought.

As Troon had promised on the Saturday evening at the cottage his steward, Stephen Bagnall, had arrived the next day to take her and Joulie away and escort them both to Mingoose Manor. Troon was there to meet them and seemed happy at their arrival. She then thought about Bagnall. He seemed a very nice man with good manners but she felt he had an inner confidence which made her feel a little inadequate. He also kept looking at Joulie and noted he always became somewhat over mannerly when she asked or wanted help. Well, if he fancies her and she him who was she to stand in their way? Maybe it was time that Joulie did have a romance. She would talk with Joulie later about it.

It was then that she felt Cuthbert, or as she always called him since they first met, Ginge, start to move. She closed her eyes and acted as if she was still asleep as he turned his body and wrapped his arms over her. But then she blurted out, "Ginge, you are strangling me, get your big arms off." Troon smiled and did as ordered saying, "Sorry Sarah." He then started to wake up a little and when he opened his eyes said in a sleepy voice, "Would you like some tea?" "Yes please," she replied in a girly type manner.

With that, Troon stretched out his arm and pulled the cord. Sarah decided to light the candle and after quickly kissing Troon on the cheek got out of bed and over to the dressing table to get herself ready. "You don't have to get up Sarah," Troon said. "Ginge I have been awake a little while and like to drink my tea around a table, not lying in bed. By the way, you could snore for Cornwall." "You mean Devon my little love." "Shhhh Ginge, you can't say that word around here." "Well, that's where your from Sarah." Troon was going to add and say about her fidgeting but thought no, he won't go there, best left alone and say nothing. He then decided that he would get up as he needed to talk.

When the maid came in with the tea and then left the room, they sat quietly together. Then after taking a few sips, Sarah said, "Ginge, I think your Bagnall man likes Joulie." "Do you have a problem with that?" "No not really, but isn't he married?" "Well Sarah, he is a good man and has been through the mill. His wife died about ten years ago and he has been on his own ever since." "So does he live here?" "Yes, he has quarters here in the Manor but also has a small town house in Truro where he goes when off duty." "Hmmm, sounds quite nice, I didn't know his wife died, does he have any children?"

"Not that I know of, so does Joulie like him?" "I don't know that either, she hasn't said anything but I will ask her." "It's a funny thing Sarah, his wife was also very small in stature." As they sat gently gossiping with the morning light coming through the curtains, Troon confirmed that their move to Bodmin was on. "So, have you sorted it?" "Yes, I got the message yesterday that a small cottage just north of the town is ready for you and Joulie to move in." "Thank you Ginge, you are a good man." Troon went silent and thought about what Sarah had just said. He had swindled many people to get large sums of money to live a life above all others. For some reason, his mind then thought back to the young family he had evicted after inheriting, due to the death of the old woman, the cottage that encroached on his Manor and laughed at their demise. He can still remember their names being Edward and Selina Killigrew and daughter, Grace. That was just one of the many bad things he had done. With his mind in silence, he lowered his head as if in some inner act of remorse, but in truth, that was far from the case. Sarah was watching and saw him lower his head and took it that he was sad at her and Joulie leaving Mingoose so said, "Ginge, it's not that we don't like it here, we just don't feel safe and very much need to get out of harm's way." "I know Sarah, I know." She then put her fingers to her mouth and blew him a kiss.

Sarah then thought about what Joulie had asked her to ask Troon. "Ginge, have you sorted things out for the Ferret?" Troon looked up at the ceiling and sighed and said, "Sarah, it's all become a complete mess but I do mean to get him out of the sisters' cottage in Scorrier and put him on a ship far away from here as possible.

Troon then knew it was time to tell Sarah of his plans. "Sarah, I think you should know I have a person coming to see the Mine in St Agnes on Saturday." "That's good news Ginge, where is he coming from?" "The message said he was coming from London." "Wow, that's a long way to buy a Mine." "Not really, when I put the word out it went around like wild fire and knew the money men in London would be interested. Tin is in." "So what's his name." "I don't know, it was signed in the name of Shanks which doesn't surprise me in the least as the London exchange works in mysterious ways. I will also ask him if he wants to buy the Manor and maybe cut a deal." "Well let's hope it goes well." "Thanks Sarah, once the Tin Mine and this place are sold I will come to you at your cottage in Bodmin and take us both away to our Devon homeland. We can then live our lives together in safety." Sarah for the first time after meeting Ginge didn't respond to his plans and thought that was strange. Maybe it was because she had lived a single life of being on her own for so long or used by people for devious means. Maybe it was being locked up at the Chateau at Morlaix for five years. Quickly coming out of her thoughts she asked, "What are your plans for Joulie, what of her?" "If you wish her to come with us to Devon then I am happy with that but as you pointed out earlier my steward Bagnall might have other ideas." "Have you told him of your selling up." "No, not yet, I wanted to tell you first and get your thoughts." "Ginge, I think you're doing it right and yes I am nervous but I too want to get as far away from here as possible and live a life as once we knew." "Bagnall is due back on duty tomorrow and I will tell him then." "He may be a little upset about your plans Ginge as he won't have a job." I know that, but that is his problem, not ours." Sarah looked at him and thought when he wants to be nice he can, but then an inner streak of pure ego and selfishness arises.

When they had finished their tea, both got themselves washed and freshened up. Troon then suggested that Sarah get Joulie and he will take them in the buggy to the small coastal town of St Agnes and treat them both to something nice to eat at the local Inn. "Thank you Ginge, but I don't feel at all comfortable being seen in the open." "Sarah, you are over analysing things, St Agnes is a fishing village completely out of the way, you will enjoy it." "Would you buy me and Joulie a bonnet?" "As I said Sarah, St Agnes is just a simple fishing village, there are no shops like that there." Sarah went quiet and thought about how she was now going out into an open village without any care like any other normal person would. But her life wasn't normal. For some reason, her mind then thought back to the Sniper and how simple and easy he was compared to Cuthbert Troon who was very intelligent and devious for his own gain. She then pondered and thought about where her Snipe was now and how his life had turned out. While in these quiet thoughts, she felt her heart smile but then heard, "Come on Sarah, let's go." Sarah didn't say anything and just got up and went out to see Joulie.

Stephen Bagnall was in his town house at the top of Green Street, Truro, getting himself ready but saw that the time was moving on. He needed to get to The White Hart Inn to meet his good friend but couldn't stay out too late as he had to be on duty at Mingoose first thing.

Once fully dressed, he went out and after locking the front door, walked briskly along to Bridge Street. As he entered the White Hart he went to the bar and when the Landlord saw him he nodded and turned his head to the side table. Bagnall nodded back and after walking on further around the bar saw his good friend John Hughes sitting and drinking his cider. "Hello John." Hughesy looked up and with a smile said, "Hello Stephen, take a seat, good to see you my old friend, I got you one in."

Stephen sat himself down and after picking up his ale and taking a deserved mouthful put it back down on the table saying, "He's selling up." "What, the house or the Mine?" "Both." "Has he said this to you." "No, not yet, but I have seen messages he has sent and received and quietly heard him talk" "Hmmm," Hughes said aloud and then picked up his tankard and took a big gulp." "And what of the women and that bloody Ferret bloke?" "You mean my little sugar Joulie." Stephen, if you fancy her then go for her, we don't have a problem with it. But, what about them, what's happening?" "I am to take both women to a safe cottage in a small village just north of Bodmin. As for the Ferret, I don't know, but am sure I will find out shortly."

"Why is he selling, as he lost his nerve." "I think that's exactly what it is and also meeting his old flame from Devon." "So, he can swindle and cheat anyone he chooses and when he wants to doddle off into the sunset leaving his victims penniless and desperate, he does." "Yep, that just about sums him up." "What a bastard." "John, were not exactly angels ourselves" "I know that, but we cheat the rich and leave the poor alone." "That's a good point." "Right my good friend, it seems we have a problem." "What do you mean John." "Before we get into it let me get some more drinks and then we can talk, by the way here's yer money." Hughes then pulled out a chunky envelope from inside his jacket and slid it across the table. "How much?" "Two hundred guineas, we had a good run on the Tin." "Thanks John." "Your welcome, now let me get those drinks."

Chapter 20

It had been a long day and the time was touching ten thirty in the evening with the night dark and the stars aglow. The two assassins had reached the outskirts of Portishead and decided to rest up a while and gather their thoughts. They had discussed their plans and had the name, address, facial portrait and social overview of their next victim. Once they had checked their weapons and dusted themselves down they would move off and scout the target area. This was important to achieve their aim. Once done they would pull back and go over in finer detail how they would achieve the kill. This job would be different from the Customs man death in the latrine in Bristol two days ago as it needed to send a different message.

So after an hour of rest had gone by, it was time. Getting on their horses they gently rode out of the small wooded copse and moved to the target area. It would take them about an hour to get to the address which would mean they would hit the target area at around midnight. Just about right as not too late and not too early.

Their target was a known pirate and local hard man called Sean Wiltkins who was the leader of the lugger crews responsible for getting the smuggled ore from the Coves of Cornwall. He was married and had two young children and, when not in the local Inn drinking the night away, lived in a cottage at number twenty five, Canal Lane, just a little way out of the town.

The local Inn called the Fishermans, situated half a mile from Canal Lane, was buzzing with the fiddler playing his merry tunes and people singing and dancing. Eight men were sitting around a table and after banging their tankards together three times on the top of the table, all drank them in one and cheered aloud. "Come on Sean, it's your round," shouted one of the men and everyone again cheered. Sean waved his hand at the busy barmaid who came over with a large tray and took the empty tankards away for refill.

The two assassins reined their horses to a still a hundred yards back from Canal Lane. They weighed the situation up and both agreed it wasn't a good area to leave their horses tied up while they walked through the lane to do their surveillance. So quietly they dismounted and took out the horse's soft hoof pads from their saddlebags and tied them onto their hoofs. Once the soft hoof pads were firmly fixed on both horses they remounted and rode at a very slow pace up the lane. Being midnight most if not all candle lights were out in the cottages which was good news as it gave them extra cover in the darkness. The soft shoe pads were also doing their job well and so quietly they rode slowly on through.

It wasn't long before they passed number twenty five and as with all the other cottages everything was silent and dark. Keeping their eyes and ears sharp they pushed on further out of the cobbled street and stopped. Then, one of the men dismounted and quickly scurried back to the side and rear of number twenty five and waited. While he did so he surveyed the backyard and noticed that there was a back door and one black horse tied up alone. Other than that all seemed normal with nothing untoward. After two more minutes of quiet watching the man then hurried back to his accomplice and remounted his horse. Both then moved on to find a better place of safety to tie the horses.

It wasn't far when they saw a small green with large bushy trees which would suit their needs well, just the job. They could tie their horses and rest unseen and do what they needed to do. The man who had surveyed the backyard explained to his colleague what he had seen. The big black stallion was the key, as it was recognised as Wiltkins horse. So he was most likely in the cottage or, knowing he liked a drink, down the Inn. But, this was an assumption and working on assumptions got people killed, they needed to qualify things better in their favour. So with that, the other man nodded as it was now his turn for spying. After checking his pistol he walked off with his head down to the local Fishermans Inn while the other man held the horses.

Twenty lonely minutes then passed before the man who had gone off with his head down came back. Yes, the Fishermans Inn was indeed buzzing with fiddle and sailor songs being sung aloud. The man had not entered the Inn as it would be too risky so had sat and waited outside with the paupers. Hearing the singing and joy of a busy local Inn with many men, meant the increased likelihood that Wiltkins was in there. So, after a quiet discussion, they agreed a plan to shoot him dead on his drunken return. If it proved that he was not in the Inn then they would wait in the woods and move out just before first light and kill him in the cottage he lived which was doable but not ideal.

After tying the horses up inside the trees both men then calmly walked out and went to the edge of Canal Lane where each would sit on either side of the cobble street in the dark recesses which they had observed earlier. It was a good position as not only could they cover each other, but the little woods which they had just left was also in sight. So, with their knees up to their chests and heads lowered they waited in the shadows of the dark.

"Come on Sean", it's your round. "I'm done, the wife will kill me," Wilts replied. "Come on Wilts, just one more." Then just as he was going to repeat himself the Landlord shouted, "Time gentlemen please," It was one o clock in the morning and everyone was sozzled. The fiddler also tipsy then drank his last and started to put his instrument away. It had been a good night by all. "What time we got to be at the Luggers Sean?" "Nine o clock on the dot, we got a good job on, so let's all get out and get some sleep." With that, they all drank back the last of their ciders and staggered to the door.

When all were outside of the Inn most of the men turned right and headed down to the cheap streets. But Wiltkins and one other man turned left and headed up towards Canal Lane which was seen as a better place to live and not so rough. So, trying to walk as straight as they could, the two men swayed home to their families and bed.

After three or four minutes of this happy swaying walk they neared the corner of Canal Lane. The two assassins, lying in wait, heard the two men approaching and so, keeping their heads down and faces covered, took a firmer grip on their pistols. As Wiltkins and the other man turned into Canal Lane and both still waffling on about the team not being late in the morning was when they saw the man sitting alone in the dark recess. Feeling an inner sympathy for the down and out pauper, they slowed their pace and after delving into their pockets threw a penny down by the man's side. Both smiling at doing the right thing, they carried on down the dark street. It was then that the two assassins in unison moved out from the shadows. Although drunk, Wilts heard the movement behind him and so quickly turned his head about but it was too late. The two assassins were now very close and with pistols raised pulled the triggers. Both Wilts and the other man went down but Wilts, although seriously wounded, was still alive trying desperately to get his pistol out to shoot back. But the assassins saw all and calmly walked up to them and using their secondary loaded pistols shot Wilts and his friend in the head, dead.

The four pistol shots were extremely loud and broke the night silence like thunder. There was no time to hang about so leaving the two blooded bodies in the street where they lay, both men ran back to their horses and once mounted galloped away, fast. It had been a good job done. Once both were well away from the murder scene they rested up and talked. It would take them a couple of long days in the saddle to get to Exeter for their meeting with Shanks. So, being tired and joyous at the same time they decided to stop off half way and drink to their success.

Shanks had completed his visit to Bath and met the rich contact as Luisa had requested. He then stayed the night in a very posh hotel but had to get up early for the ride to Plymouth. However, to make things easier for Shanks and in good will to Luisa, the rich man had assigned a buggy and a driver to take Shanks, with his horse reined to the back. It had taken a full day to get to Plymouth but he was there and now sitting quietly by the fireplace in a warm and cosy Inn overlooking the harbour. His good horse was also stabled and being well cared for. He was to meet the new customs man tomorrow at ten in the morning to agree terms.

Their plan was simple. This new customs man was to give safe docking and manage, for an agreed sum of money, a cargo ship laden with tin smuggled from Cornwall. The ship was owned by Luisa and would need safe port as required throughout the year. Once the cargo of Ore was ashore and cleared from any tax, the customs man was then to organise delivery to London by land or sea. The cargo size ship would appear normal and routine with nothing untoward. The ship was at present anchored off Northern Spain and the Captain, who was a cousin of Luisa, was awaiting orders to sail to a safe holding near St Agnes. No more would the tin Ore be smuggled in dribs and drabs from dark Cornish coves. No more trying to control things on land with all the people's problems and their duplicity. This is a Luisa operation and she will use only her men. If Shanks could get this agreement in place on behalf of Luisa, he could then move on with his next job in getting rid of the Cornish scumbags who have caused much loss.

While sitting and looking out through the window over the harbour he thought about his two hit men and how they had got on in Portishead. He trusted all had gone well and that he will see them in a few days in Exeter where he would again send message update to Luisa in Mayfair. She liked to be kept informed all the way. So, with spare time on his hands this night, he decided to drink up and go to the brothel area where he could have his wicked way as he wanted and also have more drinks. He deserved it.

Chapter 21

And so, as planned and on schedule, the two assassins and Shanks, were now safely in the City of Exeter. They were in the Kings Head Inn resting up for their next move into Cornwall. Plymouth had gone well and as explained by the assassins Portishead had too. Shanks was pleased to hear this and so all were happy and in fine spirit. So after positive messages were sent it was a good time to relax and enjoy. They would have a good hearty breakfast in the morning where they could go over last minutes details and once packed and ready, get themselves off. Shanks had got himself to Exeter from Plymouth by the ease of sitting in a buggy. He had been advised by Luisa's contact in Bath that should he want, he could carry on and use this facility after his Plymouth run for as long as he wanted and as he saw fit. Shanks was happy with this as the buggy driver, who was well trained and armed, could also act as Shanks's guard and even better, had been fully paid. This he found most excellent.

The next morning after a good night of drink and sleep had been had by all, the four men were up at the table having their breakfast. Shanks went over the finer details confirming that he will meet the two assassins again in four days at the Dragon Inn on the eastern outskirts of the city of Truro. It would be their base of operation and was located out of the way which suited their needs very nicely. Their rooms had already been booked and paid and also confirmed that another two man team would be there waiting.

After again thanking the two men for their successful kills in Bristol and Portishead, Shanks told them that he and they were now to separate. They were to quietly and without speed make their own way to Truro. This was not only a wise move but also four men seen together riding in daylight could bring unwanted attention. Also, Shanks and his guard had an important meeting with a man called Cuthbert Troon at his manor in Mingoose. So with breakfast finished they all got up and went to their rooms. It was around nine thirty when all were ready and waiting outside that Shanks and his driver said their farewell. They were off.

The two assassins watched the buggy go out of sight and after nodding to each other flicked their horse's reins and followed on. They had discussed things before hand and agreed that they would stop overnight for a rest at a town called Okehampton twenty miles away. After all, as Shanks had pointed out to them, there was no rush.

As the day moved on and the nights rest at the town of Okehampton done, the assassins pushed on and entered the land of Cornwall. It was after a further two hours of gentle riding through the green and village countryside they came to a vast emptiness of nothing. It stretched all around for miles and they felt very open and vulnerable. They had seen nothing quite like it and so putting two and two together realised that it must be the Moors of Bodmin that they had been told about. Maybe it was their experience in the field of close killing that they felt exposed and so stopped to talk. "I don't like this at all," said one of the men. "I agree, its making me feel very nervous." Then seeing and pointing to a clump of trees four hundred yards away one of them said, "Why don't

we go over and get into those trees and discuss things."
"Well at least we will have some cover, yeah why not.".

As they got close to the trees they dismounted and with horse reins in their hand walked in. Then on tying the horses loosely up, they sat down to rest and talk. They noticed the horses were breathing and sweating heavily and so maybe it was just as well they did this as they too needed some rest and water. They thought about taking the horse's saddles and side bags off which were holding all their gear but thought no that's going too far. Then as they settled down, two small butterflies flew out.

The time was only nearing seven but unusually the sun seemed to be drifting down quickly. They both agreed that the vast openness made them feel very uneasy and was not good for their safety of possible Snipers. So they decided to rest and wait for the early darkness to fall then get out and gallop at speed to the closest Inn. It was just over an hour later when the moon had risen and the dark of the night had fallen that the horse's ears flicked.

Zoar and his brother Zareb had now been watching both men for some time while lying in the undergrowth close by. With the information gained from the butterflies they now knew what to do. Zoar would go for the horses as their reins had been only loosely tied to the branches of the trees and not the solid trunks. Zareb would distract and give cover. It had to be done quick and fast.

After two more minutes of waiting, it was time to move. Zareb crawled without sound around the opposite side of the wooded copse and when in position laid down in silence. Then as planned with his brother, Zoar, he drew a deep breath and opened his massive jaws and roared a thunderous roar.

The assassins felt immediate shock and went straight for their pistols. As they did so, Zoar rushed in from the opposite side and jumped cleanly over onto and off the backs of the reined horses. The horses were terrified and shrieked aloud and kicked violently and as they did the branches holding their reins broke. With their freedom given, they galloped out and away as fast as they could from the beasts that would eat them alive.

Zoar didn't stop and was out of the copse as fast as he had come in. Once clear he and his brother quickly got ran off to find the scared horses. When they would find them, they would talk to them and calm them down and lead them far away into the moor. The horses would be fine and live a good life as Zelahnor would love them and introduce them to her ponies.

All happened so fast that the two assassins didn't have time to get a shot off and so sat in total confusion. One minute they were resting and the next minute they were in fear of death. They decided that whatever those beasts were, they were simply not going to hang about. They again tried to make sense of it all but it just didn't make any sense. So, what were they to do? Well, the first thing they needed was to get their horses back as without them they couldn't do anything. But that depended on where the horses were. Or they could walk. But the horses had all their equipment and they were in the middle of bloody nowhere. They decided to check their pistols and move out to look for the horses. It was their only option but then that bloody beast or beasts could still be outside. So they changed their plan again to stay put and wait with pistols ready for ten minutes before they did anything.

As the ten minutes ticked by the assassins were starting to calm and get their instinct and boldness back but, they had to be careful. So, slowly with pistols in hand, they crept to the edge of the wood and looked about.

As they peered across the dark vast open moor they saw nothing but total emptiness. Then one of the men said, "Right, you ready, let's go and find the horses." Then taking the lead he moved his body forward but the other man grabbed him and said, "Stop, this is just not good, something is very wrong." "Look, we just agreed, we have no choice, the horses have all our stuff, we gotta find them." "We do have choice and my gut feeling is to let them go." "And then what, we have little money, no food or ammo." "I know that, but I say we withdraw and get back to the main track and get away why we're still alive." "Then?" "Then we find the nearest village and work it from there."

Chapter 22

It was a beautiful morning when Joulie, still lying in bed heard, "Joulie, are you awake?" She opened her eyes and replied, "Yes, I am." "Are you alright, would you like me to make you a cup of tea?" "That would be lovely Stephen, thank you."

So Stephen got out of bed and poked the embers of the fire to get some glow to heat the pot. Then getting back into his side of the warm bed said, "I think your lovely Joulie; I fancied you as soon as I saw you." "Stephen, I like you too but it is early days."

They were in Bagnall's bedroom at Mingoose Manor and both of them and Sarah have a busy day ahead. First, they had to get themselves ready, then the buggy, and then get off to Scorrier. Then once they had picked up the Ferret and taken him to the port, the three of them would push on to Bodmin. It was going to be a long day.

"Stephen, can I say thank you for last night and thank you for being a gentleman." "Joulie, I won't push myself on you, when you are ready then I will gladly, but only if you wish." Joulie liked him for this and thought more of him. "Would you like to meet up again sometime and maybe come over to my place in Truro, it could do with a woman's touch." Joulie smiled and said, "Where in Truro do you live?" "It's called Green Street, in the City Centre, at the back of the Quay, by the beautiful River Kenwyn." "Joulie looked at him in quiet thought for a few seconds to let her inner feelings come forward and decided why not. "Yes, I would like that, I will send you word and you can come and pick me up from our safe house in Bodmin." "I will do that with pleasure."

Troon was getting anxious as he had the meeting with the man called Shanks at ten o clock and Sarah and Joulie were still here which just shouldn't be. He had pulled the cord for his steward ten minutes ago but still he hadn't come. He was just about to pull it again when the door opened and in walked Bagnall.

"Stephen, where have you been, time is pushing on and both the women are still here." "Yes, I know, Sarah is taking ages to get ready. I have knocked on their door again but Sarah shouted that she and Joulie are talking and will be out shortly." Troon was going to get up and go and talk to Sarah himself but then thought he rather not and so stayed where he was saying, "Sorry Stephen, but I do have an important meeting with a gentleman from London in thirty minutes." "I understand, I will go up and knock again." "Is all else ready." "Yes, all is done and packed with horses reined for the off." "Well good luck and see you in a few days." Troon had not told Bagnall anything of his plans to sell up or who he was meeting although he had promised Sarah he would.

Once again Stephen went back to the women's bedroom but as he approached the door it all of a sudden opened from within. Sarah then looked out and seeing Stephen said, "Arr you're here, good, where ready now, could you help us with our bags."

As he walked in he saw yet another pile of gear in which he had to help load. He also saw Joulie and so smiled a loving smile. Joulie saw him do this and quickly lowered her head in shyness. Yes, he thought, she is lovely. Sarah caught sight of this quiet exchange of silent endearment between them and said, "Right, now can we get on with things, we are late and have to get going."

And so, the lifting and carrying started and as the last of things were packed aboard the buggy the two women got on and got themselves comfortable. The buggy was small and geared for two people but at a squeeze could take three. Stephen, still on the ground was just about to jump aboard up front and take the reins when he heard another buggy drive in.

So, with curiosity he stopped and started to walk around the buggy as one would to check for anything untoward before driving off. But, while doing this and making sure his face was not seen he kept an open eye on who was coming in and what they looked like.

When the incoming buggy stopped by the steps to the front doors of the Manor, Shanks got out. Stephen saw him but carried on with what he was doing. However, with keen eye, he took a mental image of the man's face and stature so he could report to his friend. He also took a mental image of the driver who quite clearly looked to be able to handle himself. When Stephen had visualised in his brain what he wanted he jumped up on the buggy and gently whipped the horse and buggy away. Shanks turned his head and looked on as the buggy and people inside left the grounds of the Manor but just shrugged his shoulders in unconcerned contempt. It was then the large front door to the Manor house opened with Troon standing tall. "Mr Cuthbert Troon?" said Shanks. "And you are Shanks, the man from London to talk about the Mine." "That is me, Sir."

So with a welcome smile, Troon escorted Shanks into the Library. With the two of them now alone and sitting comfortably, Troon asked, "Gin or Brandy?" "A brandy, thank you." Troon then poured the brandy and offered the glass and as Shanks took it, Troon asked, "Is Shanks your true name?" Shanks gave a giggle saying, "No, my real name is David King and work for the shareholders of a Company in London." Troon didn't believe this was his true name but it didn't bother him, as this is exactly how he worked. "And how was your journey." "It was fine, thank you," Mr King replied.

"Right shall I get the map out and we can go over the Wheal Coates Mine and the land it sits on." "That would be good." King was playing the game and didn't tell Troon that they had already done their own searches of the records and were quite happy. So as time went on Troon became content that this man in front of him and the Company he worked for had money. Troon could feel it in the man's manner and so was considering when to ask this Mr King about also buying the Manor. It didn't bother Troon in the least about who he sold it to as long as they had cash. It was that simple. "So, we now get down to the bottom line Mr Troon, what price you ask?" "Would you also be interested in buying this Manor?" This added question didn't bother King at all as he knew he was with a man who manipulates others for his own gain. He also remembered the name Troon being mentioned by the now dead customs man in Bristol. But, it was interesting as Luisa had always said she would like a bolt hole in the Cornish Country. "Well, we may be, it depends on the price and how you want to be paid." This was music to Troon's ears and so replied, "Shall we say ten thousand for the Mine and thirty thousand for the Manor in cash." "Before, I agree or not agree, may I ask why you are selling up." "I have had a wonderful time here in Cornwall but wish now to retire to my lovely Scotland." This was a complete lie but then Troon thought it sounded convincing. Shanks also knew differently but kept quiet and let the silence take its toll on his answer. After a minute of silent thought Shanks then replied, "Shall we say thirty thousand for both the Mine and this Manor." "In cash?" "Yes, in cash." "Make it thirty five and we have a deal." "Thirty two." Troon was in his element and loved this wheeling and dealing. Thirty two thousand pounds in his pocket when he had got both for near nothing. Troon then put his hand across the table and when King took it in his hand, Troon said aloud, "Deal."

With that, Troon with a broad smile on his face poured both of them another large brandy. King took the refilled glass and after leaning back said, "We would like the contracts to be completed as soon a possible, do you agree." "Absolutely, what Solicitors will you use?" "Our Solicitor is Mr Wright, the senior partner at Wright & Co in Queens Square, Bath." Troon straight away knew that this deal is going through as Queens Square in Bath was like a rich Mayfair in London and so replied, "Fine, I will get my Solicitor Mr Shaw from Shaw & Shaw in Truro to draw up the deeds of transfer and get things sorted." "Good, then I will get message to Mr Wright as he has the power of signature for all the shareholders." Shanks had done his job and wasn't going to stay any longer than he needed. It had been a good day and now they had the Mine and the Manor they could operate as Luisa wished.

Chapter 23

As the buggy rumbled slowly on towards Scorrier, Sarah carried on, "So he didn't do nothing." "Sarah, I told you, we just kissed, that's all." "So what next?" "He has asked me to his place in Truro." "And?" "And nothing; Sarah, I got to be careful, look what happened to the Ferret." "Talking of the Ferret, are you still alright with Stephen taking him away for sail?" "Well, yes and no really but with the situation we are in I think it would be best if he got away from these shores." Sarah hadn't told Joulie that Troon had suggested that she could just poison him but then had reconsidered and said no, it was best get him away. Joulie then asked, "So you and Troon, sorry Ginge, are still in love and getting it on." "Yes, we are Joulie," Sarah replied, but again something inside didn't feel quite right. "Sarah, I feel so happy we are finally getting away from all the strife and worry." "Joulie, we are so lucky and I too can't wait to live a life we have never had." For some reason, the Sniper again slipped into her mind. "Guess what I'm going to do when we get to our safe house." "What are you going to do Joulie?" "I'm going to buy some flowers." Sarah then leaned her head forward and shouted at Stephen, "How long before Scorrier." Stephen turned his head and shouted back, "About an hour." "Can you pull over I need to go for a widdle?" Stephen sighed but nodded his head while Joulie said, "Sarah, you're so embarrassing."

After Sarah got back in the buggy from relieving herself in the small woods Stephen again flicked the reins. Then as they rode on and the hour mark passed, the sister's cottage came into view. Stephen turned his head and said, "Get yourselves ready ladies, we're nearly there."

Just before they reached the gates, Stephen pulled the horses to a still and got down to talk. Sarah and Joulie sitting comfortably side by side on the buggy looked at Stephen who said, "Before we go in, are you both alright with what we have agreed to do with the Ferret as if you have any doubts, now is the time to speak up."

Sarah and Joulie looked at each other and although Joulie felt a deep sympathy towards him knew it was the right thing to get him away. So with a lower movement of her head said, "I have none, I know it's for the best." Stephen smiled politely knowing it was a difficult time for Joulie and then looked at Sarah who said. "It's our only choice for everyone's safety." "Right then, after I go in, if you could both take care of the two sisters, I will get the Ferret out and away. A message has been sent so he should be all ready to go and I will see you both in a couple of days."

Stephen felt more comfortable knowing that he had the support of the two women, especially Joulie. So, with that, he walked forward and opened the gate and then got back on the buggy and drove it forward up to the front door. Getting down once again, he asked if they could gather their things and get down and wait over by the side. He felt it wise that he goes in first without any distraction and get the Ferret out and away sharpish.

So, with both women standing off to the side watching, Stephen knocked the door. Expecting a quick response he turned to the women and smiled. Then after a minute of hearing nothing, he knocked again but this time a little harder, but again, nothing. He decided to knock one more time and while he did so leaned forward and shouted the sister's names. Again, hearing no response, he tried to open the door but it was locked. So, with no movement or sound coming from inside, Stephen turned to the women saying, "This is not good, wait here, I will go around the back."

However, again he saw and heard nothing, all was still and quiet. Stephen walked back round to the front and went straight to the buggy to fetch his pistol. Then with pistol loaded in hand he went close to the front door and shouted, "Stand back." Turning his face away from the blast he fired at the door lock and then shoulder barged the door. The door swung open but before he went in he pulled slightly away, off to the side and knelt on one knee to recharge the gun. He then stood up and again looked at the women and said, "I'm going in." Sarah quickly replied, "I have a small pocket pistol, shall I wait by the door, just in case?" "Is it loaded?" "Yes, I just need to pull the flintlock back." Stephen was not at all surprised that she had a gun and said, "Yes please Sarah." "Be careful," Joulie said to them both. Once Sarah was by the side of Stephen with her small pistol at the ready, Stephen went in.

With his eyes alert and pistol forward he looked about and saw nothing but an empty room with the fire out. He searched the ground bedroom and the scullery and all were empty. Sarah, still standing just outside the open door, was watching what he was doing and when she saw him pointing up the stairs she nodded and walked into the cottage. Then, after getting up the stairs and opening the first bedroom door was when he saw one of the sisters tied and gagged on the bed. When she saw him, her eyes opened with both joy and fear and struggled frantically as if pleading with him to help her. Stephen quickly went in and untied the gag around her mouth and as he did so she cried, "My sister, my sister, is she alright?" "I don't know, where is she?" "I don't know, please find her." "I will don't worry, all will be well, just hang on." Stephen went out along the hallway to the second bedroom and when opening the door saw the other sister tied and gagged. When he again untied the gag she cried. "Thank you, thank the Lord, where is my sister, is she alright?" "Yes, she is, please hold on, I will get help." Stephen went back down the stairs and talked with Sarah. On hearing what he had found, she quickly went out and got Joulie. Both women then ran back in and up to the bedrooms.

It took a while but now all were downstairs and calming down by the warm fire with tea in hand. The sisters sat close together holding each other's hand while Stephen was asking many questions, trying to get a grip on what had happened. Sarah and Joulie were by each of their side giving them love and comfort when needed.

It seems that the Ferret became very agitated when the sisters showed him the message they received yesterday saying that he was to be taken away this day. He said he had to get away and took their two horses and gig and the money they had saved for their later years. Stephen asked if he had been physical with them to get what he wanted. The sisters shook their heads that he had not but had used a loaded pistol towards them and told them he would shoot if they didn't do what he said.

Sarah didn't say anything but got up and put the water pot back on the fire to make all another tea. "Sarah, do you have any of that gin," said Janet. All smiled and realised that it could have been a lot worse and that they were safe. "Yes I do," she replied, "I will go out and get some for you." "And me please," said Fay.

While the gin was being sipped by all, Stephen asked, "I don't suppose he said where he was heading for." "No, he didn't, he just kept on saying that he was scared and had to get away for his life depended on it." Stephen thought upon this and concluded that maybe he had a point and probably he would have done the same. You couldn't trust anyone. He also realised that there wasn't much he could do about it. If the Ferret had left around nine last night then he could be anywhere, even out of Cornwall. Maybe this was a blessing in disguise and saved him an awful lot of trouble.

"So Stephen, what are you going to do?" "Well Sarah, I do need to get you and Joulie to your safe place in Bodmin but think I better inform Troon before I do anything." When Fay heard Stephen say this she asked, "Could you ask Mr Troon to give us back the money the Ferret has stolen from us." "Yes, of course, how much did he take?" "He took it all, one hundred pounds of our life savings." That wasn't quite true as it was near fifty but her sister Janet didn't say anything. "I will ask him." "Thank you, and if you could also mention that he stole our horses too." "Yes, I will do that also." "Thank you."
With everyone now calmed, Stephen said, "Right, well I better be off back to Mingoose and report to Troon, I will see you all tomorrow" "What time tomorrow?" Sarah asked. "I would say around mid to late morning, is that alright." "Yes, that would be fine." He didn't tell them

that on his way to Mingoose, he would first go via Truro and see John Hughes.

Troon did not find the news of the Ferret's escape at all amusing and became quite loud. Stephen just sat there and took the abuse as though it was his fault. "And you say he took all their money and horses." "Yes, that's what he did."

Troon marched up and down by the window huffing and puffing. What a mess and thought the sooner he and Sarah were gone from this bloody Cornwall, the better. Then standing still by the window he turned around and said, "By the way Stephen, I must inform you that I have yesterday agreed on the sale of the Manor and the Mine and so your services will no longer be required." Troon said this in an authoritative type manner as though he rules but Stephen kept his calm as he knew this would happen. Stephen then thought on how different this man acts in front of Sarah. "I understand Mr Troon so when will I be finishing." "We will probably complete in three to four weeks and so wish you stay on till that time but first I want Sarah and Joulie taken away to the house in Bodmin and quickly." Stephen noticed that he didn't say one word of thanks for his five years of service but again kept quiet. The day was now pushing on and getting very late in the evening but Troon wanted him to get back to Scorrier this night. So, after Troon had given last minute orders and the money for the sisters, Stephen got himself away.

As Stephen rode off he thought about going to his town house in Truro and sleep the night but decided he had better play the game and get back to the sister's house.

Troon remained sat in his comfy chair in the drawing room looking up at the ceiling in disbelief. That bloody Ferret has caused nothing but problems and deadly ones at that. He took another swig of the brandy and shook his head from side to side.

Sarah and Joulie were still up when they heard the noise of the gig pull up outside. It was passing two in the morning but both had decided they weren't taking any chances in simply going to bed and sleeping. That would leave them very vulnerable should anything or anyone come back after the Ferret's escape. So moving quietly and peeking out from the front curtain, Sarah saw it was Stephen and breathed a sigh of relief.

While the sisters were upstairs safely in their beds and sleeping the Gin off, Sarah, Joulie and Stephen remained downstairs. After explaining what Troon had said, they each got themselves comfortable in their seats and began to nod off. Stephen thought about going over to Joulie and giving her a cuddle but then thought better of it.

The morning light soon came and all had slept well with nothing untoward happening. However, that didn't stop Stephen and Sarah from sleeping with loaded pistols by their side, just in case.

Being refreshed and relieved, it was now the turn of the sisters to help their guests. So making a big breakfast for all they sat down and ate heartily. Whilst doing so, Fay and Janet thanked them for the help and the one hundred and twenty pounds which included the loss of their horses, from Troon. With breakfast now eaten and bags packed the three of them were now ready to move off and Sarah and Joulie couldn't wait. Even Stephen felt a sense of freedom of getting away. However, Joulie did feel a little dismayed at not having the opportunity to thank the Ferret for all he had done for her and to wish him all the very best.

As they rode away from the cottage, the thankful sisters stood outside the front door and waved them off. After a gentle one hour ride had passed Stephen stopped the gig outside a small Inn in a village called Indian Queens. He felt they needed to have a break and relax a little. Whilst sipping their drinks Sarah asked, "Can you now tell us where we are going." "Yes, I can now Sarah, I am to take you both to a place called St Tudy, a small village a few miles north of Bodmin." "What's it like," said Joulie. "I have no idea Joulie, when I went there to sort things it looked just like a normal village but it did seem quiet." After ten more minutes of chatting and glasses of drink empty, all got back on the buggy and drove off to their new safe house. All were in good spirit.

The Ferret however was the complete opposite and in total turmoil trying to make sense of his situation. He had got himself to the bustling port of Falmouth and was tucked up in a small room at the back of the Sailors Inn. He had this morning sent message to his trusted people in France and so would remain there unseen and await reply for safe sail. He was also still alive which he had to be thankful but then thought of his beautiful Andre, who was not. Cornwall had been a disaster.

.

Chapter 24

It had been a couple of days since Rebecca met Jacques in the Halzephron. He looked awful but she had listened to him and now her mind was made up that she would tell her Mother. Jacques remained in the Inn as agreed with the Landlord and prayed that she would.

Mrs Stephens kindly agreed to have the two children while Joshua escorted Rebecca to Lady Street. As they arrived outside the cottage on their own horses, Rebecca leaned over and kissed Joshua goodbye. Joshua bid her good luck with her Mother, Jeanne, and then galloped off as he had to get to the Bolventor Inn for the meeting with his two team leaders of Bedruthan and Mevagissey. Normally he would meet them routinely every quarter but the information from Kernow meant he had to bring things forward. But then they could also have a drink together and get merry with the fiddler and his music. It was also about time they all had a bit of fun and let their hair down.

Rebecca walked her horse into the back courtyard and as she was tying her up next to her Mother's horse, Jeanne saw her through the window and waved. Jeanne wasn't expecting to see her daughter today so wondered what was up. So, after unlocking the back door, Jeanne went over to the fire and put the pot of water on for boil.

As Rebecca walked in, Jeanne went up to her and after kissing her on the cheek asked where the children were. Rebecca explained that Mrs Stephens at Cury had them and then asked if they could both sit down. So, sitting by the fire waiting for the water in the pot to boil, Jeanne asked, "Are you alright Rebecca, you look strained." "I am fine Mother but I would like to talk to you about something." "Well, talk away my dear." "Mother, would you mind if we could have a brandy instead of tea." "O it's like that is it, of course we can." So, taking the water pot off the fire and brandy now in their hands, Rebecca went for it. "Mother, I need to tell you something." Jeanne was just sipping her brandy when Rebecca said this and immediately felt an inner concern. "Rebecca my dear, whatever it is you need to tell me, then tell me." "Mother, Jacques is alive and here in Cornwall." Jeanne dropped her brandy glass and stared in utter shock at what Rebecca had just said and with eyes and mouth open, she fainted.

Rebecca quickly ran to fetch some cold water and with cloth in hand started to wipe her Mothers face. After a few seconds of doing this, Jeanne started to come around and as she did, Rebecca said, "Mother, are you alright." "I'm sorry my dear, what happened?" "You passed out, that's what happened."

After sitting back up again and refilling her Mothers glass of brandy, Rebecca told all that she knew. Jeanne listened in silence but couldn't believe it. After all this time and thinking he was dead or injured or something awful. "And you saw him?" "Yes, Joshua and I met him two days ago, and Mother, he looked awful." O my dear Lord, O my dear, all this time and he just turns up, just like that."

Rebecca explained that as Mrs Stephens has the children she could stay here in the cottage or, she could get the gig ready and she will take her to him. "Rebecca, can you stay, we could go over to the Blue Anchor to relax and talk, I need to get my head around this, I am in shock." "Yes, we can Mother, you must be sure, there is no rush, we can go whenever you want or not go, it's entirely up to you."

Joshua and his two team leaders were in the corner of the Bolventor Inn and their meeting behind closed doors was completed and gone well. It was now time for the three of them to relax and enjoy the night. The Bolventor Inn was in fine swing. The fiddler was there playing good tapping music and the atmosphere was one of merriment and drink. Yes, there were also many shady characters about but that was not unusual in this Inn. For some reason, Joshua always felt at ease and safe in this Inn than in any other in Cornwall. But, could never quite understand why that was.

It was near midnight when his man from Bedruthan said, "I'm done, my missus will kill me if I don't get some sleep." "Joshua and the other team leader from Mevagissey laughed aloud but understood, as men do. Joshua then said, "Well, I say we've had a good night so let's all drink up and see each other at breakfast."

It was seven thirty in the morning while Joshua was still sound asleep in bed when he heard the knocking on his bedroom door. "Who is it he shouted." "Urgent message for Joshua Pendragon."

Sluggishly and reluctantly getting out of his bed, Joshua walked to the door in just his underpants. Halfway across he then switched on and went back to get his pistol and cocked it ready for firing. Then standing close but just off to the side by the wall he stretched out his hand and unlocked the door and pulled it ajar. It was then that a hand with the message appeared. Joshua took it and after saying a quiet 'thank you' closed the door shut and relocked it. He then went over to his bed and plonked himself down. Looking closer at the sealed message he knew the handwriting was George Kernow's and so carefully opened it.

The message read:-

Joshua
Two known tin smugglers killed.
Portishead.
Amber+.
GK

Well, that's two more people killed in the tin game he thought. So alert Amber plus it will be, something is up. He had better get himself freshened up and ready for breakfast with his two team leaders.

Jeanne and her daughter Rebecca were now both side by side in the gig being pulled by Jeanne's horse. Rebecca's horse was tethered to the rear and following along quite happily. They were off to Gunwalloe to the Halzephron Inn to see Jacques. Their night in the Blue Anchor had been good for both of them and Jeanne had made her mind up that she would indeed see him, she had to. The time was near midday and Jeanne had her new dress on and had also asked Rebecca to do her hair. She even put lipstick on. Jeanne felt good and looked happy which led Rebecca to say, "Mother you look like you're going on your first date." Jeanne didn't respond but just laughed and took in the beautiful air and the refreshing breeze.

It took a couple of hours but, they reached the Inn and stopped the buggy outside the front entrance. Rebecca suggested that her Mother wait in the buggy and she will go in to organise things. Although Rebecca's love and loyalty were to Jeanne she had to put her defensive head on. This wasn't just a game of love, this was a serious thing between two people and so she had to play things with care. Joshua had given her his backing should Jeanne wish to pursue things which was good and made her feel a lot better.

Jacques was in his bedroom in deep thought when he heard the knock on the door. He quickly jumped up and opened the door and on seeing it was Rebecca, he smiled brightly and asked her in. He thought it may have been Jeanne so was a little disappointed but once they started to talk he could not have been happier.

After ten minutes or so of talking, Rebecca then went out to her Mother. However, before she did, she went to find Peter the Landlord to explain things and for him to keep a careful eye on them.

As Rebecca walked out of the Inn and got to the buggy, her Mother turned to her and said, "Where have you been Rebecca, I've been waiting for ages." "Mother, are you ready, it's all been sorted." Jeanne went quiet and after taking a big gasp of fresh air slowly got down from the gig. Rebecca explained that it was best if the two of them met in a cosy corner out of the way in the bar area and she would wait outside. "I understand Rebecca, we have to be careful. After having a quick hug, Rebecca said, "Good luck Mother."

As Jeanne went in through the entrance door, Peter saw her and quickly went over to talk. "Hello, you must be Jeanne, Rebecca's Mother." "Yes, that is me." "Pleased to meet you, I am Peter, the landlord and good friend of Joshua's. The man you wish to see is over there in the corner would you like a drink sent across?" "Yes please, two large brandy's would be nice, thank you." Jeanne then walked over to the corner and spotted Jacques straight away but he looked half the man she had once known and loved. Getting close to his table Jacques saw her and stood up as gentlemen do and couldn't believe the feeling of happiness and joy at seeing Jeanne again, the love of his life.

Chapter 25

After getting off the Moor safely and stealing two horses from an out of the way village the two assassins arrived at the Dragons Inn in Truro. Shanks, although had said there was no rush, was very concerned as it had been near five days since he last saw them in Exeter. As soon as they had arrived the assassins went and knocked his bedroom door to explain their delay. Although annoyed at being woken so early in the morning Shanks quietly listened but couldn't believe what he was hearing. He had just presumed they had got drunk and skived off somewhere. "So, let me get this right, the reason it took you five days to get here was that you were in a wood on Bodmin Moor and were attacked by two giant lions?" They both nodded their heads and said, "Yes." "And you lost both your horses and all equipment." "Yes, that is correct." Shanks didn't reply but looked on in despair and bewilderment. He was going to ask more questions but decided against it as it was so far fetched. He then told them both to get some sleep and he will give them money to re-equip. He then slammed the bedroom door and walking back to his bed shook his head in disbelief.

That was four days ago and after reequipping the two assassins and introducing them to the other two man team; all were now doing their job well. It was a slow process but that was fine. They needed to use their skills to find who the main men are and once found, eliminate them. But that was easier said than done as it needed good planning without drama or suspicion. Luisa wants a clear path for her smuggling and would not accept anything less. Shanks also had to be ready in a couple of weeks for the exchange of contracts and money for the Mingoose Manor. This was an important part of the total plan and would need to go exceptionally well.

It was the next morning while in his bedroom having tea that he received the message from London. Once read he then thought about what to do. His two teams were still out scouting and would not be back till later this evening or the next morning at the earliest. It wasn't a big job just one person to be taken out. The message also read that it had to be done without delay. Shanks didn't have many options so decided he would ask his driver, come guard man, to do it. Also, the target was located quite close in the port of Falmouth. Yes, that's what he would do. If it all went wrong and he got killed then he had lost only a buggy driver who can be replaced. But, if it went well he could maybe use him for other jobs. So with his mind made up, he got himself washed and dressed.

When a few quiet moments had passed after Shanks and his driver had sat down to eat their breakfast, Shanks approached the subject. "It would seem we have a little problem to sort out and would ask if you could help." The driver looked up and after swallowing a piece of sausage said, "Yes of course, what is it you require." "I would like you to go to Falmouth this day and kill a small man by any means you see fit. I have his full description and the address." The driver looked at him without fear or surprise and in a calm voice answered, "Thank you but my orders are to drive the buggy as you require and to help where I can, that's it." "So, you are saying you can't do it." "I didn't say I can't, I said my orders are my orders." Shanks was not used to people refusing his orders and was going to raise his voice and say, "How dare you refuse me, you do what I say." He then thought better of it as the man from Bath who had given him this driver was himself a powerful person and also was very close to Luisa. After a few silent seconds of taking in what the driver had said and the calm way he said it, Shanks smiled with a reluctant acceptance of being told no and quickly tucked in his ego. The driver didn't seem at all fussed and just carried on eating his breakfast. Shanks then started to ponder on who exactly is this man in front of him. Anyway, that was by the by. So, the only other options were, to do it himself or, wait for one of the teams to come back. He thought about doing it himself which he was capable of but then thought he hadn't come this far in life to go back to the scrag end of killing. No, he wouldn't get his hands dirty or get involved so would wait till tomorrow and assign one of the teams. With decision made both men quietly and without word got on with eating their breakfast as two normal people would.

The Ferret was laid on his bed with the morning candle aglow in the far back room of the Sailors Inn. It had been ten days since he sent the message but still had no reply of sail. Yes, he had the money from the sisters who had agreed to give him it to him as long as he promised to pay it back. Ten days of doing nothing in a small room was not good for the brain. There was only so much he could take. But was else could he do, he had to lie low. And so he decided that he would lie low a further four days which would be two weeks of self confinement and if nothing came back he would take sail to somewhere else, he had to. Swinging his legs over onto the floor and sitting up on the side of the bed with head down and hunched shoulders he took another large gulp of the gin. It was going to be another long day.

Later that same afternoon two men in smart dress found the Sailors Inn and boldly walked straight in. On finding the landlord they asked if a man of very small size by the name of DuPont was staying there and if so, could he please tell them what room he is in. The Sailor Inn was built on the quayside and the Landlord was used to people coming in asking questions about other people. Or people just barging in and causing problems through drink or fighting. So, as a measure of client safety and Inn security the door to the upper bedrooms was always kept locked and only he, the maids and the guests had keys. The landlord knew of the man they spoke so after weighing the two men up said, "If you would like to take a seat I will get someone to check." "If you could that would be very kind and please tell him that we have come with safe sail." The landlord nodded and went off to talk with a maid.

Ten minutes later the landlord came back over to the two men and said, "The small man you talk off is here but has asked if you could name me his close associate?" "Yes, of course, her name is Joulie." "Thank you, that's what he said. I don't usually get involved with this sort of stuff but he has been a good guest and I think he is not very well." The landlord handed over the keys to the Ferrets room and the door saying, "Good luck." "Does he owe you any money?" "No, he has paid in full"

As the two men entered the Ferret's bedroom they saw him on his bed and so went over to talk with him. They noticed he was drunk but trying his best to act sensible.

The two men were not surprised by this and so helped him with his gear, which wasn't much, to get him out and away. The ship would not be ready for sail until the high tide at eight tonight but thought it best to get him out of the Inn now and onboard into his cabin. So once all was ready, they got him up and all walked out of the Inn across the quay to the awaiting ship. The landlord watched them through the window and giggled as the two men tried to keep the Ferret upright.

The two man team from the Dragons Inn in Truro rode into Falmouth arriving at the quay side just after seven thirty that evening. The sun was coming down and the old men with flame were about lighting the street lamps. They saw the Sailors Inn but decided to pull back out of the way a little to discuss what to do. They had got back to the Dragons Inn this very afternoon which was earlier than they thought they would and so were expecting a well earned drink and rest. So the last thing they needed was new orders for another assignment. But, Shanks was insistent that this job had to be completed this day. So, pulling back and sitting down out of the way both men moaned saying, 'it's alright for him to say but taking a life is not easy when it has to be done without capture.' But then they accepted that these moments crop up and so they had to do what they had to do. What they knew was this man was staying in the Sailors Inn and was a mere midget named Francis Du Pont. So how were they to do it, that was the question? They both sat quietly thinking by the edge of the quay with their horses tied. The time was now nearing eight and the stars were starting to appear.

"I think the first thing we should do is see if he is actually in the Inn." "Yes, but even then we don't know what he looks like." "We have a description and name." "Yes, I suppose and there can't be many midgets about the place, can there." "Tell you what, why don't we put say five silver coins in a purse and one of us go in acting all respectable saying, something like, "Please could you give this money to the small man, Francis Du Pont?" The other man thought on this and after a few seconds said, "That's very good, we will then at least know if he is in there and then pull back and work out how." So with minds made up, they got the money purse together and after tossing a coin to see who goes in they both walked over to the Inn. While one of the men stayed outside by the door holding the horses the other quickly rubbed his face and dusted his clothes, walked in.

Keeping his head and stature high he walked through to the bar area with eyes alert looking for someone like a manager or landlord. He then spotted a man behind the bar talking to a staff member who looked exactly like the person he needed to talk to. Knowing his mate was outside watching his back, he confidently walked to the bar and with posh voice said, "Excuse me my good man, are you the landlord?" The man behind the bar stopped talking to his staff member and turned his head saying a little sharply, "Yes I am, can I help you." Keeping things very simple and assured the man held up the purse and said, "Please could you give this purse of silver coins to the small man Francois Du Pont." "Sorry, Mr Du Pont no longer has room here, he left this afternoon." "Do, you know where he went?" "He went to that ship." Then after pointing his finger at the front window said, "Which has just set sail out from the port." The man turned his head to the window and saw the ship in question with full sail catching the tide. Then on turning his head back to the landlord said, "Thank you, sorry to disturb you." Without hesitation the man put the purse back in his pocket, turned and started to walk to the front door. After taking a few steps the landlord said aloud, "What do we do about his horse, he has left it here?" "Keep it."

Chapter 26

It was a lovely sunny morning and the sun was shining through the curtains with warmth and love. Troon was awake in his bed and in good spirits thinking about the day ahead. It had been nearly a month since he and the man Shanks had agreed to the sale of Mingoose and the Mine at St Agnes. It had taken a while but today was the day that all will be concluded. The Manors furniture and chattels had been sold or were in storage for later use and all of the staff had been sacked and paid off the day before. The only servant he kept on was the young maid who was to keep him satisfied as he wished and to serve the tea as he wanted.

The young maid was still asleep next to him having given her best for most of the night. Troon with his arms behind his head and looking up decided it was time to make a move. He had a lot to get on with and the meeting between all parties was to start at twelve noon. Once this meeting was completed he would make his way in his carriage with the gold coins to the cottage at St Tudy. He had thought about keeping Bagnall on for a few more days and get him to sort a couple of outriders to protect the gold. But then thought of the expense and really what's the point? It's only a two hour ride and no one knows what's going on and it's always best to keep things close and quiet. He will sort things out when he gets to the cottage. So, with a joy in his step, he elbowed the young maid awake and jumped out of bed. He went over to the large window and after pulling back the curtains and standing tall and upright allowing the sun on his naked body said aloud, "Good morning world."

Shanks and his two teams were in the Dragons Inn at Truro going over last minute details. He wanted nothing to go wrong and questioned everyone in detail. The time was eight in the morning and with everyone agreeing on what they had to do, Shanks ended the meeting and wished them good luck. He now had an hour to freshen himself up ready for his next meeting with his Solicitors who had specially come down two weeks ago from Bath to get everything sorted for their meeting with Troon and his Solicitors at Mingoose Manor. All the paperwork had been prepared and agreed and now only needed the signatures of all parties with witnesses to complete the sale of transfer. Also, the coins of gold in the Solicitor's vaults in Truro had now been inspected and approved the day before and just needed to be picked up.

Stephen Bagnall was in his town house in Truro thinking of his lovely little Joulie. He had been over to the cottage at St Tudy a couple of times on behalf of his employer Troon but now he had been sacked things wouldn't be so easy. But they had talked a lot and got on really well even though Sarah huffed and puffed at their silly love talk. They had kissed a lot too but nothing more. Joulie wanted to take things slowly and Stephen had agreed. On his last visit there a few days ago he saw the message from Troon saying he would be with them on this day and all will be well. Hmmmm, Stephen thought. Joulie had told him that Sarah always seemed to get fidgety when the name Troon came up. Maybe, as Joulie and Sarah talk a lot, that it had something to do with him mentioning how his employer really acts away from Sarah. They had agreed that she will send message to him as soon as she knows what is happening after Troon's arrival. Stephen couldn't wait to see her again but when and where was the question? He had to be patient for her sake. He then thought about the day ahead and his meeting with his mate in the White Hart.

The cottage in St Tudy was lovely and Sarah and Joulie were indeed getting excited about Troon's arrival later that day. As both were sitting around the table eating their early morning breakfast Joulie asked, "So, are we going to Devon?" "Joulie, that's the fifth time you have asked me that, and I don't know for sure, that is the answer." "But you said when we left Mingoose that we were." "I know I did but if we do or we don't what's the difference, are you thinking of Stephen?" In truth, Joulie was thinking about him and also how Devon was so far away from Truro. Sarah didn't say it but she too was thinking of Ginge but then couldn't get rid of an inner gut feeling that something felt wrong. Both women went on to chat through the day to give each reassurance that all will be well and that they were there for each other.

Shanks, who was just finishing off the meeting with the Solicitors in the Dragons Inn, excused himself and went to his room. All was ready but he needed five minutes alone. This had to go to plan and so looking out of his bedroom window in deep thought, he went over things to make sure he hadn't missed something. He thought about the Ferret and how lucky he was in getting away when he did. Luisa wasn't pleased but had accepted the outcome as Shanks had done all that he could in the time scale given. Well, that's the message he had sent her but omitted to mention that he himself was available. Then bringing his thoughts back to the here and now he stood up straight and thought, 'Right, let's get this on.' As he walked to the door he saw the gin bottle and decided a little nip would do him good.

Sitting back down in the bar area one of the two legal men from Bath asked, "Everything alright?" "Yes, all is well, were just waiting for the carriage with the gold to arrive." "Yes, we know." With that Shanks asked again if they could confirm that their visit and survey of both Mine and Manor was agreeable." "Yes, both are good and the locations excellent." "Good, then have you any last questions?" "No, as we said, we met Troon's legal team yesterday and are both in agreement that once the contract is signed and the agreed sum of money handed over then we will be the new owners from that moment." "Then I think we have covered everything." It was then they saw the carriage draw up to the front of the Inn guarded by Shank's two man teams. "Right, it is time we were off and I will see you at Mingoose."

It took over an hour to get to the gates of the Manor at Mingoose but once outside they stopped. Shanks got out of the carriage and asked that the four men of his two teams get down off their horses. While sitting in the carriage he had been thinking on which team would do the assassination and which would do the guarding. He decided that the team who had lost everything on the Moor due to some stupid excuse about lions would stay close and guard. So, after informing them of his decision the team to stay close stayed where they were and the other team moved off into the woods and waited.

Shanks got back in the carriage and asked his driver to move on. As they went through the gates and stopped outside the front of the Manor the front door opened.

Troon stood there smiling and went down to greet him. "Good day Mr King, thank you for being on time, we are all gathered inside ready." "Good day Mr Troon, good to see you again, I will leave my two guards here to protect your investment."

As soon as Shanks went in he noticed how bare the Manor had become. However, knowing Luisa as he did she would soon put that right. Then getting into the library he saw seven people around the table talking away about the sale. All were from the legal profession and the discussion bored him dearly. But, he had a job to do and so would play the game. The young maid was sitting in the corner and when Shanks had got himself seated, she came across and poured him some tea.

The meeting went on for a long time with both parties going carefully over the deeds of sale, the clauses and the plans. It was their job to get it right in the interest of their client and, would be paid handsomely. It wasn't until they got onto the subject of the gold that Shanks spoke up in a meek and friendly tone. "Yes, all the gold coins are here in the carriage outside." Then the senior partner of Troon's solicitors suggested, "I think it would be good if we all went outside and counted it and if all being satisfied, come back here and get things signed off, are we in agreement?" All nodded their heads and got up from their seats. It was while the two senior solicitors were counting the gold that Shanks, standing very close to Troon said in a most friendly and kindly manner, "Do you think you could take us to the Mine to have a quick look round?" "Well, I do really need to get away as we agreed." "Yes, I'm sorry, I thought I would ask, are you going anywhere nice?" Without thought, Troon replied,

"Devon actually." "That's a long way away, how are you getting there, are you going straight from here." "Yes, I am but may stop off at Bodmin." "Well, please be careful, that's a lot of coin aboard." "Thank you, I will." "Tell you what, when they have finished counting, my two men here will help you load it onto your carriage." "Thank you, that would be very helpful." "Well, it's the least we can do, we are very happy with the sale and wish you all the best." With the counting completed and the legal men going back into the Manor, Troon with the help of the two men loaded the gold into Troon's carriage. When all was done, Troon started to walk back in to sign and witness on the dotted lines. Shanks went with him but held back for a second and whispered into the ear of one of his men. The man then waited for everyone to go in and when all were out of sight and the door closed got on his horse and rode out quietly to talk with the other team waiting in the woods. When done, he rode back to the manor as though he had never left.

With all sitting down and everything now concluded the maid got the brandy and glasses and served all. Then when all was quiet for all to hear, Shanks spoke up, "Mr Troon, as a measure of goodwill would you like to use my outriders to help you get to your destination where ever that maybe?" All the solicitors with brandy in their hands looked at Troon thinking what a kind gesture. "Thank you Mr King but as I said before, I wish to be free and on my way, without hinder." So all with glasses raised in cheer of the deal done, they drank back the brandy in one. Then, after packing away all their stuff and shaking hands it was time for all to leave.

The first person to leave the grounds of the Manor was, as agreed, Cuthbert Troon in his gig with the gold. Then, when he was gone and out of sight it was the turn of all the legal men. Shanks and his team stayed where they were and watched all of them go. When all had gone, Shanks, his driver and his two man team went back in the Manor into the library.

The whole place was now Luisa's and it was now up to Shanks to care take the place upon her arrival. With all now sitting down Shanks saw the brandy bottle on the table and so poured each man a well earned drink. It was then that a knock on the door was heard and all saw the young maid poke her around. "Come over here my dear," Shanks said. So, as a young servant would, she dipped her head and walked in towards him. Then one of the men in the two man team nudged his mate and whispered, "Nice." His team mate started to laugh and nodded his head in agreement. "How much was Troon paying you," Shanks asked. "He pays me one penny a day Sir." "Well, I will increase that to two pennies a day if you agree to stay and keep things tidy. "Thank you Sir, I agree."

When the young maid had left the room, Shanks turned his attention to the two men. Then grabbing the large ring of keys and sliding them across the table said, "Right, you two have done well, enjoy your drink and get yourselves to the Mine." "What time shall we expect delivery?" "I would say about nine to nine thirty if all goes to plan. Once done, hand the keys over to the other team and move yourselves off back to the Dragon Inn, any questions? " "No, all is clear."

Although the Manor was now owned by Luisa she could not be seen or connected with anything untoward and that included the presence of Shanks and his associates. Therefore, Luisa's solicitors from Bath had hired a local butler and wife who were to arrive first thing tomorrow. They would live in the Manor and look after the place with the young maid.

Chapter 27

Troon was in fine spirit riding upon his gig with the gold coins loaded in the back. His next stop would be St Tudy where he will see Sarah once again. He quickly thought about Joulie and his promise to take her with them to Devon. He had lied, there was no way he would take that little imp with them and spoil what he had in mind. Two's company, three's a crowd. He would work out something and then laughed aloud. As the powerful stallion pulling the gig trotted on, Troon looked about the countryside and felt good. Cornwall had done its work and he was a very rich man, so goodbye Cornwall and hello Devon, here we come.

When the two man team, who had been waiting in the woods outside the Manor, had been given the word that Troon was going east to Devon or Bodmin they jumped on their horses and galloped away. They had done their research and discussed with Shanks that should he go east then the route he would most likely take would be this and if he went west it would be that. So after an hour in the saddle, they arrived at the position they had planned. It was a place near St Columb Major where the road slopes down and bends sharply at the bottom. It was surrounded by dense forest which gave them good cover and visual through the trees of the road coming down. So all in all a good place to do what they had to do. Then checking their pistols and getting into position they waited. The time was nearing seven thirty and the sun was going down.

Troon was trying to make good pace but knew he had to take it steady. He had been in the seat for well over an hour and at the pace he was going it would probably be another hour before he got to Sarah's. That would mean an estimated time of arrival of nine thirty. But it is what it is and he was just so glad that all the hassle was now behind him. Riding down the sloping road he saw the tight bend at the bottom so reined his horse to a gentle canter. As he slowed things to the correct pace and took the gig round the bend was when he saw the two men. Both were on horseback with scarves around their faces on either side of the road and pistols drawn. With inner fright and instinct, Troon lashed his horse hard and in a spurt, the gig lunged forward at pace. This didn't bother the gunmen in the least and while keeping their calm and letting the gig ride through their position aimed and fired their pistols.

With the sudden loud blast of the guns and the flash of fire, the horse reared up in mid gallop. Doing this made the gig jerk and lunge forward and Troon, with pistol shots to the chest, fell over the footings and dropped to the ground. The horse was still in panic and didn't know what to do so darted forward at high speed up the road. With one of the men staying by the body on the ground, the other man chased after it. After fifty or so yards of frantic gallop, the horse started to calm allowing the man to catch up and bring the gig to a halt. On checking that the gold coins were still in place and secure he turned the horse and gig about and went back to his mate. Once back by his mate, he jumped down and after hearing that Troon was dead, both picked up the body and threw it onto the gig. Being content with what they had done they covered the body over with a blanket and on turning to each other shook hands firmly. They didn't need to say anything. What they had to do now was get back to the Mine at Wheal Coates. Shanks had estimated they should get there by nine to nine thirty but that was out of the question. It would be more towards the hour of eleven.

The pace back to the Mine was taken at a steady rate, not like the gallop they had done to get to the ambush point. One of the men was up ahead leading the way while the other was driving the gig with his horse tied at the back. Both were on high alert as the cargo on board needed it. Then, as time and miles ticked by they came to Wheal Coates Mine without fault or hindrance. The gate was locked but the other two man team inside the hut heard the noise and came out. The time was eleven fifteen.

"You took your time, where have you been, down the pub?" "Very funny, now could you open the gate and let us in." Both men on the ground laughed but then did as asked and as the gate opened the horse and gig gently rode in coming to a halt just outside the hut. Both men then jumped down from horse and gig and went over to the two men. "How did it go?" "We did it as planned, he is in the gig on the floor and the gold is in the back." "Well done mates, let's have a look." All four men went to the gig but not before one of the men ran into the hut to fetch the lantern.

With all four now around the gig, one of the men pulled back the blanket to see Troons body. After a few seconds of silence, one of the men said, "Well that's what you get for being a twat and playing with the devil." No one responded to that remark and just stayed silent. Then one of the ground men leant forward and touched the body and seeing the two bullet entries on Troons upper chest said, "Good shooting lads." It was then that one of the gig team asked, "Have you any gin or brandy here?" "Yeah, we do but I think we better do what we have to do first then we can all sit and have a swig, what say you both?" With all nodding their agreement they got on with what they had to do. The first thing was to get rid of the body. "Where is he to go?" "Over in the far corner by the fence near the cliff, it's not far." So, each man grabbed a limb and dragged the body across the ground.

Just as they were nearing the fenced area one of the men said, "Just hold there a minute." He then went forward with the lantern and pulled back the iron cover of an old disused Mine shaft. Making sure all was clear he held the lantern just inside the shaft and looked down. Being happy that all was clear he turned to his mates and put his thumb up. The three men dragged the body towards the shaft and as they got close, the man put the lamp to the side and picked up one of Troons legs. All four men then started to swing the body backwards and forwards. Then as the body was swinging in good motion one of the men started to slowly count to three and when he said, "Three," they gave one final heave and released their grip. Troons lifeless body flew over into the shaft and down into its darkness like a sack of potatoes.

The next job was the gold. That was simple enough as that just needed to be brought into the hut and guarded. When that was done, the last job was to set fire to the gig. So they led the horse on with gig in tow to an open spot away from the hut. Once in position, they released the reins and took the horse out of harm's way back to the hut area. With all four men now around the gig with oil poured all over it, a lighted lantern was thrown on.

Although it was still drizzling the gig caught alight in seconds and the four men stood in silence watching the flames roar. It was now time for that well earned drink.

With the four men back in the hut one of the ground men said, "Well, we had better be off." "Why don't you both stay the night with us in the hut, we don't mind?" "Thanks, but our orders are to hand everything over to you and get back to the Dragons Inn." "But it's very late." "We know that, but you know what he's like."

So, after saying their farewells and shaking each other's hands the two ground men left for the Inn. The other two closed the gate behind them and walked back to the hut for further drink and sleep. Shanks had ordered that they were to wait and guard the gold there until such time as they were replaced, which wouldn't be long. This didn't bother them at all as they needed a good rest.

The other two men riding out then stopped their horses about half a mile away. One of them then said, "We could have stayed if we wanted you know." "Yeah I know but it's only an hour's run to the Inn and I want a nice warm bed tonight with a big hot breakfast in the morning." They both laughed aloud and galloped off.

Chapter 28

It was early morning when the Packet ship took the wind and set sail for London from Falmouth Harbour. After all that they had been through, Jeanne decided she and Jacques needed time to be alone together well away from the land of Cornwall. So, with the help of her loving daughter Rebecca, she had booked a small cabin for them both. Although Jacques was on the mend and looking better he was still not well from his past ordeals and struggles. They intended to go away to the capital city to relax and enjoy its atmosphere and architecture. She had also done her homework and read up on a little town called Epsom with its drinking waters of healing. So, they would also take a journey there to help improve Jacque's health and well being.

When they had met each other in the Halzephron Inn after five years of being apart Jeanne couldn't believe it was Jacques. He looked dreadful and half the man of courage and strength she once knew. But the glint of love and joy she could see and feel in his eyes convinced her that she too had missed him dearly. And so, she sat down and listened to his reasons and tales of why he did what he did. After thirty minutes or so of sincere talking Jacques offered his hand across the table and although hurt from his running away she could see he was in deep regret on what he did and so extended her hand too. Both smiling in deep love for each other they raised their brandies in their other hands and drank them back like they use to when they were younger. "Thank you Jeanne for being so loving and understanding, I love you with all my heart." "Jacques, I love you too but promise me now you will never leave me again." "I promise with all my heart and soul."

With Rebecca, Joshua and the two children standing at the Falmouth quayside, Jeanne and Jacques aboard the ship waved their goodbyes. "I think it will do them the world of good Joshua." "I think your right Rebecca, maybe one day we could do the same." "Maybe when the children are grown, if you're lucky," she jokingly replied. When the ship had sailed out of the harbour, Rebecca and Joshua took each of the children's hands and made their way from the quay. Joshua had to get to Truro to meet the sheriff and Rebecca needed to get to Lady Street with the children. She had promised her Mother that she would look after her cottage until such time as she and Jacques return. Having an empty cottage for a long period of time in the town of Helston was not good and would attract the rogues and paupers that walk the streets. After Rebecca got on the gig and took the reins with the children and the two little dogs beside her, Joshua got on his trusted steed Harry and escorted them to Helston. While he did so, he thought that it was just as well Jeanne and Jacques were getting away as something was up. What it was he didn't know but things weren't feeling right.

With Rebecca safely at Jeanne's cottage, Joshua rode on to Truro in good speed and after dismounting and tying up Harry, walked into the Sheriff's office. "Good to see you Joshua, would you like tea, or something a little stronger?" "That depends on what you know and tell me?" "Well, it's not a lot so why don't we have some tea." The sheriff of Truro was a good man and Joshua liked him.

After receiving the messages from Kernow in London of the killings in Bristol and Portishead, and the increase security alert to amber plus, Joshua had reacted quickly and sent messages all around. The sheriff went over the things he had become aware of since receiving this alert but really nothing had appeared out of the ordinary or of any significance. Truro was a busy town and had many devious goings on and therefore, trying to sift and filter what was off beat, out of sink or strange was not easy. What Joshua was hunting for was something that didn't fit but that was easier said than done. Joshua listened to what the sheriff had to say and although it was interesting, nothing was happening out of the norm or gave him a sense of curiosity. Yes, there was thieving, fighting and smuggling of spirits and goods but that was just the Cornish day to day living. So, once all was done and tea sipped, Joshua got up and shook the sheriff's hand and thanked him for his help and cooperation. Joshua needed to get to his cottage at Gunwalloe and rest up. He had a busy day tomorrow.

Getting back to his safe cottage and with a good night's sleep behind him, Joshua felt refreshed and ready to go. After eating some food which Rebecca had prepared, he went out and got Harry ready. He had two meetings today with the senior constables of St Ives and Penzance. It would be a long ride but Joshua was trying to spread himself about as best and as quickly as he could. He also had two other meetings arranged for the following day at Redruth and Falmouth. His plan was to complete all four meetings on time and when done would go and visit Bull at Zennen to discuss. With time at a premium, Joshua pushed Harry on into a gallop and got on with things.

Bull's missus was in a fluster running around getting things prepared for Joshua's arrival anytime now. "Bull, don't just sit there, help me with the rugs, they need shaking." Bull raised his eyes without her seeing and got up to do as told. He had learnt that when she was on a mission it was always best just to go with it. It was just past noon when they heard Joshua ride up to the farm. Bull looked at his missus and on getting the approval sign got up and went to the door to welcome him in.

"Hello Bull." "Hello Joshua, come on in." Joshua went in behind Bull to the main room and with the fire ablaze sat down around the table. As they did so, Bull's missus came in to say hello and as she did, Joshua stood up and said, "Good afternoon." "Tea or brandy Joshua?" "A brandy would go down well, thank you." "I have made us all some bacon and eggs which should be ready in about ten minutes." Joshua once again said his thanks and sat back down. "So Bull, how are things?" "All is well Joshua, and very quiet." "Hmmm, I thought that may be the case. Anyway, shall we get down to business as I would like your thoughts and ideas?"

Joshua went on to explain his sense of increased tension since the amber plus alert and the outcome of the four meetings he had completed with the officials of the different towns. Bull listened and like Joshua, was trying to understand and get a grip on the underneath meaning of things. "So Joshua, let me get this right, nothing out of the norm has been seen, heard or noted in any way." "I couldn't have put it better Bull, exactly." Both men sat quietly thinking without word and then in a quiet voice, Joshua spoke, "Any chance of another brandy Bull."

"Yes of course Joshua, let me clear the table away first and I will refill your glass." When things were cleared away and Bull was out getting the brandy, Joshua got the map out of his pocket and spread it open across the table. He wanted to go over things in more detail and visualise the ground as it may nudge or give rise to something.

Both men then analysed the map of the towns, coves and terrain, but still, nothing was coming. So it was down to Joshua to make a decision with the resources he had at hand. "Bull, I think we need to get our socks on and start the scouting process, how are your men at this time?" "Are we talking covert observing or overt street and Inn scouting?" "I'm talking both Bull." "That's fine Joshua, my team are good and can muster eight men including myself to give us four teams of two men each." "Good, then I think we should discuss where the teams are to go and see what can be found." "And what do we want to find Joshua?" Joshua had to hand it to Bull, as it was a very good question. "Bull, I gotta hand it to you, that is the very question I have been asking myself. All I know is that the messages received from Kernow show that something is afoot but as to what I know not." "I agree Joshua but the killings were carried out in Bristol and Somerset, well away from Cornwall." "That may be so Bull, but Kernow has put us on amber plus alert for some reason." "He did say one of the men killed was an HM Customs officer, did he not." "Yes, he did." "Well, then maybe we should start our covert operation around ports or known smuggling areas such as the Lizard and Poldu." "I think that would be a good start Bull, we can then tweak things as we go. Also, to try and answer your previous question more precisely, we are seeking any information no matter how trivial that could link to these deaths." "Now that I do understand Joshua." "Thanks' Bull, it took me a while." They both chuckled at Joshua's last comments. "Right Bull, I had better be heading back, thanks again for your help and good luck." "Where are you off to?" Joshua had already explained to Bull the situation with both Jeanne and Jacques and so said, "Well, I am staying over in Helston tonight to see Rebecca and the children and then up early for the Bolventor Inn to meet our North and South teams."

On his way out, Joshua thanked Bulls missus for the lovely brandy and the food. She smiled with warmth and replied, "Anytime Joshua, you are most welcome, please give my love to Rebecca and the children."

As Joshua rode off, Bull turned to his missus and said, "Right, my dear, I had better be off myself, I should be back before night fall." "Alright my love, don't drink too much and if I'm asleep when you get back you can wake me up." She then fluttered her eye lids and smiled a meekly smile." Bull got the message and gave her a kiss on the cheek knowing exactly what she meant."

Joshua got to Lady Street just after four o clock. It had been a very busy three days of riding and meetings and he was exhausted. Tying Harry up in the rear courtyard, Joshua knocked on the back door but he needn't have bothered as just as he did, little Richard had already seen him from the window and rushed out to meet his Dad. Joshua picked him up and gave him a loving kiss on the forehead and while still holding him in his arms walked into the cottage. As he entered, little Vivienne also ran towards him and while still holding Richard in one arm, picked her up in the other arm and squeezed her tight with love. So now, with both the children in his arms, he walked through the scullery into the main room. The fire was aglow and Rebecca was sitting relaxed in a soft chair reading with Cecil and Queenie asleep at her feet.

Rebecca looked up and with care and love said, ''Joshua, you look worn out, come and sit down and I will get us both a brandy.'' ''Rebecca, that would be lovely.'' ''I have also bought some fresh eggs and bacon and so will make us all some food too.'' Joshua was just about to say that he had already had this exact food a few hours ago at Bulls Farm in Sennen but thought better of it and kept quiet.

After all the joy of the children and eating the delicious food, it was time to put the little ones to bed. While getting them ready, Rebecca asked if Joshua could take the dogs for a quick walk and when done they could sit down and relax together.

And so with the children tucked up in their bedroom, it was time for Rebecca and Joshua to enjoy the company of each other in the quiet of the cottage. Joshua was quietly thinking about his meeting tomorrow and how his North and South teams are to replicate the same plan he and Bull devised in the West with immediate effect. Then without further thought, he stretched his legs out and gazed into the fire. "What a lovely little place your Mum has." "Yes, isn't it, she has done well, but then again she has worked for it." "That's true." "How was Bull?" "He is well, O and his missus sends you and the children her love." "They're a nice couple Joshua." "Yes, they are, and Bull has helped me in many ways with his honesty and experience." "What time are you setting off tomorrow?" "Well, I got to be at Bolventor around noon so would say eight o clock." "Fine, then I will make some breakfast before you go and suggest we get an early night." Joshua smiled and raised his eyebrows with a smile but Rebecca quickly replied, ''Joshua there will be none of that in this cottage, it's to sleep, and that's all." "Alright Rebecca." "By the way Joshua, is there anything to worry about, is something going on?" "That's what I intend to find out." "Be careful Joshua."

Chapter 29

The five armed men, four riding on their horses and one driving a two horse gig, arrived at the Crowns Head Inn just north of the Cornish border in the village of Lifton. They were an experienced team of quiet couriers for Wright & Co Solicitors on behalf of their client, Luisa. All lived in the Bath area and had done many jobs in the land of England, especially around the ports of Bristol and Plymouth. However, this job was different, as the location was some way out of the way Tin Mine in Cornwall which would normally be handled by a team living much closer. But orders were orders and they were not going to miss out on the good pay packet that was on offer.

Jim Coulston, the leader of the team, suggested they all stay outside while he goes in and sort things out. The Inn was very quiet which agreed with everyone. After sorting out the rooms and paying the landlord upfront, Jim walked back outside. Then after taking their horses, gig and gear around to the stables, they entered the rear of the Inn without fuss. The time was approaching early evening and so all were ready for some food and cider.

When the young serving maid had taken their plates away and refilled their tankards, all five men started to relax and wind down from the day's long journey from Exeter. "So, why didn't we stop at Okehampton Jim?" said one of the team. "I don't know, when we left Exeter I just felt we needed to get closer to Cornwall and, as we were making good time, decided to go for it, so well done all." As Jim finished talking another team member said, "I wish we could have stayed in Exeter another night, that Susie girl was lovely." Jim smiled and said, "Yes, we know, we saw you." All five men then laughed aloud. When the laughing died down, Jim continued, "But that won't happen here tonight, I can assure you, this is not Exeter, we are in a small village and we will all have an early night." "I don't know Jim, that young barmaid looks quite nice and I think she fancies me." Jim flicked his eyes to the ceiling and said in a stronger tone, "It's an early night for all, St Agnes is still a four hour ride from here." Then the quiet one of the five asked, "Jim, why are we doing this Cornwall run, I thought the Cornish did things by themselves." This question made everyone sit up and go quiet waiting for Jim's reply. "I have no idea, but a job is a job and we just get on with it." "Yes, I know that, but it seems strange don't you think?" "No, not really, things happen, you don't know what goes on behind the scenes." "Hmmm, I suppose so, but the Cornish, they put the bloody cream on top." This gave everyone a hearty giggle and paved the way for a nice evening of good spirit.

The night went well and all were up on time and fully equipped ready for the off. With Jim leading, they left the village quietly but once they hit the main highway Jim opened up his horse into a gallop. With all keeping a good pace they entered Cornwall and after a further hour of ride came to the edge of the Moor. Jim decided it was a good time to pull over for a fifteen minutes break and give the horses and his men a rest. When all the men had done their toiletries and got back together in a group, one of the men said, "I thought our Somerset moors was big but this is totally different, it feels weird." "I agree," said another, "There's also no colour, it's just a massive wilderness of gorse and granite" Jim listened with ease but then had to get things sorted so said in a rather fatherly manner, "When you two have finished do you think you could rub your horses down and check all the equipment." Although Jim had worked in the darker and more brutal side of things, he knew the four men in his team had not, but they were good men and loyal and stuck together.

Then on moving off and keeping a good steady pace for the next two and a bit hours, the front gate of the Wheal Coates Tin Mine came into view. On seeing Jim raise his hand, his team of men following reined their horses and gig and went to his side. Jim suggested they stay put and spread out and keep alert while he goes forward to talk.

The two men inside the Mine, although being in the light midday, were still in the hut lying down on their beds bored stiff. Yes, they had their pistols loaded and ready but that was about it. It was when they heard the man's voice shout 'Hello' from the main gate that they jumped up ready for action. "So, what do ya think?" said one of them. Keeping their heads low but peering out through the misted window the other said, "Well, they're here on and about the said time but let's shout the code word first and see what their response is." The other man nodded in agreement and so both cocked their pistols for fire. Then, with one of the men went by the window, the other crept forward to the front door and pulled it ajar. Then carefully kneeling himself down without any of his body or head showing shouted out, "Angof." Jim, knew this to be the code he was expecting and smiled with relief and responded by shouting back, "Anvil." Both men in the hut heard the response which was correct but, experience had taught them to double check when things are just a little too easy. So, after quietly nodding to each other, the man by the door shouted back, "What City?" Jim smiled and knew they were being cautious and so replied aloud, "Bath." This did the trick and the man by the door got up and walked out of the hut to the front gate with his mate by the window covering him. With the shaking of hands and a gentle discussion, the gate was then unlocked and Jim and his team rode in.

With all men, horses and gig gathered together outside the hut, one of the inside men said, "So, what would everyone like to drink?" "A good tot of brandy would be great," said one of Jim's men quickly. Jim smiled but quickly overruled on behalf of sensibility and said, "Do you have tea." "Yes, we do, the fire is on and will get it sorted." "That would be very welcome, thank you."

The hut was too small for seven men to comfortably sit inside, so when the tea was brewed they took their cups and sat outside. "So how long did it take you guys to get here from Bath?" Jim replied, "Just over two days, we stopped off at the village of Lifton last night and left early this morning," "Where's Lifton?" "It's just outside Cornwall, literally only five miles from the border." Jim continued, "How long have you two been here?" "We got here last week and then got the message a few days ago that you guys would be arriving to take the gold." "Where is the gold." "Inside the hut all ready for you to take away." "Well, when we finished our tea we will get it on the gig and be off if that is alright with you." "Yes, that's fine with us, cos when you go we can then lock up and get ourselves away, it's been a long week."

With all being done and the gold safely aboard the gig, the two men wished them good luck and watched them ride off. As they walked back into the hut one of them said, "Right, what say we get our gear together and get out of this bloody place." "I couldn't agree with you more, the quicker the better, I say." So, with their gear together and job done, they closed and locked the gate and quickly rode off to the Dragons Inn near Truro. Although they had rested for the past week and been bored out of their brains they were looking forward to having a good cider and maybe, all going well, a lady of the night.

Jim stopped his horse once they had ridden a few miles away from the Mine and asked his men to gather round. "Right men, I just want to check that all is well and you are ready, it's going to be a long ride and I don't want any mistakes." "When will we stop for a breather Jim?" "That's the point; I want us to get well away out of this Cornwall place while it's still daylight, so I would say not before Exeter." "Blimey Jim, that's a long run." "Yes, I know it is but we gotta get this gold to Bath and locked up secure in the vaults, without fault or delay." None of the men responded to what Jim said and accepted the task ahead, after all, it's what they do and they will be well paid. On hearing no response, Jim ordered they all get into position and get going. So, with Jim and one other up front and two men riding behind the gig, they rode off.

Riding at a steady but fair pace the miles ticked by with good timing. After an hour of riding up and down hills and going round long and tight bends on the road, the men noticed the sign for the Bolventor Inn. One of the back riders said to his mate, "Be nice to stop off for a few, I'm gasping." His mate by his side laughed aloud and replied, "I agree, but we will make up for it when we get to Exeter." "You Bet." And so both turned their heads forward and carried on.

It was when a further twenty minutes of riding had passed from the Inn that Jim's horse ears flicked up in alert. Jim noticed this straight away as he knew his horse well and looked about for what or why had made his horse do this. Normally when flies or gnats are about his horse will flick or move his head to shoo them off but this was different. Jim stroked his horse's neck in the reassurance that all was well and to calm him down. He then looked to his mate by his side and noticed that his horse too had his ears up and eyes alert. His mate turned to Jim and moved his hands away from his body and shrugged his shoulders as if to say, 'I have no idea.' Jim turned his head to the rear and noticed that all the horses, even the ones pulling the gig were fidgety. The time was nearing five in the afternoon and the location they were in was deep in the moor and its open marshes. Jim sensed something so shouted, "Keep alert men." The men did as was told but scratched their heads with confusion as all they could see around them was nothing but emptiness and granite Tors away in the distance.

Then suddenly the sun disappeared and the grey heavy clouds above let loose their rain filled bellies. With the sudden change of weather, Jim's horse started snorting aloud and raised and kicked his front legs in some kind of panic. Jim held the reins tightly and looked around the landscape but again could see nothing untoward.

Then without warning and high above their heads in the now darkened wet sky, they swooped.

Ten Hawks flew down as one flock at ultra high speed and as they neared their target split into two divisions and attacked the two horses pulling the gig. With their razor sharp claws open and ready they went straight for their heads. The horses squealed and snorted aloud in fear and reared their bodies up to defend themselves. The four outriders looked on in amazement and even pulled out their pistols to try and shoot these attacking birds. But while their horses were reeling and kicking it took all their effort just to remain saddled. It was total chaos as they had never seen the like before. The two horses pulling the gig were doing their best to hold it together but they just couldn't take the onslaught any further. So frantically they surged forward to get away but as they did, the gig swayed to the side and slipped down the wet muddy embankment. Seeing their job was done without casualty the Hawks flew off heading south by south west.

The driver of the gig had no option but to jump for his life. The gig carried on forward down the embankment still being pulled by the terrified horses. As the gig hit the lower marsh area it rolled itself over and came to a sudden halt. The horses, even with their strength, could do nothing as they too were being pulled down the embankment. With the horses now on their bellies but still desperately kicking the gig became stuck solid in the bog and ever so slowly started to sink.

Jim was trying hard to create a workable rescue plan but everything was happening so fast, so before anything, he and the gig driver rushed down to help the stranded horses. They quickly attached ropes to the horses from their horses to help pull them out but it didn't help as they were still strapped to the sinking gig. "Cut them free Jim," shouted one of the men." "What about the gold," said another. Jim stood up and shook his head in sheer disbelief at what had happened. Again, he was trying to think quickly about what to do. He decided that if he did cut the kicking and terrified horses free, it would at least steady the gig. He could then get one of his men, with a safety rope attached, to reach the gig and try and salvage some of the gold before it was lost. So, with decision made, he cut the horses free and helped them back on the track. Then, after quickly asking for a volunteer, one of the men raised his hand. With ropes tied to his waist, he crawled down onto the sinking gig to try and get the gold.

After ten minutes of this futile action, Jim with his head down in an acceptance of defeat, rubbed his face with his hands and said aloud, "That's enough, let it go." With that, the two men pulled the man out from the bog area back up to the track and safety. With one of the men holding all the horses away from the embankment, Jim and the three other men looked on in silence as the gig sunk out of sight.

"What are we going to do Jim?" "I don't know, but I tell you what, let's all get on our horses right now and ride away from this open wasteland to a safe spot where we can talk." "Where's that, not Exeter?" "Look men, we are all in trouble losing the gold so what say we ride to the Crown Inn at Lifton an hour away and work this out together." "Jim, it wasn't our fault." "I know that, and you know that, but you try telling that to the money men in Bath." All the men looked at each other and in unison turned to Jim and said, "Agreed." "Right, then let's all get saddled up and get to Devon." "Jim, I don't have a saddle," said the rider of the gig. Jim looked up to the sky in utter despair and replied, "Then you have to go bareback and tow the other horse while you're at it, now let's get going."

The Crown Inn took them just under the hour to get to but all the while whilst riding, Jim was trying to work out what to do for the best. He could simply lie and tell everyone that they were attacked by armed robbers and although they fired in defence and did their best they were overwhelmed. Or, he could tell them the truth. But saying that the sun went down and heavy rain clouds burst open and a flock of eagles or what they were, flew out of the darkened sky and attacked the two horses of the gig making it veer off into the bog and sink without trace sounded just pathetic. More to the point it wasn't logical but then that was the truth.

After booking his men in with the Landlord, all five men were now sitting around the table by the fire waiting for their drinks in the Crown Inn. The time was now eight o clock and the night was closing in.

Although Jim was the leader of the team and the buck stopped with him, he wanted to ask his men what they felt should be done. His team were not just a team of couriers they also lived close to one another and knew each family well. So this was a matter for all and they respected him for this.

With the drinks now served and all feeling a calm relief, Jim started. "Right men, there is no question that this has been a disaster but we are all still alive, what say we do." While drinking his cider, Jim listened carefully and allowed each man, in turn, to tell him how he felt and what he thought should be done. When all had their say it became apparent that the truth needed to be said. "Well, thank you all for your thoughts and in truth, I agree with the decision but, you must be aware, we will more than likely not be paid and probably also lose our contract with this employer." One of the men then said, "Jim, we have done our best and if that's the way they want it then stuff em, we can find work elsewhere." "Hear, hear," said the others. "Alright, but if any of you start to struggle with money issues, let me know." All raised their tankards in salute of Jim's kindness. "So you know, I am to meet our employer in two days and will let you all know the outcome." "Good on yer Jim."

True to his word, two days later a meeting between Jim and Mr Wright, of Wright & Co Solicitors in Bath, was on. The time was ten in the morning and Jim was sitting nervously in reception waiting to be called in. Mr Wright had been asked to invite one of Luisa's cousins into the meeting who was also a Company shareholder, which owned the gold. However, experience had taught him to get information first and then discuss things. So, he had booked a table for two at one o clock after his meeting with Jim at an Inn on Old King Street. He and Luisa's cousin, called Jose, could then go over things alone. It was a wise move.

Then, making Jim jump out of his quiet thoughts, the receptionist's bell rang and Jim was politely asked to go in. Jim got up, and without notice, gently slid his hand into his side pocket to check the small pistol, just in case.

Entering the opulent office and being warmly greeted by Mr Wright, Senior Partner, Jim was asked to take a seat. Mr Wright was in fine spirit as he was looking forward to taking the gold and putting it in their vaults.

Once the niceties were over, Jim took a deep breath and explained all that had happened, in truth and as agreed with his team. Mr Wright was not expecting this and couldn't comprehend what he was hearing. "And you want me to believe that the gold is gone, gone, sunk into the bog on Bodmin Moor." "I have told you the truth, and yes that is exactly where it is." Mr Wright lowered his head into his hands and couldn't believe it. Jim sat there waiting for a response, of what, he didn't know but was ready. Mr Wright, with his head still in his hands, was in utter dismay, shaking his head from side to side. What was he to do? If Luisa, his firm's best client, ever got wind that her vast amount of gold to buy Mingoose and the Mine was gone, he would be dead. He needed to get his head in gear but to do that he first needed to rid his office of this urchin in front of him and then get the firm's partners together for an emergency meeting, now.

Jim was then asked to leave and so without fuss got up and walked to the door. Just as he was about to walk out, Mr Wright said in quite forceful manner, "We will be in touch." Jim turned himself about and replied, "Is that a threat?" "I didn't say that." Jim kept his mouth shut and didn't respond but carried on out of the office closing the door behind him. Once out of the building, he quickly got on his horse and rode away heading for the comfort of his wife and home. He had done what he said he would and now he and his team had to wait for any repercussions which may well come their way.

The time was nearing twelve fifteen and the emergency meeting between the partners and the treasurer was now completed. It had been a very difficult meeting but they simply had no choice, if they wanted to keep in business and stay alive. After seeing the treasurer's report of their cash flow, reserves of gold and value of their share stock all then reluctantly agreed to finance the loss of the gold themselves. There was no other way and all had to be done in secret and without word to anyone.

Mr Wright now had to quickly get to the Old Road and talk with the Bank manager. Being one of his best clients, the Bank manager met Mr Wright and although he had raised his eyebrows with the large sum involved, he did as was asked. Once this meeting was over, Mr Wright thanked the manager for his understanding and headed off to Old King Street. Just as he got outside of the Inn he stopped and took some deep breaths to calm him down. Then putting on a false smile and pulling his shoulders back, he opened the door and entered the Inn. Seeing Luisa's cousin sat at the table in the corner, he casually walked over showing no signs of worry.

"Hello Jose," he said in a happy tone. Jose was known as a confident fellow with good brains but never, ever to be crossed. As Mr Wright sat down and started to make himself comfortable, Jose smiled and replied, "Hello Mr Wright, good to see you, how are things, or more point, how is our investment." Without word, Mr Wright bent down and opened his brief case and pulled out one file and one envelope. Putting both on the table and pushing them forward to Jose, he then poured himself a brandy and waited. Jose picked up the file first which had the signed Transfer Deeds of ownership for the Mingoose Manor to include the Wheal Coates Mine. After quickly scanning these official deeds he put them to the side and then picked up the envelope. This made Mr Wright twitch inside a little but never the less he kept his calm appearance of confidence. On opening the envelope Jose looked at the Legal Bank Note, signed by the manager of the Old Bank of Bath for the amount of twenty eight thousand eight hundred pounds. This was the agreed sum to be paid after taking out ten per cent share to Wright & Co Solicitors. Without saying anything, Jose put the Bank Note on top of the Deeds and then raising his glass of brandy in salute said, "Well, that all seems to be in order, we now legally own two Cornish Wheal mines at Tye and Coates and now a Manor at Mingoose. All is going well as planned, Luisa will be very pleased, what say we have some lunch and a little more brandy," Mr Wright smiled and picked up the menu.

.

Chapter 30

It had been five long days since that bloody Troon said he would come and make everything good. Their food had run out two days ago and they had no money, no means of ride, nothing. At first, they thought he must have got delayed somewhere and accepted that, but as the days went by they knew that something was wrong. No message and no communication at all, not even from Stephen bloody Bagnall, Joulie's so called new love. Two women on their own in a far out cottage in the middle of nowhere without any means of living was not right and both felt extremely vulnerable. Also, if they stayed in the cottage they would simply starve to death or something even worse which Sarah just couldn't do.

It was then that Sarah's survival instinct started to kick in. They needed food and money no matter how they got it that was for sure. Once achieved, they would then have choice as what to do next. They had devised a plan and practised many times whilst in the cottage to get it right and very soon would act it out.

It was near midnight and all around was still and dark except for a few stars way off in the night sky. Sarah was standing quietly looking out the slightly open back door inside the cottage at St Tudy. Joulie, with candle lit, was upstairs putting on the last of her warm clothing. With everything done as best she could she blew the candle out. Then being very careful and holding onto the walls she shuffled her way in the dark out of the bedroom and down the stairs.

Hearing Joulie walk down the stairs, Sarah looked about and when she was close enough whispered, ''Are you ready Joulie.'' ''I am Sarah, but are you sure we need to do this.'' ''Joulie, we have discussed this over and over many times, what else can we do.'' Joulie knew that Sarah was right, they had no other choice. Sarah gently hugged Joulie in reassurance and then turned, picked up her bag and walked out. Joulie followed and closed the door behind her.

After trudging slowly for over two hours southwards to their target area of Bodmin, Sarah saw a wooded area up in an isolated position so turned off the track and led the way towards it. It was nearing three in the morning and they needed to rest up and gather their thoughts.

Once both were safely in the woods and sitting down by a large tree, Joulie said, ''Sarah, I cannot believe it has come to this.'' ''Joulie, I am lost for words and cannot for the life of me comprehend how we got into this mess. We are fighting for our very lives and I intend to keep it that way.'' ''Sarah, you are so strong, I would have given up by now.'' ''Don't be silly Joulie, you are strong, we will get out of this, trust me.'' Both then closed their eyes to rest their souls and body. Just before they nodded off, Joulie moved her hand towards Sarah's hand and held it with a sense of comfort.

It was as the sun shone through the trees that Joulie felt an itch on her nose. With her eyes still closed she flicked her hand to shoo away whatever it was but every time she did it came back. She had no choice and so opened her eyes from her sleep and saw a butterfly flapping its wings right on the bridge of her nose. Startled, she shook her head from side to side and calmly without any rush the butterfly flew away. Joulie looked at Sarah but saw she was still asleep so she got up and went to relieve herself in the bushes nearby.

As Joulie came back, Sarah opened her eyes and looked about. "Sarah, you never guess what." "What?" "A butterfly just landed on my nose and woke me up." "A butterfly what." "A butterfly was on my nose, I think it wanted to talk." "Joulie, have you been drinking?" They both laughed which they hadn't done for a long time. "Right Joulie, I will just go to the toilet and then we had better be off. "How far to go?" "I would say a couple more miles that's all, we are nearly there."

It was just past nine when the town of Bodmin came into view. "Right Joulie, let's get ourselves over into those trees and get ready." When in the trees they quickly got undressed and after delving into their bags put their clean clothes on. Then, kneeling down facing each other they put some make up on and combed each other's hair. When all done, it was time for Joulie to get the sharp knife out. "Now be careful Joulie, don't rush it." Sarah put out her hand and while Joulie held it tight, slit the end of her thumb. Holding a small bag underneath, Joulie squeezed the thumb and the blood dripped into it. Joulie then applied pressure to the small slit and after two minutes put a small bandage over it. Sarah then tied the little bag tight and put it into her pocket. With both women now looking rather smart and fresh, although starving and penniless, they packed up and went into the town. It was now ten thirty and the street market was busy just as they had hoped. As planned they both walked hand in hand like Mother and sweet daughter.

As Joulie was so small and cute looking no one would know any difference. If only they knew. It was when they were passing the butcher's stall that they slowed their pace down and looked. Once passed, they sped up and walked down the high street to the bottom. "Now don't forget Joulie, I will meet you by the side of the White Hart Inn at the top of the street as soon as I can, are you ready?" "I'm ready Sarah and I'm starving."

Joulie went first back up to the Butcher's stall but hung back and waited close by until the two sellers were busy. Sarah with the small bag of blood in hand also did the same but held back just a little further. Then as the two butcher men became busy with some customers, Joulie turned and nodded her head and went forward. Sarah did the same but went to the other end of the stall. When both were in place and a few seconds had passed Sarah screamed aloud and swished her arms up in the air and fell forward smashing into the meat table and dropped to the floor face down. As she did this, she smacked the little bag holding the blood from her thumb against the top of her head. Everyone looked on in panic as the two butcher men ran to her aid which is exactly what they had planned. While both butchers went to tend Sarah, Joulie snatched the lump of belly pork and slid it inside her coat and then turned and walked away.

It was a good ten minutes later before Sarah got away from the stall up the street to the side alley of the White Hart Inn. As she arrived Joulie smiled brightly. "Did you get it Joulie." "Yes, I did." "Right let's get out of here and back to the woods where we left." "Sarah, you still got some blood on your forehead." "Well that can wait let's get that fire going and eat our hearts out."

So with a spring in their step, they both walked back onto the main street to walk away from the town. Just as they got out of the alley and turned right, Sarah saw a tall man with one arm walking towards them wearing a dirty vest with the words 'Jesus Saves' scrawled on the front. She stopped in her tracks and with her mouth open wide in utter astonishment said, "My God, it can't be." Joulie heard what Sarah had just said but, more to the point, the way she said it and so quickly responded, "What's wrong Sarah?"

The man didn't see them as his head was held high in the air and was singing aloud, 'Jesus Christ! Come all ye to him, Hallelujah, Hallelujah!' Sarah was completely taken aback and stood motionless. As the man got ever closer, Joulie got hold of Sarah's arm and started to shake it as she seemed to have gone into some kind of trance. Sarah turned and put a hand on Joulies arm in a reassuring way that all was well. As the man was just about to pass them by, Sarah jumped her full body in front of him which made him stop in his tracks and look down. As he did so, Sarah looked up into his face and said with a most happy zest, "Snipe, it's me, Sarah." At first, he thought it was a mad woman but then the penny dropped and realised it was his Sarah from many years ago. Without any thought, he just said, "I should have married you." Although she felt a loving warmth from what he had just said she replied, "Snipe, we are in trouble, can you help us." Again without any thought or question, he replied, "Of course I will." He then pointed to the Inn they were outside of and said, "Let's go in there and talk." "Do they do food, we are starving and haven't eaten in two days." "Yes, they do." "Can you pay as we have no money." "Yes, I can."

As all three sat around a snug table in the White Hart Inn, Snipe asked what they wanted to drink. ''What are you having,'' Sarah asked. ''I think I will have a cider.'' ''I thought you were with the Lord.'' ''I am Sarah but he allows me to have this refreshment if I take care and not have too much.'' ''Then I will have a cider too.'' Snipe and Sarah both looked at Joulie, who had kept rather quiet since meeting this Snipe fellow, but nodded her head saying, ''Same here.'' When the young maid came across to take their order, Sarah asked if they could have some food which she replied, ''Yes, my lady, we have mutton stew with dumplings, would that be alright and how many bowls do you want?'' Sarah looked at Snipe who shook his head to say no, so Sarah ordered two bowls, one for her and Joulie. After the maid went away, Joulie, said, ''Sarah, I need to go to the latrine, can you help me?'' Sarah was going to say, 'You're a big girl, go on your own,' but sensed that Joulie wanted to talk, so said to Snipe, ''We won't be long.''

When both women went in the latrine, Joulie turned and said, ''Sarah, what are you doing, who is this man?'' ''I told you about him, it's the Sniper who I used to work with.'' ''Is he the man you use to have sex with and then tried to poison.'' Sarah, looked up at the filthy ceiling in remorse and thought, how the world turns, but then lowered her head back down saying, ''Yes that is him.'' Joulie shook her head in disbelief and said, ''Sarah is there any man you haven't dropped your knickers for.'' ''Joulie, that's not fair.'' ''So, what are you thinking?'' ''I am thinking of telling him everything and hopefully, he will help us out of this bloody mess.'' ''But how do we know we can trust him.'' Joulie, he is with the Lord and if we can't put our trust in him, then who can we trust.''

"Well, alright, but what should I do with this bloody lump of pork?" "Give it here." Joulie handed over the lump of meat which Sarah then quickly threw out the back door onto the long grass under a tree.

It wasn't long after they both got back to the table that their food was served. Snipe was going to start asking questions about their situation but saw they just couldn't stop eating and so left them in peace until they finished. When they were done and drank back the last of their cider to wash the food down, Snipe said, "More cider girls?" Both saying yes, Snipe waved his hand and as the maid came over, he ordered more drinks for all. It was then that Snipe asked, "So, what has happened Sarah, how can I help?" "Before, we go into that Snipe, do you live in Bodmin?" "Not in Bodmin but close by in a small barn a few miles North West of here." "And do work?" "Yes, I work at the Asylum four days a week and when not working I walk the streets praising the Lord, who saved me." As he said this, Sarah's mind drifted back to Cuthbert Troon and all the money and riches he had which he believed would give her future happiness. If that was the case then why did she feel so much warmth and comfort from Snipe's very simple way of life in a barn? She once again couldn't quite believe that Snipe, who with one arm, and looking calm and at peace with his life, was now by her side, sitting at a table in a cosy Inn in Bodmin. Sarah, without a word, then looked at Joulie in such a way as to say, shall I tell all?" Joulie had watched Snipe closely and listened to what and the way he talked and felt, yes, she should, and so nodded her head in approval.

They had now been at the table for over an hour yet still they talked and listened to one another. It was when Joulie had described her life and her ways of work that the Snipe's ears pricked. "So, you would probably know the man called the Ferret." Joulie couldn't believe what she had just heard and turned to Sarah for help. "Tell him the truth Joulie, that's what we agreed." "Yes, I do know him, why do you ask." "Joulie, I mean nothing by it, but as I explained, I worked in the arena in which you worked for many years and once did a job for him a long time ago which I now deeply regret."

After a few more minutes of talk and their ciders nearly finished, Snipe suggested that he go to the bar and pay the bill. It would then give the two women a little time to decide what they wanted to do. As he got up, Sarah asked, "What do you think we should do Snipe?" "I am unsure Sarah, let me go and pay the bill and we can discuss further on my return, what say you Joulie?" "I agree, but am also at a total loss on what to do." Snipe nodded his head in understanding but went to the bar to pay the bill. While he was away from the table Sarah asked Joulie, "Shall I ask if we can stay with him at his barn, I don't fancy living in the open woods or hanging about here." "Yes, why not, anything is better than that, we have nothing to lose."

When Snipe came back and sat down he said warmly to them both, "Had any thoughts on what to do?" Sarah replied, "Snipe, can we stay at your barn for a while?" Without a hint of doubt, Snipe replied, "Yes, of course you can, it's not a palace but I do have a little water well and a fire place to keep us warm." "So, how far is it, do we walk?" Snipe laughed and said, "Funny you say that

Sarah, as today I decided to ride into town in my little buggy, normally I would have just ridden on my horse. So, no, you don't have to walk and it will take twenty minutes." "Thank you Snipe, thank you."

While still sitting around the table before getting ready to move off, Joulie said, "Snipe, the more I think about it, the more I think I need to get word to Stephen Bagnall." Snipe scratched his chin and replied, "In my experience Joulie and knowing the position you're in, I wouldn't send word to anyone as this could give away your very existence and location." "Then what would you do?" "Do you know where he lives?" "Yes, he lives in a town house in Truro, a place called Green Street by the Quay." "What number in Green Street?" "I don't know, he said it backs onto a river but I have never been there." Snipe quietly thought a while and then said, "What I would do is go to Green Street and observe without notice and then act when you have the information, you got to play this carefully and not endanger yourself." Joulie replied in a warm but resolute way, "But how can I do this, I have no money, no food, no horse, nothing." While Sarah kept quiet, Snipe replied, "I will help you, let's all get back to my place where we can talk further on how best to do it."

The barn was as the Snipe had said, it was no palace, but it was dry and snug. After showing the women about, Snipe lit the fire and put the water on for boiling. It was now getting late but, they had eventually agreed a plan. Snipe would take them in the buggy to Bagnall's place of residence where they would scout without rush. Then and only then if all looked safe and well and the time right, Joulie would make contact. Sarah asked not to be left alone, and so at all times would stay close to either Joulie or Snipe. That's really all they could do at this moment and, as Truro was a two hour ride they would need to set off late tomorrow afternoon to arrive in darkness. So, with each having a blanket they nestled on the floor and slept.

Chapter 31

With Rebecca being in the cottage in Helston, Joshua sat alone by the fire in his cottage at Gunwalloe eating his breakfast of two over cooked sausages and burnt toast. Queenie and Cecil were by his feet waiting in earnest for any scraps. Joshua was in a thoughtful mode, staring out through the window, thinking back to the time he first came to the cottage some ten years ago. He smiled at the thought when he first saw Rebecca standing at the gate twiddling her fingers. He started to chuckle but then got distracted when he saw a man on the horse ride through the gate up to the front door. He quickly put his plate to the side and went for his pistol. Then getting up he went to the window and glanced through to see who it was. On recognising the horse and rider he calmed himself and went to the door but cocked his pistol just in case.

The courier had galloped at pace to get to the cottage. As soon as he arrived he reined his horse, dismounted and ran to the front door.

As Joshua opened the door, the man spoke up with an efficient clarity saying, "Mr Pendragon, urgent message from the sheriff." As he handed over the message Joshua asked the man if could wait while he goes inside to read. The man nodded and as Joshua closed the door, the rider went back to his horse and took out a bottle from the saddlebag and took a well earned drink of water. He then walked his horse over to the trough so he also could have a drink. While his horse was busy slurping, the man sat down and lit a pipe. The ride from Truro had been hard with no let ups, on strict orders from his boss, the Sherriff. Joshua stood back from the door and while leaning against the wall opened the message. It read:-

Joshua,
Suspicious activity at Coverack.
Require your help and advice.
Sherriff

Joshua closed the message and put it in his pocket then went outside to speak with the man. On seeing Joshua coming out the man got up and as they got close Joshua said, "Thank you, could you tell the sheriff that I will ride to his office this afternoon." "Yes, Mr Pendragon, I will get on my way now."

With the man gone, Joshua headed back into the cottage to get organised. It had been over three weeks since he received the message from Kernow and although he had put everyone on alert, not much, if anything had come back. But, a lead is a lead and he must do his duty to follow things up when asked. The first thing he needed to do was to get his horse ready for the ride and also get his gear together. He also decided that as Helston was on his way back from Truro he would, time permitting, visit Rebecca and the children in Lady Street. The trip to Truro may be a waste of time but then again, it may not. So, he would drop the two dogs off at Mrs Stephens in Cury, just in case. He needed to have a clear path to do what had to be done, if anything.

When all was ready, Joshua decided he needed to take a few minutes out and have a pipe to gather his thoughts. So, sitting back down by the dying fire he sat back and drew in the smoke. Queenie and Cecil had seen Joshua do this before and knew he needed some space, so with heads down they walked over to the front door and lay down without fuss. Joshua carried on in quiet thought and with eyes closed rested himself.

Joshua got to Truro late in the afternoon. He could have got there earlier but he didn't want to push Harry, his horse, and also had to be careful with the two little dogs in the side sacks. As always, Mrs Stephens was lovely and took the dogs without any fault. The Sheriff's office was up at the top of Lemon Street and as he got close he slowed Harry to a walking pace. Just as he entered the Sheriff's front yard he looked down the wide street and thought of the Red Lion at the bottom on the right. It made him think back to the time that he and the three others had stayed there after the poisoning episode in Helston. He shook his head in disbelief and looked up to the sky in thanks to the Lady for their survival. Then walking Harry to the front of the building, Joshua got down and after tying tied his horse up, went in.

The man inside greeted Joshua and escorted him up the stairs to the Sherriff's office and knocked the door. As Joshua walked in, the sheriff, sitting behind his desk, smiled brightly and said, "Good to see you again Joshua, take a seat, how are you?" "I am good, thank you, how are you?" "Well, that depends on how you look at things, but all in all, not doing too bad thank you, would you like a drink." "That would be nice." "What will it be, a cup of tea or something stronger." "A cup of tea would be just fine for now but maybe some stronger stuff after we finished." The Sherriff got up and walked out the door to order the drinks and when he came back and sat down, pushed the clay pipe on the desk towards

Joshua saying, "Please Joshua, I don't mind in the least, I know you like a smoke." Joshua smiled with warmth and after the tea was served and his pipe lit, the good Sherriff got on with the meeting.

With Joshua listening quietly without word, the Sherriff went on to explain all that had happened. It appears that movement of unidentified men had been seen going into a disused tunnel. This tunnel had been dug many years ago and was used by smugglers and escaped prisoners. Due to this criminal action of route, the tunnel was ordered by the authorities to be sealed off. The tunnel maintains a level of three feet under the ground and weaves itself around the hills from the cove of Coverack ending at the small village of Zoar on the main track to Helston. While the Sherriff was explaining this, he pulled out a map and showed Joshua exactly where he was talking about. As the sheriff took a breath, Joshua was thinking whether all this was just another matter for the police, or maybe was it something more serious and so asked, "May I ask how you got to know about this?" "Yes, of course, it was by sheer luck. A local fisherman got blown off course by some freak wind storm which he said, he had never experienced before. It was one early morning two weeks ago. He noticed the small ship being very close to the rocky cove and men were being taken ashore and going into the tunnel. The ship wasn't local and had no sign of anchorage. The man also noticed that all the people going in were not coming out." "Hmmm, so what are your thoughts," said Joshua. "Well, my initial thought was that it's a smuggling ring, so would organise the capture of the ship and its people but, these people were not carrying goods or load which is strange. "Have you put anything in place?" "Yes, I have two men watching from the cliffs with scopes." "And when did they last report?" "They reported yesterday and it seems the ship comes in on the early morning tide, off loads and when done, simply sails away. Since we got the tip off, the ship has come back twice." "Have you any men watching at Zoar, where this tunnel ends?" The Sheriff looked at Joshua in dismay saying, " Joshua, I just don't have the manpower or the reserves to do this, so the answer is no." "Well, I think that's the first thing we need to sort." "You may be right but there are many pop ups along this tunnel so Zoar may not be their route end." "Sorry, you lost me, what are pop ups?" "Pops ups are covered escape holes, dug out along the tunnel roof in strategic places where the people inside can push open to either look out or get out." "Hmmm, that's very clever." "Yes, it is and very hard and time consuming to observe." Joshua sat back and rubbed his chin with thought. Then after a minute or so of silence had passed Joshua asked again, "So what do you think these people are up to?" "Well, if they are not carrying any heavy goods it can be either a people smuggling ring or preparation for a raid or something but whatever it is, it's just not right." "I agree with you Sherriff, so on that information, I think we need to act and get ourselves into a position of strength so we have choice to do what we want to do. You say the ship has been seen twice on the same day which could mean a pattern. If so, then the next time for its arrival would be in six days." "Yes, that would be correct Joshua." "Right then, this is what I suggest." Joshua went on to propose and explain his joint plan of action which would include the use of Bull's team and the Sheriff's men.

Chapter 32

Shanks was used to high profile meetings but this house in Mayfair was something else. He was sitting in one of the finest chairs he had ever seen waiting quietly in the opulent lobby, gazing around at the marbled walls. It was like being in a palace of a Queen. It had taken over two days to get to the London Hotel from the Dragons Inn at Truro but, he had slept well through the night in a comfy bed, care of Luisa, and was now ready for the meeting, as ordered. He had left his four assassins in the Dragon Inn in Truro to carry on with their duties and find the two men that needed erasing. He also told them not to drink too much and to keep their heads down. When he arrived and entered the house, the butler took his hat and coat and then apologised as the meeting that Luisa was in was running late and could he wait in the lobby until called. That was an hour ago and he was still waiting. However, the time passed quietly by as he just couldn't help but keep looking around at the splendour.

Inside the Library room were Luisa, her cousin Jose, and two other men. All four had been in the meeting since the stroke of eight and after heavy discussion were now going over the finer details. Luisa had kept rather quiet throughout, listening to all three men give their up to date reports. But now it was her turn to recap on things so a decision could be made. "So, Jose, the delivery of the Tin is running well?" "Yes, our smuggling ring from around the Cornish Mines is doing very well and all on course for full delivery and more." "And your men have landed safely to occupy both mines in full readiness to convey the Tin to our Ship on its arrival on the last day of this month?" "Yes, that is correct my good cousin." "Well done Jose, thank you for being clear and precise."

She then turned her attention to the very handsome and well dressed man known as Peter Williams, a Somerset man of birth. Peter Williams was now, after six months of undercover work and persuasion by Luisa's contacts, now the Deputy Production Manager at Wheal Gof in St Austell, the largest Mine in Cornwall. "And you Peter, you say that subject to our man Shanks help, all is ready for the disaster at the Gof Mine, in the time discussed?" "Yes, all is ready Luisa." "Thank you, I am sure when we have finished this meeting and Shanks comes in, he would do as asked."

She then turned to the third man, who was a good friend, in more ways than one, and an executive of the London Metal Exchange. It was his job to influence the Exchange when any precious metals become in short supply which would rapidly escalate the share value. "So, listening to all that has been said, if we can achieve what we have planned on the last day of this month, can you assure me that a great deal of money will be made?" Without hesitation, he answered, "Yes, and more if you can carry things on." With three positive answers being given, she raised her glass containing the very best red wine, and said with a smile, "Then I think gentlemen we are on." All three men then raised their glasses and cheered, "Hear, Hear." Luisa then got up and pulled the cord for her butler. Within a few minutes, the butler arrived and as he entered the room, the London Metal Exchange man got up. After shaking Jose and Peter's hands in goodbye, he walked around the table to Luisa. As Ladies do, Luisa held out the back of her hand and with courtesy, he gently took it into his hands and bent down and kissed it. As he did so, both looked into each other eyes and without notice to the others, gave her a knowing wink. Luisa smiled, as a lady does, and pulled her hand back onto her lap. With the formalities over, the butler then escorted him out of the room which left Luisa, Jose and Peter.

When the butler had escorted the Exchange man from the library and out of the front door of the house, he turned and walked over to Shanks. "If you are ready Sir, Luisa will see you now." With that, Shanks got up and went with the butler into the Library. At first, he was a little taken aback at seeing two other people in the room as he was expecting his meeting to be confidential with Luisa only. However, after sitting down around the table he relaxed and sipped the tea in the finest china. It was then that Luisa politely asked Jose and Peter if they could explain to Shanks what part of the plan they were responsible for. When they had done this, Luisa asked Shanks to do the same.

When Shanks had finished, Luisa said, "Right, my good loyal men, firstly, I would like to congratulate Shanks on doing a fine job in taking out the people in Bristol and Portishead, who could have interfered with our plans for success." Luisa, with Jose and Peter, picked up their glasses and drank the toast. As they drank and put the glasses back down on the table, Luisa light heartedly said, "O and thank you for my twenty eight thousand pounds and the Mingoose Estate, that was a very good piece of work." "My pleasure," replied Shanks." Luisa lent down over to her side and picked up her handbag and, after pulling out a roll of bank notes and putting them on the table, pushed them over to Shanks saying, "Here you go, your two thousand pounds in cash, as agreed." "Thank you, my Lady, my men will be pleased, as I am." "By the way, how did Troon get it," asked Jose." "Two of my men ambushed him just after the sale of the Manor and shot him in the chest." "Excellent, and where is he now." "He is at the bottom of an old disused Mine shaft at Wheal Coates." Luisa listened to how Shanks had clinically answered Jose's questions and couldn't help but feel a sense of elation pass through her body. She just loved the inner power and thrived on her dominance and wealth. "Well done Shanks." said Jose, "your men have done good." Thank you, Jose, much appreciated." "By the way, do we keep calling you Shanks or do you have a real name?" Shanks looked at Luisa and after giving him a smile, turned his head back to Jose and said, "Yes, I do, my real name is Samuel Shankbottom, from Stepney." Jose and Peter started to chuckle as Shanks added boringly, "Yes, I know, I've heard all the jokes."

Once again, it was down to Luisa to get things back on track and so raised her voice and asked Shanks to give an up to date situation report. Shanks took a long breath and after taking a sip of the tea got on with what Luisa had asked. Jose and Peter listened with much interest as this man's words could affect their overall plans. Shanks went over everything that had occurred from his start point at Bristol and Portishead and once getting things up to date, emphasised the two outstanding kills which needed to be done. When he finished, he reached for the teacup and sank a large gulp. Luisa saw this and was disgusted; as you sip the tea, not drink it like a pint of ale. However, she kept quiet about that and asked, "So who are these two men you need to take out." "One is a minor smuggler, known as Fin, living in and around the area of Scorrier who in the past has taken Tin from your Mine at Wheal Tye. We are on his trail now and he will be eliminated very shortly. The other is a hardier known smuggler with a reputation in South West Cornwall by the name of John Hughes. We know his address in Truro and so sent one of my team in for the kill, but he has disappeared from the face of the earth. We are in the process of tracking him down." It was then that Peter Williams said, "I have heard of this man and you are right, his reputation precedes him." Jose, then added, "If you fail in killing this man Hughes, could he affect our plans." "In truth, I would say I don't know, all I know is that he has very close links to the smuggling trade, especially Tin, and my job is to wipe these people out to ease the way for your success." "He may have got wind of your killings in Bristol?" "That's True Jose, and if so, he has probably gone to ground." "Well, if I heard that some people in my line of work had been killed that's what I would do." "I agree with you there." Luisa then interrupted as she wanted to get to the point if Shanks would help Peter at Wheal Gof, so asked, " Peter could you explain to us again the situation with the powder kegs to blow up the Gof mine?" "Yes of course my Lady, as I said, it took longer than I thought and was hard work but all are in place, waiting only to be put down the shaft and the fuses lit, the day before the end of the Month." For some reason, Luisa then started to fidget in the chair and so sitting back and getting herself comfortable turned to Shanks saying, "Shanks, this is where Peter will need your help." "What do mean my Lady?" "As you heard, Peter has bravely without being seen and single handed placed ten barrels of gunpowder in an old entrance shaft at Wheal Gof. And, to get them into position for denoting they need to be lowered down the shaft. But, all being roped together are too heavy, far more than Peter can do himself." This was the first time Shanks had heard of this and was somewhat flummoxed so turned his attention to Peter in such a way for him to explain things. Peter looked at Luisa and after nodding her head said, "Shanks, this is all part of the overall plan and has taken me many weeks in the dead of night to get the kegs to where they are now. All is ready but need at least two men of strength to help me lower them down the shaft." "Have you not got any men you can use?" Before Peter could answer this, Luisa stepped in and said, "Yes, we do, but this job is highly secret and we just cannot risk anyone outside of our inner circle to do it." Shanks understood and so turning his attention back to Peter said, "How much weight are we talking?" "Each barrel has forty pounds of powder making a total of four hundred pounds in dead weight to be lowered." Luisa then added, "What we are asking Shanks is that you release one of your team to help do this." Shanks thought before answering, trying to work out if he could do it and, after a brief moment of silence said, "Yes, this can be done but I would have to let the minor smuggler at Scorrier off the hook and reorganise my team." Peter kept quiet as he knew that Luisa had the final say and so she said, "That's very good of you Shanks, if after the meeting you and Peter could get together and discuss the finer details that would be excellent. "Yes, of course my Lady," Shanks replied." "Well, having listened to you all, I think we should all push on with our plans and let Shanks here reorganise his teams and also carry on with finding and killing this Hughes fellow just in case, what say you two?" Jose and Peter both agreed and so

Luisa turned to Shanks and said, "Good, then I think we are all done". Then after a brief moment of silence, Luisa said, "O, by the way Shanks, you didn't manage to kill the Ferret then?' This short statement of fact stunned Shanks into silence but also gave him time to think of a reply. He noted that all three people for waiting eagerly for what he would say. "That is correct my Lady, when we got to the Sailors Inn in Falmouth he had already sailed to France." "Yes, we know." Shanks was puzzled and asked, "Sorry, how do know?" "My dear Shanks, we intercepted the message he sent to his people in France and the two men that picked him up, work for me." "So, do you know where the Ferret is now." "Yes, I do, he is at the bottom of the sea where the little squirt belongs." Shanks didn't have a response to this and so grimaced with a smile and kept his mouth shut.

After another brief moment of silence between all, Luisa spoke, "Right, I really do need to get myself ready for lunch, are there any last questions before we say our goodbyes?" Peter and Jose replied, "No," but Shanks said, "I have one." "Then speak up, we are all friends here." Shanks, feeling a little nervous at being seen as weak, turned his eyes to Peter and asked, "When you and my two men set off the explosion at the Gof Mine, are you expecting many casualties?" Peter glanced at both Luisa and Jose then turning his head back to Shanks said, "The casualties will be minimal as the day before the last day of the month is a Sunday so most of the workers will be at Church." "Thank you Peter, I just wanted to get the scale of things, that's all." Luisa then said, "It isn't about scale, it's about stopping the mining of the tin and causing sheer mayhem to the south coast giving us much freedom to maximise profit on the north coast." "I understand, thank you." "Good, I'm glad you understand, now I really must get going and Jose and myself look forward to seeing you both again at my Manor in Mingoose on Friday in six days. This will be the final meeting between us so please do not be late as I will be leaving for London the very next morning, before sunrise." With that, Luisa again got up and pulled the cord for the butler.

Chapter 33

They had ridden all through the night and the following day and the horse pulling the small gig was exhausted as were Shanks and his driver. However, they reached the Dragons Inn without fault and now looking forward to having a beer and sleep but, before Shanks could close his eyes, he needed to talk with his two teams. He had, as requested by Luisa, discussed things with Peter after the meeting back in London and agreed that one of his team will be at his house in St Austell in the next few days. However, which one, he was yet to decide on?

It was late but the four men were still in the bar having a few ales when they saw Shanks walk in. The driver had remained outside taking care of the gig and giving the horse a well earned rub down. The time had just passed the hour of eleven.

Shanks went over to the table where the four men were sitting and slumped his body down in the spare chair. "Shanks, you look exhausted," said one of the men. "I am, I could sleep for a week but I need an update from you four first and, while I am it, what are you lot doing still drinking at this hour?" Before anyone could answer, Shanks waved his right hand towards the bar and when he got the young waitress's attention she came over and took his order for a well deserved tankard of ale. When the young waitress left, the leader of the first team said, "Shanks, we have good news, we found the Inn where that small time smuggler called Fin drinks. It's called the Plume and Feathers in Redruth and we have also located a good place to kill him." "Good, and what about you two, did you find Hughes?" "No, we did not, we tried everything we could but he has just gone, vanished." Shanks was not surprised by this but didn't say so, only saying, "Hmmm." It was then that the young waitress, who was also very pretty, came back over with tray in hand and laid the tankard of cider on the table. Shanks thanked her and paid the money saying, "Keep the change." "Thank you Sir," she replied, and walked away but not before all of the four men eyed her up with smiles. Shanks picked up the tankard and sank his first gulp with absolute pleasure feeling it slide down into his tummy. The four men didn't speak while Shanks was drinking and just sat there watching him.

When taking a couple more large gulps he put the near empty tankard back on the table and got serious. So, after wiping his mouth with his sleeve said, "Alright, first of all, I want to say well done to you all for what you have done so far." He then went into his bag and pulled the wad of bank notes out and gave each man one hundred and fifty pounds saying, this is yours for now and the bonuses will be paid when we are done, which hopefully won't be long." With smiles all around the four men pocketed their money and then picked up their tankards. After clinking them all together they each took a large swig. While they did this, Shanks looked on and made his mind up on which team would stay and which one would go to St Austell. He would send the team which killed Troon in Cornwall to St Austell and keep the team who killed in Bristol and Portishead with him. "Right men, there has been a change of plan. Two of you are to go to St Austell to help one of our colleagues." All four men went quiet in wait for Shanks to tell them which two are to go. He then added, "It has also been decided that the smuggler man called Fin is of little importance so to keep things on track, team two, will stop what you're doing and head on to St Austell." "What are we to do in St Austell?" "I will tell you all about it in the morning but suggest you both be ready to leave after breakfast." He then turned his attention to the other team and said, "This Hughes fellow has got to be found and taken out, is there anything we can do to help?" The leader of the team thought for a quick second and replied, "Well, just a thought, if we could question this small time smuggler Fin, he may know something." Shanks thought on this and said, "Hmm, that sounds interesting and maybe worth a go, why don't you men get yourselves together and talk but time is running out and Hughes must be killed by Friday." None of the four men was fazed by this time limit but asked, "It doesn't give us much time, is there any particular reason why it has to be by Friday, and not Saturday or even Sunday?" Shanks could have lied and said something out of the blue but he needed to be honest as best he could without saying too much, so said, "Good question, it's because it fits with what has been agreed in London, I can't say anymore than that." "We understand, Shanks." Shanks leant back in his chair and once again raised and waved his hand for the waitress to come across. He then spoke to all four men saying, "Well, I think we are done for tonight so are there any last questions?" While all four men remained silent, Shanks saw the young pretty maid start to walk over to their table and quickly said, "Right then, what say you let me buy each of you a cider then get yourselves off to bed and have a good night sleep."

So, while the four men and Shanks supped their ciders in the Dragons Inn, a few miles away on the other side of the city were the two women, Sarah and Joulie. Both were in the middle of a dense wood having travelled two hours in the dark from Bodmin and now sitting patiently in the gig waiting for Snipe to return.

When they arrived at the wood and the Snipe was sure they were safe and warm, he unstrapped the horse from the gig and rode off into the city to check out the area of Green Street. It would be a long night for both women, so sitting close to each other up in the gig, they huddled themselves under the blanket. It was then that Joulie asked, "Sarah, is Snipe armed?" "No, he isn't, I asked the same question before we left his barn at Bodmin." "But he might get caught or shot at?" "That's what I said, but he said to me that he doesn't do guns or harm anymore and just trusts in the Lord." "Are you armed, do you have your gun with you." "Yes, I do, and loaded and ready." Sarah then touched the side pocket of her coat to confirm where her pocket pistol was." "Right," said Sarah, "Let's both try and get some sleep." As both closed their eyes to rest it wasn't long before the silent eeriness of the trees took over.

It was around four in the morning with the darkness still all around that they heard the sound of a horse. It was the Snipe, so with smiles of relief, they welcomed him back. "How did it go Snipe," Joulie asked. "All went well, let me dig a hole and make a fire and I will tell all."

The Snipe had indeed done well. His experience of his past work had not left him. He told them all what he had done and how Green Street was laid and, although it wasn't a thorough way, he found a way to observe. "Did you see Stephen?" Jouilie asked. The Snipe raised a smile at her naivety and said, "Joulie it's not as simple as that, even though you described him, I don't know what number he lives and also it was the middle of the night. I have to be careful, it's just a small cobbled street with terraced houses on both sides." "So what do we do," "What we do is play it calm and not rush things. I have checked all around the area and have found a good place for us to observe behind the terrace houses down by the riverside." "But how can we see the street from there," Sarah said. "You can't from the ground, but there is a dense forest close by with very tall trees and if you girls can climb then we can, as well as my casual street walk, watch and wait without being seen." Both girls went deadly silent at the thought of what the Snipe had just said about them climbing a bloody tree. Snipe saw this and so asked if any of them had any questions and, after receiving a no from both said, "Right, then let's get our gear up and get going before the day dawns."

With all their gear packed and the horse leashed back onto the gig, they were off. With Sarah and Joulie sitting in the back, Snipe took the reins and gently led the horse out. The first thing he wanted to do was familiarise both women with Green Street. So keeping the horse at an easy walk it took thirty minutes before the turn off into Green Street came into view. As they passed the street, Snipe reined the horse to a slow pace and turned around to the women pointing up the street for them to get a visual of what they had to observe. Both women put their thumbs up and with a nod of his head pushed the horse on.

Keeping things as quiet as he could, Snipe then eased the gig around the back of the street and onto the grass area leading down to the river. He then turned left heading to the dense woods with the tall trees. All went well and they reached the area inside the woods as Snipe had wanted without being seen and the timing good. But, experience had taught him, that to cover their tracks was important and so all three went around making sure that all looked natural. When all was done as best they could, and now sitting down quietly together waiting for the dawn to break, Snipe quietly asked which one of them would like to observe first. "I will," said Joulie. Snipe looked at Sarah, who quickly responded, "Yes, we have already chatted about it and Joulie wants to go first as I haven't climbed a bloody tree in years." "Alright, the sun will be up in about an hour, I suggest we all rest ourselves until then but first I will go and tend to the horse and make things ready just in case we have to get out fast."

With the hour passing quickly and the sun trying its best to rid the dark, they were ready. Snipe briefed Joulie on how to observe and gave her a small set of binoculars. He also, to keep her steady, gave her some pieces of rope to tie around her waist and loop around branches where she could. So, when she was ready, Snipe bent down on all fours by the trunk of the tree and waited for Joulie to stand on his back. The good thing about Joulie was her size and weight as being very small and light made things a lot easier. Holding Sarah's hand for balance, Joulie got onto Snipe's back and when standing on the back of his shoulders and holding onto the tree, Snipe raised himself up. Getting to his full height allowed her to grab a branch and start her climb. As she scrambled up, Snipe then walked out from the woods to start his overt surveillance. It was now up to Sarah to stand guard on the ground to look after the horse and gig and support Joulie where and whenever she could.

It took a while but slowly and surely Joulie climbed to a position about thirty feet from the ground and tied the rope around the branch to keep her body steady. The position was excellent as Snipe had said as not only could she see the back of the houses, but she could also look over their roofs into the Street. Once she had got herself comfortable she pulled out the binoculars and started her observation.

Snipe had walked the long way around to the entrance of Green Street where it joins the main road into town. Finding a little spot where he could see down the Street and over to the high trees in the woods beyond, he sat himself down and, with his one arm missing in full view, took out his bowl for begging. With his head down but his eyes alert, he took off his scraggy hat and scratched his head. Joulie, looking through her tiny binoculars saw him do this and smiled thinking, what a clever man. Now both were in position, it was time to be patient and watch.

After sitting on the high branch for a good two hours, Joulie was getting tired and was thinking about climbing down. But then she saw the back door of a house open and a man walk to what seemed like the latrine. She picked up the binoculars and honed in but noticed, to her dismay, it wasn't Stephen. She made a mental note of where and what she had seen and with a heavy sigh carried on watching.

Many people, horses and gigs had come into view and gone by off no consequence. But then around ten o clock the Snipe, hearing the sound of more hoofs coming from his right ever so gently moved his eyes and saw it was the man Bagnall as Joulie had described. The man and horse didn't stop and turned right into Green Street heading for one of the houses at the end. Snipe watched on until the horse stopped outside the end house on the right. The man then dismounted and walked the horse around to the back. Snipe didn't waste any time and so packed his stuff, got up, and walked calmly away back to the woods. Joulie also saw what the Snipe had seen and smiled knowing it was her Stephen. However, he then went out of sight for a while but reappeared at the back of the same house where she had seen the other man an hour ago. She thought he lived on his own and was a little confused but then seeing Snipe pack up and head off, she did the same and untied her anchor rope to start her descent.

When Bagnall had tied his horse up in his back yard he quickly unlocked the back door of the house and went in. "Hi Stephen, how did it go, did you find her?" "No, I didn't, she wasn't there, the cottage was empty, bloody strange." "Come in and sit down, I will pour us both a drink." "Thanks John, I need it." "She said she would send word but nothing and now vanished." "Well, she may have gone off with that Sarah woman and that rich Troon fellow and forgot all about you." "I don't believe that John, something is not right." "Come on Stephen, chin up, life works in mysterious ways."

Snipe, Sarah and Joulie had now packed up their things in the wood and were now in the gig getting very close to Green Street. On getting as close as he could the Snipe then pulled the horse to a halt. Then turning his head he looked at Joulie and said, "Now, are you sure you want to do this?" "I am sure." "Alright, but if all shouldn't go well, you know where I and Sarah will be." They had agreed on a simple plan that while Joulie goes on alone to the house, Snipe and Sarah will wait in the gig at the end of the street to watch and wait for her signal. After squeezing Sarah's hand one last time, Joulie let go and stepped down out of the gig. Sarah felt the hope and happiness coming from Joulie which quickly made her reflect on her own life. She looked at the back of the man Snipe, who was sitting busy holding the horse still and thought, could she live in a wooden barn in the middle of nowhere with a man who had one arm and walked the streets praising the Lord? He wasn't rich in money and worked part time at the asylum. She then looked up to the heavens and, after closing her eyes and asking what she should do, started to laugh aloud and felt a wonderful warm feeling flow through her body. Snipe heard her giggle and looked around saying, "Are you alright Sarah?" She looked at him with a smile and said, "I'm fine Snipe, just thinking that was all." He looked at her as if knowing what was going through her mind and said in a kind simple voice, "Sarah, I don't have much but I know we will be happy together." She smiled with a true inner warmth and replied, "Thank you Snipe, you know me well." And, she meant it.

With a spring in her step and her heart beating faster, Joulie headed up Green Street. On reaching outside the front door of Stephen's house she stopped and brushed her hands through her hair. She then turned her head back towards Snipe, who was watching and waiting at the end of the road with Sarah in the gig. Then taking a long deep breath she stood up straight and knocked on the door.

Stephen and John both heard the knock and quickly put their drinks down. John quickly ran up the stairs out of the way in full readiness to escape through the rear window should he need. Stephen got up and went to the door but before he opened it said aloud, "Yes, who is it?" "It's me Stephen, Joulie." On hearing Joulie's sweet voice, his heart raced and so opened the door as fast as he could. Seeing his lovely Joulie standing there in full smile he could not stop the love and warmth shine from his eyes and heart. He then quickly stepped out of the doorway and picked her up in his arms and kissed her lovingly on the lips. Joulie responded and hugged his neck with joy.

When their lips parted but Joulie still being held high in his arms, she turned her head up the street and waved at Sarah and Snipe. Stephen turned his head towards the direction Joulie was waving and seeing the gig at the end of the street said, "Who are they Joulie?" "That's Sarah and her old flame called Snipe?" "Sarah, I thought she was with Troon, Joulie, what's going on?" "Stephen, I will tell you all but first is it safe to come in?" Stephen quickly thought of his friend Hughesy who was upstairs in the bedroom but said, "Yes, of course, my darling." "And can I stay here as Sarah and Snipe are waiting for my signal that all is well?" "Yes, you can, I have been searching all over for you, where have you been?" "Stephen I will tell you everything when I come in but first, you must put me down and both of us must freely wave our hands to Sarah and Snipe." Stephen started to get it and so did as Joulie asked."

Sarah and Snipe saw them both waving and as planned, waved back. Then putting the reins in both his hands and slightly adjusting his seated position said, "Are you ready Sarah?" "Yes, I am ready Snipe." With that, the Snipe flicked the reins and after turning the gig about headed back out of Truro to his small isolated barn near Bodmin. Once they were safely away from the city and driving slowly through the lanes across the open land, Sarah sat back and thought, 'they haven't two pennies to rub together but never has she felt so at ease and free.' So, with her mind made up, she put her hands in her pockets and took out the small pistol and the bottle of deadly nightshade. Then with a most happy laugh at her new life ahead, she threw them both far away

Chapter 34

While in the meeting with the Sherriff in Truro, Joshua had sent word to Bull for them to meet up in the Red Lion in Helston later than afternoon. He wanted to discuss a plan of joint action on how best to observe the tunnel at Coverack before he met the Sherriff again the following day. Once he had finished with Bull at the Red Lion he could then nip down and see Rebecca and stay the night.

So, after having a good meeting with Bull and on both agreeing a plan, Joshua got on his trusted Harry and rode on down to Lady Street. Rebecca was surprised to see him and greeted Joshua with warmth as did the children. She then poured him a brandy and made him a pipe which he lit while sitting in a comfy chair by the roaring fire. This is what he needed, how lucky he felt to have met such a strong faithful woman. As Joshua puffed on the pipe and sipped the brandy, Rebecca came over and handed him a message saying, "Joshua this came for you yesterday." As ordered by George Kernow, Joshua had to give an alternative contact address now that Rebecca was away from their home. "Thank you, Rebecca, I will just finish this brandy and pipe in peace and then read it." "As you will Joshua but I must say the man looked exhausted. Oh, and also, I had a message from Mother. It seems she and Jacques are sailing back from London in a few days so with a little luck we will all be back together as a family at Gunwalloe very soon." "That would be nice Rebecca, I've missed you very much, it seems ages since you and the children were home." Rebecca smiled but left Joshua in peace to read the message. The message read:-

Joshua,
Urgent need of your help.
Waiting - Bolventor Inn
Signed LM

Joshua let slip his pipe as he leant forward in surprise at the content and so read the message again. It was from his man at Mevagissey known as LM on signature. What could be wrong? Joshua got up and went to find Rebecca who was sitting in the yard with the children. "Rebecca, I got to be off, seems there is a problem at Mevagissey." "What right this minute, you have only just got here." "I know but the message said urgent so I must go straight away." "Will you be back tonight." "I don't think so; Jim wants to meet at the Bolventor Inn so I will get a room for the night and take things from there. I also better get to the constable's office here in Helston and get message to the Sherriff at Truro to postpone our meeting for tomorrow." "Alright Joshua, but let me make you something to eat first and maybe a little nip to help you on your way." Joshua bent down and gave his wife a kiss and said, "Thank you Rebecca, I will just go and see to Harry and get him ready."

The ride to Bolventor went well but took over four hours with a little stop here and there to give both rider and Harry rest. As always with Joshua when getting a few miles to the Inn where the Moor starts to open, he feels an inner feeling of depth. There is just something about the Tors and the vast openness with its granite underlay that gives one an inner feeling of beauty yet harsh way of life.

With his horse being cared for by the stable boy, Joshua entered the Inn and immediately heard the fiddler in the corner and the air of song. Dusting himself down he went over to the bar to find the landlord. "Hi Smithy," said Joshua. Smithy looked up from pouring the cider and with a big smile replied, Hi Joshua, how goes it?" "All well thank you, I've come to meet a friend which may take a while, any chance of a room tonight." "Yes, of course," and then pointing over into the corner said, "He's over there." "Thanks Smithy, could you send over a couple of ciders please."

As Joshua walked through the busy Inn over to Jim, he noticed a lot of men in groups in quiet discussion and others singing and laughing aloud with the fiddler. He also noticed some women of the night plying their trade. As he got closer to where Jim was sitting he saw his friend looking down at his tankard in deep thought. "Hello Jim," said Joshua." Jim looked up from his heavy thoughts and said, "Hello Joshua, thank you for coming, good to see you."

Joshua sat down and while making himself comfortable said, "I've ordered a couple of ciders, they should be here in a bit." "Thanks Joshua, it's been one of those days." Jim was fifty two years of age, of large build, and had a big bushy beard. Joshua liked Jim very much and respected his work ethic. He also found him very loyal and worked hard in keeping the Cornish people safe. Jim had worked in his job role as Team leader on the east south side of Cornwall for a long time even before Joshua came along. He was then working with Henry Hosking, who sadly was no longer after being hanged in Bodmin for treason. While waiting for their tankards of cider, both chatted lightly away about their families and going's on. When the drinks arrived, both picked them up and after tapping them together and taking a swig, they got down to business.

"So Jim, your message said urgent, what's up?" Joshua, we have found ten barrels on gun powder with fuses set for igniting at the Gof Mine in St Austell." "What, who found them and how?" As always, Joshua needed to know the ins and outs of the situation. Jim told Joshua that on receiving his increased alert status, he made every effort to contact people in the areas he knew that could be vulnerable. One was the high producing Tim Mine at Wheal Gof, so he went to visit his good and long term friend who is the Senior Security Manager. Joshua while sipping his ale stayed quiet and listened intently.

Jim carried on and explained, "Although my friend has a security staff of twenty men who man the site twenty four hours a day, two days ago he decided to do an outer fence patrol himself. He doesn't know why he just felt he needed to. As he was half way round the outer perimeter he stopped and looked over to where the old entrance to the Mine used to be, many years ago, before it was sealed off and relocated to its present position. It is now fully overgrown, and completely out of the way by the edge of the new tree line. Being the inquisitive ex-army man he is, he went over to take a look. The first thing he noticed was the area by the entrance was all trampled down and so looking closer saw that the small security seal on the top of the door was broken. So, getting his bunch of keys out and finding the one marked 'Old Entrance' he unlocked the big old padlock and went in. As he walked up to the end of the shaft he saw the kegs all tied together and placed by the opening of the down shaft." Joshua kept quiet but the first thought that came into his head was Guido Fawkes, the English, Spanish traitor, of a hundred years ago.

"What did the Security Manager do?" "He was going to raise the alarm for complete evacuation but, as it was in the light of midday, decided that before he did anything, he needed help. So, he ordered one of his men to ride over to me for my urgent presence. He then went back to the shaft with pistols ready for fire and waited out of sight, on guard." "You say that was two days ago, what is the situation now." "On arriving at the Mine, I met with my friend who told me everything and so we sat together, in the woods, and worked a plan. Our main thoughts were the safety of the workers and so whatever we did that had to come first." "That's good Jim, so what did you come up with?" "Well, although risky, my friend said he would attempt to diffuse the kegs by going back into the shaft alone and take out the fuses. If he could achieve this, we would then, after the night sky had fallen, take the kegs out one by one and empty the powder into the earth far away from the mine. We would then place everything back as we found it, but without the powder inside and cover all tracks." "Did you succeed?" "Yes, we did Joshua, and I take my hat off to my friend for his bravery." "Very well done Jim, we could use men like your friend, a good man." Joshua noted that both their tankards were empty and so asked, "Would you like another drink Jim." "Yes please Joshua, I could do with another one or two." Joshua waved the bar girl over and after ordering two refills asked Jim, "Right Jim, so what is happening now?" "Well, after sending word to you, I got my team together who are now dug in pairs, spread around the edge of the wood. "How many men do you have in place and do they have weapons and ammunition?" "Altogether I have eight men and yes all are well equipped." After taking a swig of his cider, Joshua asked, "Jim, who knows of this and who knows what you have done?" "Just me and my team and the security manager." "Has he not reported it to his superiors?" "Good question Joshua and one which we discussed at length, and the answer is no, he has not reported it to anyone. We felt, now that the kegs had been diffused and the entrance guarded out of sight it would be best to keep things quiet and wait for your advice. We also went around and checked the complete area just in case. But Joshua, what is bothering us is someone must have had a key to open the padlock as apart from my friend having one, the only other one is held in a safe in the production office."

As Jim leant forward and picked up his cider, taking a thirsty gulp, Joshua sat back and rubbed his chin with thought and then said, "Right Jim, first things first, your men will need relieving soon so I suggest I send rider with message to John at Bedruthan for him to get here by sun up tomorrow. Us three can then get on and discuss a plan of action, are you alright with that or have you other plans?" "No, Joshua that's fine with me, does the Landlord have a spare room?" "I am sure he does but let me go over and talk with him and also organise the rider to Bedruthan."

Joshua quietly talked with the Landlord and when done and his tankards refilled went back to the table. "All sorted Jim, I suggest we have a couple more and then get ourselves off to bed, what say you." "Couldn't agree more Joshua, I am tired and it's getting late." "I am also tired but let's carry on and talk. You say that only one other key could fit that padlock, could it not have been just picked open? "That's what I asked my friend but he is adamant that due to the padlock's complexity and size, it was most unlikely. Has your friend any ideas?" "He hadn't when we last spoke but he is looking into things now." "While also keeping things quiet?" "Yes, very, he is a good man Joshua. He knows of my meeting here this night and is waiting for my return."

Joshua took a sip of his drink and again rubbed his chin but knew it was now time to enlighten Jim on what has been happening on the West side, especially over at Coverack. After a couple more drinks and further talk, the time soon reached the hour of ten in which they both had agreed would be the time to retire up to bed. The message to John at Bedruthan had been dispatched and both needed to be refreshed for the early morning meet.

All too soon Joshua heard the knocking on the door and the young maid repeatedly say aloud by the keyhole, "Mr Pendragon, seven o clock, Mr Pendragon, seven o cock." "Joshua roused himself awake and knowing she wasn't allowed to stop until he answered said, "Thank you young lady, I'm awake." She replied, "Thank you, Mr Pendragon," and walked off to the next room.

Joshua shuffled out of bed and after filling the bowl with fresh water and washing his face and hands, got himself dressed and ready. Although the stable lad would look after his horse Harry, he decided to go and see him and say good morning. He then went to the cold wet latrine and when he was done went into the warm, log fire area of the bar.

"Good morning Joshua," said John who was sitting at the table close to the fire. Joshua replied, "Good morning John, good to see you my good friend and thank you for getting here so quickly." What's up Joshua?" "I'll tell you all about it but first, let's wait for Jim to come down, he shouldn't be long." "What, Jim from Mevagissey is here?" "Yes, we all need to talk, things are afoot." As Joshua sat down and got cosy by the fire, Jim appeared and joined them and as he did he shook John's hand in greeting. The young maid then came across to take their breakfast order of mutton stew.

Joshua knew that using John's team from Bedruthan to intertwine with Jim's team at the Gof Mine was a risk and would leave the North Coast weak. But, he had thought things through carefully and made the decision that the Gof Mine had to be reinforced to achieve the worker's safety and also uncover or stop what was going on. Therefore the cost and risk were justified.

With a brief overview of the situation given by Jim, all three men now openly discussed how best to sort out the threat. Also, due to the severity of it all and in keeping the workers safe, it started to become clear that the firing of weapons was becoming a reality. So Joshua confirmed to them both that should the enemy or whoever they are, show any risk or cause for harm, they must shoot to kill. He also confirmed that he would inform the Sheriff that he had authorised this. It would be nice if the enemy just put their hands up on being asked and then taken away but that was a fairy tale and didn't happen in real life.

This was serious. They also surmised that if the people were to come back to ignite the powder, it would most likely be in the dead of the night or the dark of the early morning. If this was the case, and the shaft entrance being at least fifty metres from the woods edge, visibility of the enemy would be near zero. Joshua then asked Jim, do you still have those new Fire Flares I sent you some months ago?" "Yes, I do Joshua, there stored away in my bunker at home." "Do your men know how to use them?" "No, but they will by tonight." "Good, that's the spirit. And John, are you alright to bring you and your men down and help Jim?" "Yes, of course, it will take me a while to get things sorted but I would say we could be at Jim's late tomorrow afternoon." "Are you alright with that Jim?" "Yes, that would fit well, thank you John." With all being done, Joshua asked both, "Now, is there anything else either of you need?" With both men answering no, Joshua wished them and their teams the best of luck and asked they send message immediately should things escalate.

Chapter 35

After riding for two hours through the dead of the night, John Hughes reined his horse in at the end of the small cobbled street. He had to be careful and so without noise dismounted and waited. Then, after checking his pistols, took the horse's rein in his hand and walked through the street to number twenty five, a small mid terrace cottage where his smuggling friend lives. Hughesy could have stayed in Truro with Stephen Bagnall but after Joulie arrived he felt uncomfortable at putting a lady at risk by his very presence, especially one whom Stephen loved. Stephen and Joulie had both said that he could stay and that all will be well but Hughesy just couldn't do it and also felt that two was company and three a crowd. And so after talking with Stephen, Hughesy would, with the use of Stephen's horse, move off that night to Scorrier and get shelter with his friend, Fin. He had to keep a low profile until such time as he felt or knew it was safe.

As he got outside number twenty five he saw the light of the candles through the curtains which meant someone was up and about. So while still holding the horse's rein, he slowly looked up and down the street and seeing no one around, knocked the door. He then heard the inner door bolts being pulled back and when the door opened saw Emily with a candle in hand. "Hi Hughesy, how are you?" "Hi Emily, I thought you lived two doors down with Fred." "I do but Fred's gone away for the week so I moved in with Fin to give him and me a bit of company.

Emily was Fin's older sister and a good woman to boot. "Emily, where's Fin?" "Where do you think, down the pub as usual with his mates, they all came knocking two hours ago.'' ''Emily, I need a safe place to stay for a few days, can you help?'' ''Of course we can, why don't you go down to the pub and talk with Fin, you can stay here or at my place, I don't mind at all.'' ''Thank you Emily, I owe you one.'' ''Hughesy, all the men have walked to the pub so give us your horse and I will tie him up with ours at the back.'' With Emily taking his horse around the backyard, Hughesy set off to the Plume. It wasn't that far about a mile or so just at the top of Redruth. Although his friend was in the pub, he still wasn't taking any chances and so pulled his hat over his head and kept his eyes and ears alert.

As the Plume came into sight Hughesy slowed his walk to give him time to think. Yes, he was a known smuggler but never had he felt so nervy. After he had got wind of the killings at Bristol and Portishead, both linked to the Cornish Tin trade, he had no choice but to run. And so he would until he found out what the hell is going on.

Getting just outside the front of the Plume, he stopped and checked his pistols. Everything around looked fine and clear but he decided to go round the back through the stable yard and enter from the rear, just in case. As he walked through and got to the darkened end of the stables, which was close to the filthy latrines, he saw two fine stallions with saddles and gear looking all ready for the off. This was strange and got his attention as the Plume was just a local Inn for the low paid workers and, was in Redruth, not Truro. He stopped and retreated to a dark corner and hid out of sight to watch.

As the minutes ticked by nothing changed and all stayed still and quiet so he started to then think that maybe he was over reacting a little. But, he still felt edgy and so decided not to go any further forward but to go back out and enter the Inn from the front door where he could see and have choice. Better safe than sorry. Little did he know that this decision to pull back would save his life, as only twenty minutes ago the two assassins had got themselves in position just out from the stables by the latrine in wait for the man called Fin.

The two assassins had, four hours ago, completed their scouting and intended to snatch Fin by his cottage but, unlike Portishead, the area was just too tight and the risk too high. So they decided to get him as he walked to the Inn where the track curves close to a small wood. It was an ideal point of snatch and grab and their target would simply not see it coming. But after being saddled up on their horses waiting in the wood for three hours there was still no sign. Then, as planned he appeared but unfortunately for them, but lucky for Fin, he was not on his own as five other men were with him. So, they had no choice but to let him pass and rethink what to do. They had thought about letting things be and leave the area and regroup but, they needed the information to get their main target, John Hughes. Their spirit was low and had even talked about chucking it all in and riding far away from Shanks and his plans but then, he owed them three hundred pounds in bonuses. So, as they sat in the wood talking about their options, one of them said, "This Fin bloke may not even have any information, it was only a suggestion we discussed at the Dragons Inn." "This is true, but on the other side of the coin, he could have." Both went silent and knew they had no choice but to carry on and snatch him. What else could they do, they had no idea where Hughes was and he had to be killed by Friday. The likelihood is that this Fin fellow would know something, so they simply had to get him. They knew Fin was in the Plume, albeit with his mates, so that's where they would go and use their latrine method as they had done in Bristol. However, to reduce risk they would keep their stallions close by just in case things went pear shaped. With that, they shook hands, checked their gear and pistols, and got back on their horses. As they got close to the Inn they dismounted and quietly walked their horses around the side. The Plume was a large Inn and the stables and latrine were close together which was good. So tying up their stallions they got themselves into position and waited.

As John Hughes went in the Plume from the front door he felt a lot less fidgety and noticed straight away that the Inn was not busy apart from a few locals at the bar and six men sitting around a table laughing and joking. The landlord at the bar saw Hughesy come in and straight away raised his hand in greeting. Hughesy did the same and walked over to the far table. All six men saw him coming and as he got close, they cheered and raised their glasses in salute. Fin stood up and put his hand out and as Hughesy took it said, ''Where you been John, I've been searching everywhere, got some lovely tin from the Tye Mine for you?'' ''Good to see you Fin, I've been about but before I go into that, have you seen a couple of strangers in here tonight?'' ''I saw one, he came in about twenty minutes ago.'' Fin then looked about trying to find him and then said ''Funny that, he's not here, but he was, I saw him come in.'' ''Just hold on there a minute Fin, I'll' be back in a bit.'' ''What's going on John?'' Hughesy didn't reply but turned and walked to the bar. ''Hi Hughesy, what can I get you?'' Hughesy leant forward on the bar and quietly said, "Sam, have any strangers been in tonight?" Sam knew Hughesy well and so answered with truth, "Well, we had one just a while ago who ordered two beers, saying it was for him and his friend who would be along any minute." "So, where is he?" "I don't know, when he paid he asked if I could put the tankards on a table while he went to the latrine." "What table?" The landlord pointed to the small table just off to the right and noticed the tankards were still in the same place as he had left them and the chairs hadn't been moved either. Hughesy saw this and said, "So, you say he went to the latrine." "Yes, and I haven't seen him or his so called friend since. He might have a problem if you know what I mean." "Did he look like he had a problem." "No, not in the least, in fact, he oozed calm and confidence if you know what I mean?" "I do know what you mean, thanks Sam." "John, there's not going to be any trouble tonight, is there?" "In truth, there might be Sam, but I will take it away from the Inn." "Thanks Hughesy, I don't want any more of those bloody constables snooping around here again."

John Hughes walked back to the table where Fin and his friends were and while he did so, he thought on the two fine well equipped stallions in the stables and the two confident men outside in the latrines who have not been seen for twenty minutes, was strange and spelt trouble. As soon as he sat down the men stopped talking and looked his way. "Right, my good men, it looks like we may have a problem." On all putting their tankards on the table they leaned forward to hear what John had to say. John knew that whatever he had to do had to be done now, time was ticking by and there was no time to lose. So, explaining quickly what he wanted them to do, they nodded their approval and got up. As John led the way, he inwardly smiled at the thought on how loyal the Cornish working men are. Hughesy kept things simple and suggested the pincer method was the best solution. So, with neck scarves pulled over their faces, two men would go with Fin out via the front door and through the stables and three men led by John would go via the back through the bar area. Just before the two teams split, John asked Fin if he was armed which he replied, "Yes," and then tapped the left underside of his chest.

The two assassins standing close by each other were, to the outside eye, acting all normal and relaxed, chatting away with each other but with eyes and ears peeled. It had been nearly thirty minutes and apart from a couple of old men, they had yet to see their prey come out. Fin was definitely in there as when one of them went into the Inn to order two beers he saw him with five other men. So, it was just a matter of time but, time was not on their side and they were getting fidgety. Maybe they should just pull back and regroup. As they thought this, their two stallions just off to their rear started to shuffle their hoofs which made both men twitch and turn. Just as they did this the back door of the Inn crashed open and four men rushed out. Quickly turning their heads back around and seeing these men coming straight at them, they went for their pistols. But, as they did, the three men from the stables sprinted forward and jumped on their backs. It was all over in seconds and the two assassins were taken completely by surprise, exactly as Hughes had wanted. After each assassin had his wrists tied behind his back and held firmly on the ground by two men, another man searched them from head to foot and threw out everything he found onto the floor. While he did this, Hughes and Fin stood with their pistols aimed at the assassin's heads. All the men watched in silence at what was being pulled out of their pockets and raised their eyebrows at the pistols, ammunition, knives and wads of cash. When the search was done and all their personal belongings were piled high by the wall of the latrine the searcher pulled back. The assassins were then picked up and moved into the sitting position with their backs against the wall. While all this went on both of the assassins did not say a word. So, with the two assassins sitting in silence on their backsides with seven men with scarves around their faces looking down at them, Hughes spoke, "So, tell us, what are your names and what are you doing here?" Neither of the men answered and just kept quiet, knowing if they started to talk, it could get very serious if it wasn't already. Again, Hughes asked the same question and again both men kept quiet. Hughes wasn't fazed by their silence and so just looked at them with patience, keeping his pistol aimed. Also, Hughes and his men were smugglers not interrogators of torture.

After a couple of minutes of silence had passed without word from either party, one of Hughesy's men spoke up saying, "So what do we do with them?" Hughes heard the question and noted that the man who asked this did not look or openly speak his name. This was the way it was when they were around people they didn't know. However, when the question was asked, all men looked at Hughes for an answer. Hughes thought for a moment but before he could answer the question, Fin interrupted and said in a bemused voice, "Well, I think that question has been answered." "What do you mean?" Hughes said. Fin then pointed his finger at the two assassins and on each of their foreheads were at least thirty ladybirds fluttering all around. Everyone from Hughesy's team, including Fin, looked on and blew a gasp of air in quiet disbelief as they knew the old Cornish ode: -

Ladybirds of many seen on the Foe
Then to the Tor they must go.

After handing his and Fin's weapon over to two of the men to keep guard, Hughes and the others went into the corner out of ear shot. "So what do think men?" Fin answered first by saying, "Well, I know I've had a few but there is no way we can go against her." Hughes then looked at each man in turn and all said the same. "Right, then this is what we will do." He then went on to explain his plan of action that he and Fin will take them to the Tor but first split all the bounty gained from the assassin's pockets and saddlebags and then tie each of them bareback to their horses. He then looked at Fin and asked, "It's quite a ride Fin, are you up for it?" "John, we can't go against what we have seen and if this is what the Lady wants, then yes, I am." "Good, then I suggest you quickly get on home and fetch our horses and let us all make ready." So, with the decision made and all in agreement, they got on with things in haste and, with all going well, they should reach Rough Tor on Bodmin Moor before sunrise. While all this took place, the two assassins remained stony silent.

As the morning hour hand turned passed four, the dark silhouette of Rough Tor on the far left and the Bolventor Inn on their front right came into view. So it was time to veer left off the track and onto the Moor. Hughes and Fin had travelled for four hours without stop each with an assassin tied to their horses in tow. They now had to be very careful and stick to the hard ground as best they could. After a further forty minutes of steady riding, the rugged height of the Tor stood before them. Thankfully the early morning sun was starting to rise which gave some visibility through the misty dawn.

Hughesy pulled his horse close to Fins and said, "Well we're here, if you could hold my horse and keep your pistol on the men, I will get down and look around for a place to put them." With Fin in agreement, Hughesy dismounted and walked off, but not too far. He was looking for a nook or something like that in and around the large granite stones, somewhere dry where they couldn't be seen and out of the way. It didn't take long and when he found it forty or so yards away, turned and went back to Fin to organise things. But, unlike back at the Inn where there were seven of them to overpower and guard two men, now there were only two of them to guard, so they had to be very careful and alert. So with Hughesy holding two loaded pistols for covering fire, Fin untied the first assassin and got him down off his horse. With his hands still bound and mouth gagged he was told to sit and wait while Fin went back and got the other one untied. All the while Fin did this, Hughes stood back ten feet with pistols aimed at both prisoners. When both assassins were sitting down in the desired position, Hughes gave back one of the pistols to Fin. Then making sure all horses were safely tied, Hughes ordered both men to get up and, with pistols at their backs, were steered towards the granite overhang. When both the assassins were in position and sat down sat down, Hughes and Fin stood back and looked at them. Then Fin turned to Hughes and said quietly without the assassins hearing, ''So what do we do now.'' ''Well, we have done exactly what the lady wanted so I guess we leave them here and push off.'' ''Shall we untie them?'' ''I don't think that is a good idea Fin, but I do think we should move the wrist ties from their backs to their fronts and take off their mouth gags.

When this was done and Fin was again standing safely by Hughesy's side, Hughes said to both prisoners, ''We don't know who you are or what you've done but for some unknown reason the Lady has given us the sign to bring both you here, so I suggest you stay where you are and wait, do you understand?'' Again the assassins kept their mouths shut and didn't say a word. Hughes waited for some kind of answer but again on getting nothing, turned to Fin and said, ''Right, our job is done, let's go.'' So leaving the assassins in the crevice both men walked away back to their horses. Just before they mounted, Fin said, ''Do you think we should give them give water and blanket?'' ''Hughesy squiggled his mouth from side to side in a, shall we, shan't we thought, and said, ''Hmm, I suppose we should really. You take it over to them and I will just double check their horses are securely tied to ours.'' While Fin was sorting out the water and blankets, he looked up at Hughesy who was by the stallions and asked, ''How much will we get for them?'' ''Well, they are fine looking stallions and with their leather saddles included I would say at least fifteen guinea's each.'' This put a smile on Fin's face. So, while Hughesy gave pistol cover, Fin took the water and blanket to the assassins. When all was done and Fin was back on his horse they both rode off at a pace away from the moor. Once safely out of sight, Hughesy took off the scarf from his face and breathed a big sigh of relief. Seeing his smuggling friend do this, Fin did the same and then steered his horse closer to Hughes saying, "Just thought, those two men will probably untie each other from their bonds and run off." "Yeah, you may be right Fin, I did think of that when we changed the position of their ties but that's up to them mate, that's their choice, we have done as told." "Alright John, but what say we ride to the Bolventor Inn for a few jars and stay the night?" Hughes grinned but replied, "Sounds good my friend but I don't think so, we should stay low and get ourselves home as fast as we can and then have a good drink in the Plume."

The two assassins watched both Hughes and Fin ride off and when out of sight and far away, did exactly as Fin had said and untied each other from their bonds. With both shaking their heads in disbelief at their situation they talked at length about what do. This was the second time they had been discarded on the moor and just couldn't make sense of the reality of it all. They tried to reason out the Ladybird thing but again just shook their heads in bewilderment. No horses, no pistols, no nothing but, unbelievably they were still alive albeit on the moor in the middle of bloody nowhere again. Both talked about the two men who had brought them here from the Plume Inn and, with the descriptions and other intelligence they had been given, knew one was John Hughes and the other was the man, Fin. Just so ironic, as these were the two men they were meant to kill and, the very reason they were in Cornwall. So what were they to do? Should they stay and wait as strangely suggested by John Hughes or run for it? But run where? They couldn't get their heads around any of it and so decided it was best to rest up and wait, at least for the rest of the day. If nothing happened then they would go, what else could they do? With the time just gone seven in the morning and the sun half aglow, both men, sitting side by side with blanket over them, leant their arms forward onto their knees and dropping their heads forward, closed their eyes to sleep.

With both men being totally exhausted and the silence of the Moor, sleep reached their bodies very quickly. Then after only ten minutes had passed one of the men felt the need to open his eyes. In doing so he raised his head and just couldn't believe what was in front of him. The shock made his whole body jump back in fright which then woke the other man who instantly did the same. There, standing only a few feet in front of them were their two horses which they had ridden into Cornwall and who had run away from the fright of the lions a month ago leaving them stranded. Both men looked at each other in total confusion. The two horses looked bright and well and both had their saddles and reins attached. Both men got up and went to their horse's side and while holding their reins looked around the Moor and saw nothing but vast emptiness which just didn't make any sense. Where had the horses come from? It was all so very strange.

Then one of the men said, "I think someone is telling us something." "I agree," said the other. "What say we get on our horses and get out of Cornwall and go home." "I couldn't agree with you more." With that, both men did as said and while riding away kept shaking their heads in total disbelief. If only they knew.

Chapter 36

It was Thursday evening and Luisa was sitting at ease with wine glass in hand looking around at the walls of her new dining room at Mingoose Manor. She arrived with four of her staff from London the day before and now waiting for her cousin Jose to return. He had left the manor in the early morning to visit both Mines at Wheal Tye and Coates to make sure all was well and change things if needed. On realising her wine glass was empty she pulled the cord for her maid to come and refill it. The old butler and his wife who had been looking after the Manor were called in upon Luisa's arrival, where she sacked them on the spot. This confused the old couple as the Solicitor had sworn that the job was permanent. They tried to reason with her but Luisa would have none of it and while turning her head to look out the window, flicked her fingers for them to get out as if they were dust. Accepting their dismissal with quiet dignity they both turned about and while holding each other's hand walked out and away to their small cottage, fearing how they could now afford to pay the rent.

It had just passed the hour of eight that evening when the dining room door opened and in walked Jose. Luisa looked up from her book and smiled saying, "Hello, my good Cousin, how did things go?" "All went well Luisa, is there any food I'm starving?" "Yes, of course, take a seat and I will ring for the maid, would you like a drink too?" "Yes, very much so, thank you." Jose knew that his cousin was not interested in the finer details of things so while they talked he kept things brief and to the point. In truth, he did have to change a few things at Wheal Coates in readiness for midnight on Sunday but didn't tell her as it would bore her silly. What was important was the knowledge that his team of men had all arrived safe from the cove at Coverack and were doing a good job. Also, the correct weight of Tin had been delivered and was being packed and put in place in time for pick up.

When the maid came in, Luisa gave orders for her to fetch more food and a large bottle of the best cognac. As the young girl left the room, Luisa handed Jose a sealed message saying, "By the way Jose, this came for you this morning." Jose took the message and after leaning his arms forward onto the table broke the seal. It read:-

Jose
Ships Clearance Registration Details
Name – Celtic View
Number – PL0016609
Type – Open
Dock Location – Plymouth
Amigo

As Jose finished reading the message a broad smile came across his face. Luisa saw the smile and said, "Good news?" "Very good news, we have got the clearance at Plymouth." "That is good news." Jose closed the message and after putting it in his pocket said, "I must admit I was getting a little anxious." "Well, you have it now so have a brandy and calm yourself." While Jose smiled at Luisa's response she added, "Now tell me, is all running in accordance with our longer term plans?" "Yes, now we have full clearance, absolutely, this is just the start." "That's excellent news, and what of the man Shanks?" "All is ready, your two security men have arrived and I have spoken with them this morning as we discussed." "That's good Jose, he needs to be taken out, now that all is in place. So it just remains for us all to meet tomorrow and finalise the go ahead. I have sent word and arranged the meeting for twelve noon." With those last words spoken, a gentle knock on the door was heard and in walked the maid with the food and drink."

As Jose tucked into his food and drank his large cognac, Luisa remained silent but had an inward smile on her face thinking of her success in life. Jose felt this and so briefly stopped eating and said, ''Is the Manor to your liking?'' ''Well compared to my Chateau and Hacienda, O, and my House in Mayfair, it's rather nice actually and I will tell you my Cousin, I do love the sight of what wealth and power brings me.'' ''That's funny, because I love the feel of it, especially the wads of cash, loads of it.'' They both laughed and raised their glasses.

As the Friday morning sun arose, Jose opened his eyes but decided to have a lie in, he deserved it and also it was going to be a long day. Luisa on the other hand was up and getting herself ready. She had also pulled the cord for her maids and when they went in she ordered both to clean and freshen the room up. Also, she wanted them to prepare a hot bath for when she returns at one o clock. As the time passed eleven, Peter Williams, from St Austell, was the first to arrive and rode through the front gates of the Manor in fine spirit. However, as the time pushed on to eleven thirty there was still no sign of Shanks.

Shanks had got to within one mile of the Manor but then had ordered his driver to pull over and stop. The driver thought this was strange but did as asked and waited patiently. Shanks was in deep thought and needed time to get his story right. Two of his men were at St Austell with Peter Williams to help move the powder kegs at the Gof Mine which was fine. The other two men, who were to kill John Hughes, should have reported back at the very latest yesterday, but nothing. They knew he was on a tight schedule but had not even sent message, nothing. What had happened, where were they? More to the point what should he say to Luisa? He knew they liked a drink and if he found that this was in any way the case he would terminate their contract immediately with no pay. Not only was his reputation on the line but Luisa's plans could be put on hold and also his one thousand pound bonus would not be paid, so he had to make a decision, one way or the other. He then thought 'sod it, he had to look after himself,' and shouted to the driver to push on.

So, as arranged and on time, the four of them were now sitting around the table in the drawing room watching the maid pour the tea. Luisa had earlier told the maid that all alcohol was to be taken off the table and not to be served unless she and she only, gave permission. The meeting itself didn't take long as all that was needed was for each man to confirm to Luisa that all was good to go as planned. Jose went first saying positively, "All was good." Next was Peter Williams, who after firstly thanking Shanks for his two men, confirmed that all was ready. It was now the turn of Shanks, who in a self assured manner, mirrored the other two by saying, "Yes, all was good." Luisa smiled on hearing all three men's approval but was interested in Shank's reply as his job was to wipe out anyone who could affect their plans, so asked, ''So, did you get Hughes?'' ''Yes, we got him and the other one too.'' Jose, Peter and Luisa looked on in quiet applause with Jose asking, ''Where are they, how did they get it?'' Shanks smiled and replied, ''Well let's put it this way, the sharks won't be hungry for a while.'' No one responded to Shank's reply rather all went a little quiet until Luisa said, ''By the way Shanks, it seems a couple of Jose's men at the Wheal Coates Mine think they have seen some smugglers around the outside of the fence. It may be nothing, but it would be helpful if you could go over with Jose this afternoon and have a word with them, and get it sorted.'' Shanks had planned that after this meeting he would get himself back to the Dragons Inn and get drunk but stayed calm and replied, ''Yes, of course Luisa.'' Luisa smiled and pushed over the table a heavy roll of bank notes saying, ''Thank you Shanks.'' ''Thank you my Lady.''

Luisa then said to all, ''Are there any last questions?'' With all three saying 'No,' she leant across and pulled the cord and said, ''Right, now I do need to go and have my bath. May I suggest we all now have a cognac to our success and I will see you again at my Mayfair house in London in two weeks.''

After the cognac had been drunk for success and the meeting closed, it was time for Jose and Shanks to get to the Wheal Coates Mine, as agreed. Jose led the way on his horse while Shanks was following in the buggy behind. Shanks thought the meeting had gone well and although he lied, they would never find out and more importantly, she had paid him his bonus money. Now he could do what he wanted and, what he wanted was to get out of Cornwall as soon as possible, he was done.

Yes, he would go back to the Dragons Inn this evening and wait a couple of days, but that's it.

The ride to Wheal Coates didn't take long as just after twenty minutes of riding the main gate came into view. Jose talked with the guard and once the gate was open rode on through with Shanks in the buggy close behind.

The two men who worked for Luisa were standing close together and saw Jose and the buggy enter. They were waiting off to the far left as had been agreed with Jose the day before. Jose, although knowing they were there did not look over, but just carried on to the main hut and got down from his horse. When the buggy stopped close by, Jose went over and said to Shanks, "I will just go in and ask where these two men are, I won't be a moment." After a brief two minutes had passed, Jose reappeared and then pointing over to the far left by the fence said, "There over there by the fence, let's take a walk shall we." As Shanks got down, Jose turned to the driver and suggested he go to the hut to warm himself.

As both men walked over to the fence, Jose started to casually chat away saying, "So how's it going Shanks?" "All's going well thanks Jose." "That's good, I'm glad." Making Shanks feel relaxed, which Jose wanted, Shanks then asked, "So, who are these two men?" "I don't know them that well, but they seem good guys and work hard." This open and calm answer was anything but the truth but again it done the trick in keeping things looking normal. As they were getting closer, Jose, without notice to Shanks, then lifted his thumb of his right hand down by his side. The two men saw the signal but carried on acting as if it were just another day at the Mine. When the four men were together, Jose put out his hand and shook hands with both men and then calmly introduced Shanks. Shanks then also shook their hands and asked, "So what exactly have you seen which has caused you concern?" They were just about to talk when Jose butted in and pointed off to the side saying, "Is that the old Mine shaft were Troon was thrown?" Shanks turned his head to look and said, "I have no idea, I didn't throw him down." As Shanks was looking across taking his attention away from the two men was when they leapt forward and jumped him. Getting him to the floor and holding him down one of the men then drew his blade and slowly pushed it deep into his chest. It was quick and lethal and when done and Shanks had breathed his last, Jose bent down and went through his pockets to find the roll of bank notes Luisa had given him only two hours before. When the wad of notes was found and put safely in his pocket the three men picked up the body and took it to lip off the old shaft. When the iron cover had been pulled back they pushed the body over and let it drop down into the depths of darkness.

When Shanks had disappeared deep into the dark shaft, Jose said to the two men, "Well done, good job." "Our pleasure Jose, anything for you or Luisa, you know that." After putting the cover plate back in position, Jose then quickly dusted himself down and went back to the main hut to speak to the driver of the buggy. As he opened the door and went into the hut he saw the driver sitting comfortably drinking some hot tea. Seeing Jose walk in, the driver looked up and as he did so, Jose said, "By the way, there has been a change of plan." "What do you mean?" "I mean, Shanks has decided to stay at the Mine and you are wanted back by your employer in

Bath, so I suggest you make haste and get going." The driver, with the tea cup still in his hand, was somewhat baffled but then as he looked around the room saw that all four men he was in the hut with had now drawn their pistols. Jose again said, "Do you understand what I am saying?" The driver got the message straight away and replied, "Yes, I understand." He then gently put the cup back down on the table and after slowly getting up, walked toward the front door without word from his lips. As he neared the doorway, Jose said, "Just a minute my man." After then peeling a hundred pounds from the bankroll he had just taken from Shank's pocket, walked over and put them in the driver's hand. The driver took the money and carried on out to the waiting buggy and after climbing up on the seat, flicked the reins for the off. Not once did he look back and when out of the main gate, he pushed the horse onto a fast gallop. It was the driver's lucky day as Jose had wanted to kill them both. But Luisa saw things differently as the driver's employer was powerful and rich and needed him on her side, just in case. After the driver rode off, Jose sat down with his men in the hut and after pouring a brandy, thought on how Luisa will be well pleased.

Luisa was upstairs in her bedroom at Mingoose Manor and after having her warm relaxing bath was now sitting by the bay window. Both maids were by her side with one brushing her and the other painting her nails. While the maids were doing this, Luisa was looking out over the grounds of her new estate. She saw the deer running, big oak trees swaying and flowers of all kinds spread across the lush grass. While Luisa sat there feeling very content, the maid brushing her hair looked at the other maid and, without Luisa seeing, showed her the brush.

The other maid, who was kneeling on the floor, saw the brush with all the loose hair on it and moved her head from side to side silently miming, ''Don't say anything.'' So, as Luisa carried on looking over her estate, the maids got on with things without a word. When done, it was then time for them to get Luisa's facial make up on and then get her dressed. All in all, it took well over an hour to get her ready, as she liked. When all completed, Luisa walked over to the full length mirror and after turning her body and head from side to side seemed happy with what the young maids had done. She then turned about and told them they could both leave and that she will be down for her cream tea shortly. Once the two girls were alone outside Luisa's bedroom they started to natter. ''Did you see all the hair that come out of her head.'' ''Yes, I did, where is it all?'' The girl put her hand in her pocket and pulled out a huge amount of Luisa's hair.'' The other girl then said, ''Well, while I was doing her nails, I saw white spots on her fingers.'' ''Did you cover them up?'' ''Yes, I did and also as I took off her bodice I saw them on her back, did you see them?'' ''Yes, I did, but as you saw, I quickly put her shift over to cover them up.'' ''What do think, has she caught something?'' ''I don't know, let's talk with the butler, he will know.''

With the maids now gone from the room, Luisa went up to the mirror and looked deeply into her eyes. They use to be bright blue but seem to have lost their sparkle and the whites of her eyes didn't seem to be that white either. She also noticed that the young maids had done a good job on covering up the white spots on her skin. She had noticed these spots while soaking in the bath tub. Maybe she had just caught a cold or something when she had gone for a walk around the grounds, after all, it was cold and wet. Whatever it is, she will get her good doctor to come and check her out when she gets back to her house in Mayfair. As for now she was hungry and so quickly spun about to head for the door but as she did so, her head went giddy and her whole body started to sway. Quickly grabbing hold of one of the bed posts she then steadied herself but even after a good three minutes had passed she still felt light headed. So, she decided to sit down on the side of the bed to try and clear her mind. Without rush and letting time run its course she then started to feel better and so after briskly rubbing her face with her hands she got up and walked to the bedroom door. It was only after taking a few steps that she lost all consciousness and fell to the floor.

Chapter 37

Joshua was trying to work things out but every time he put two and two together he came up with five. It was nine o clock Saturday morning and he was on Harry, his good steed, riding to Helston. The weather was poor with the wind and rain coming in heavily from the south west. He had stayed overnight at the Red Lion in Truro after a busy day of discussion with the Sherriff and his man Bull. As he gently pushed his horse on, he was in deep thought.

Bull and his team had been dug in observing along the tunnel for nearly a week but nothing had been seen. The Sherriff's team had been tasked to watch and wait on the cliffs at Coverack for the ship to enter in the dark hours of Thursday morning, but that didn't appear either. And so bravely both teams had reorganised and decided to enter the tunnel from different directions, one from the exit at Zoar and one from the entrance at Coverack. But finding it completely empty with nothing untoward seen the Sherriff gave orders for the tunnel to be resealed.

While in the meeting with the Sherriff and Bull, Joshua had informed them of the serious situation at Wheal Gof Mine in St Austell and although Joshua had authorised the use of weapons, it was good to get the Sherriff's approval. Joshua then thought about the times when he was on the front line abroad in some foreign country, as when he had to fire, he didn't need to ask permission. But now he was Head of Security in Cornwall with three teams to manage reporting directly to George Kernow in London, Joshua was learning that diplomacy and tact very much help. He then thought that maybe he should tell Rebecca how he is growing in maturity. But then thought if he did she would probably hit him round the head with the frying pan. He started to laugh at the very thought.

Getting his mind back into serious mode, Joshua had agreed with Bull that his team should now continue with normal duties but with an emphasis on the Mining areas in line with the alert status. Joshua had considered using Bull and his team to help over at St Austell but decided against this as he did need to keep a flexible eye on the South West. Also, he had already drafted the other team in from the North at Bedruthan. Although only nine in the morning, Joshua started to yawn and knew he was mentally and physically tired of the long hours of riding and the pressure of the heavy meetings over the last few days. He now wanted, after seeing Rebecca, to get back to his cottage at Gunwalloe where he could rest up and recoup. So, with that in mind, he flicked the reins for Harry to speed up.

As Joshua rode into Helston and turned into Lady Street, he immediately saw a horse and buggy outside Jeanne's cottage. He saw it wasn't Rebecca's buggy or her horse Lilly, so assumed that someone must be in visit. Joshua halted his horse and dismounted and after tying him up securely walked forward and knocked on the front door. He would normally have gone around the back into the yard but thought he better play things safe. Within a moment, the door opened with Rebecca smiling brightly. "Hello Joshua, come on in, guess who's here?" "I have no idea Rebecca." "It's, Mother and Jacques, there back from London, come on Joshua, come in and close the door." Joshua did as was told and as he entered he saw both the children on Jeanne's lap, all with loving smiles and laughter. He then looked across the room and saw Jacques and couldn't believe how well he looked from the last time he saw him. So, after acknowledging both Jeanne and Jacques and giving his two children a quick cuddle, Joshua sat down while Rebecca made him a cup of tea. "How are you Joshua?" Jacques asked. "Am well thanks Jacques, how are you, I must say you look a lot better than when I last saw you." Jacques turned his head to Jeanne and smiled and then looked back at Joshua saying, "Thank you Joshua, I feel much better." As Rebecca came over to hand Joshua his tea, she asked him, "Joshua, what are your plans for today?" "Well, I was only going to stay an hour or so and then push off to our home in Gunwalloe." "O that's good, cos I was thinking now that Mother and Jacques are back, why don't we leave them in peace to settle in and I and the children go home with you." Joshua could think of nothing he would like more and said, "That would be lovely Rebecca." Jeanne watched and listened to the two of them talking and smiled at her daughter and son in law's love for one another."

Chapter 38

John, the Bedruthan Leader and his team of six men had as agreed joined Jim and his team at Wheal Gof on the Saturday afternoon. After introductions were over and all had little drink, Jim took them all around the outer woods of the Mine to get them acquainted with the area and to know what was what and who was where. Jim's team had been on guard observing for a week now and were in need of rest. So, after seeing all that needed to be seen, John and Jim sat down and talked things through. "Any thoughts John?" "Well Jim, my first thought after seeing the old Mine Shaft entrance and the location of the woods around was maybe moving the men into two pairs but placed more evenly on either side of the woods inner path. I think it would give us a better balance of fire should things become aggressive. Also, it would be good if we had some string tied between each pair to give alert if either of them hear or see something, if you know what I mean." "I know exactly what you mean John, and thanks, I will get on with it. John then asked, "Jim, when would you like me and my team to take over cos maybe it would be better if we could half mix our teams together, say four of your men take the left of the path and four of mine take the right." "Sounds good and fair to me John, how about we start the new mix before sunset this day and get into a routine of shift change say every twenty four hours?" "Sounds good, let's get to it." With both agreeing the new tactics, they shook hands and got on with things.

It was pitch black in the early hours of Sunday morning when the three men left the cottage some twenty miles away on the outskirts of Trenarren near St Austell. Once mounted on their horses, Peter Williams took the lead while the other two men followed. Their plan had been discussed many times and now all were ready. The two men, care of Shanks, were a little nervy doing this kind of job. They were more used to working on their own in finding their prey and then work out how to eliminate as they see fit in a covert way. This was an overt role, albeit in the dark of the early morning, with the simple use of their brawn, not their brain. They had discussed the risk of being caught in the act but had been assured that all was well and they only need help him lower the kegs into the ground before he lit the fuse. Once done, they would simply ride back to Peter's cottage and have some lovely brandy. It was that easy, nothing to worry about. However, the two men were not taking any chances and made sure their pistols and muskets were ready. Also, they both didn't like this man Williams as his ego was way out of his head. But, Shanks had said that their help was vital and that it must be done, and as he paid their wages, what else could they do?

The ride to the woods took just over the half hour and once they were by the path that led into the wood they reined their horses to a halt and dismounted. Williams, as they had discussed, then started to walk with his horse in tow into the woods on the small path. This is what he had done several times when planting the kegs. As he got into the woods he turned his head to check on the two men behind but noticed they were still outside by their horses and hadn't moved. Without any thought, Williams spoke out, ''Do you think you two could hurry up?'' 'Shhhh, keep your voice down,'' replied one of the men. Williams did not like being told what to do but bit his tongue and didn't respond and just waited without voice till both men were ready. Then, on checking their pistols once again and putting their muskets over their shoulders they gave the thumbs up and entered the wood. Williams just shrugged his shoulders and keeping hold of his horse's rein walked on deeper into the wood. Slowly but surely, all three carried on in line as quietly as they could until they reached the end of the woods on the outer edge of the Mine area. Williams then stopped and while pointing his finger, spoke, but not too loud, "There it is, over there, I suggest we tie the horses here and walk across." The two men saw the openness of the area between them and the shaft entrance and looked at each other. Both knowing what to do, they put their pistols back in their holsters and took their muskets from their shoulders Then holding them in both hands, with flint hammers pulled back and fingers on the trigger in readiness to fire, they nodded their heads for Williams to lead on.

It was John and his mate, dug in on the right of the path that heard the voices coming from their left. John turned to his mate and after quietly putting his finger to his lips pulled the string tied between him and his other pair of guards. Jim, on the left of the track, also heard the rustle and faint voices coming from his right and so did exactly the same to his men. So gently without noise, all eight men in the four dug outs got their muskets and pistols ready. Jim also got the fuse Flares ready as it was down to him whether he should use them or not. If he did, then there would be utter chaos and more importantly his position would be compromised. If he didn't then they, whoever they are, could escape through the cover of the darkness. It was a double edge sword. Jim looked up at the dark sky and although the moon was out and the stars a glow, visibility was minimal. After lowering his eyes and looking forward, he saw three shadowy figures walking across the open grass from the woods heading to the entrance of the Mine shaft. So now he had to make a decision whether to use the flares or not. His mind quickly thought of the hard working Miners and the Bal Maiden's safety and with that, he knew he had to do it. So, he stood up and with outstretched arms he held the flare in both hands. Once his hands were steady and aimed up to the sky, his mate struck the flint which lit the fuse for ignition. The noise of the flint smacking down on the metal broke the silence of the dark and so the three men walking to the Mine shaft stopped and turned. Seeing the fiery glow of the lighted fuse at the edge of the wood made one of the men move his rifle to his shoulder and on aiming at the red glow, pulled the trigger. Just as he did so the fuse lit the flare and up into the night sky it went. Jim took the shot in the upper side of the chest and fell to the ground gasping for breath and bleeding heavily.

With darkness still all around the three men in the open field looked up at the stream of red trace going further and further up into the night sky above their heads. The two men from Shanks's team knew what was going to happen and so dived to the ground with one of them trying to reload his musket. Peter Williams just stood in amazement and didn't understand a thing. It was then, as the flare burst open with white light, that the men in the woods could see their target and without any delay opened fire. Peter Williams was struck twice in the chest and being thrown back off his feet, fell to the ground, dead. One of the two men lying on the ground took aim and fired back and went into quick reload. While doing so the other man who had completed his reload aimed and fired. It was after the second salvo of fire coming in from the woods that the man lying on the ground who was still in the process of reloading was hit directly in skull. With the blood and bone being thrown all about his lifeless body simply slumped to the earth. With the fuse of light above still glowing brightly and a brief lapse in the noise of gun fire the other man lying on the ground threw his musket away and with his arms up in the air shouted, "I surrender, I surrender." On hearing this plead of surrender the man next to Jim shouted aloud across the woods to John, "Jims been hit, Jims been hit." John knew he had to take control of things and so shouted to all four teams to stop firing. The time was four fifteen in the morning.

And so, at two thirty that same afternoon, the worn out horse and rider entered the front gate to Joshua's cottage at Gunwalloe. Joshua was sitting quietly by the open fire after just coming back from a refreshing two hour walk along the beach. Rebecca was in the other chair reading a book aloud with the two children snugly on her lap and with their ears glued on her every word. On hearing and seeing the rider and horse enter the gate, Joshua got up and went to the front door but not before getting his pistol. Rebecca, without word, closed the book and took the two children upstairs. Joshua, didn't recognise the rider and so after hearing him knock the door, shouted aloud, "Who is it?" "Message, Joshua, urgent." "From whom, speak up man" "From Wheal Gof, St Austell, man named John from Bedruthan." That was exactly the reply Joshua had ordered and so opened the door. On taking the message, the rider asked if he was to wait for reply. Joshua asked him to wait outside and refresh his horse at the water butt and will let him know as soon as he has read the message. The message read:-

Joshua,
Require your person urgent Wheal Gof.
Shooting – two killed and Jim seriously injured.
Prisoner taken.
JM

After reading the message, Joshua quickly opened the door and said to the rider, ''Are you returning directly to Wheal Gof?'' ''Yes Sir, that is my intention.'' ''Have you eaten?'' ''No Sir, I was told not to stop and ride with all haste.'' ''I understand and you have done well. If you stay there we will bring you some hot stew and tea.'' ''Could I have a brandy instead of the tea?'' Joshua raised a smile and replied, ''Yes, of course, you can.'' ''So is there a message for me to take back?'' ''No, there is no message; I am riding back with you.

Once the rider had been refreshed with food and brandy and Joshua had talked with Rebecca, both got on their horses and galloped away. With a couple of brief stops to rest the horses, Joshua made it to the main gate at Wheal Gof at nine that evening. Harry, his horse, had done well. The gate guard had been advised of Joshua's coming and so on his arrival was signed in and escorted to the side office. John from Bedruthan was waiting outside and when seeing Joshua went to him and after shaking his hand in greeting said, ''Thanks for coming Joshua, come in.'' Joshua followed John into the office which had no windows and was located away from the main building.'' As he entered, Jim's friend, the security manager stood up. With the three of them around the table and the door closed, John got on and explained what had happened. Once the detailed briefing had been completed, Joshua leant back in his chair and after a brief moment of pause asked, ''So where is the prisoner now?'' John replied, ''Next door, handcuffed and guarded by two of my men.'' ''And you say Jim will make it?'' ''Yes, that is what we have been told by the surgeon, who operated this morning. He is in bed over at the Mines treatment centre.'' ''And the two dead men, where are they.'' ''They are also at the treatment centre, in the lower morgue.'' ''Do they know that one of them is the Deputy Production Manager?'' ''Joshua, I think the whole work force knows, everyone is whispering and gossiping all over the place.'' This didn't surprise Joshua in the least as this is one trait that the Cornish had never lost. ''Alright, first let me say well done on doing a good job, what say you take me to see Jim and the two corpses and then we come back here and question the prisoner. We can then discuss and agree what to do. By the way, before I forget, is there any place where I can get a room for the night?'' ''I already thought of that Joshua and have talked with the Landlady at the Stags Head a few miles from here who has kindly kept open a room for you, should you need it.''

After seeing Jim and the two dead bodies, the time was now touching past the eleventh hour. Joshua wanted to see the prisoner but after the long ride he was very tired which could affect his approach when talking with him. He needed to be on his toes. He didn't want to rush things but then again he couldn't delay things either. As the three of them were walking back to the side office, Joshua went quietly over things in his mind. They had prevented the explosion and saved lives and captured one of the assailants. Very importantly, Jim would live. Also, the Mine was now back in full operation. The only thing needed now was to question the captive and get as much information from him as they could. But then he thought if anyone should do this, George Kernow and his team were really the people to do it. Unlike Joshua, who would without force, simply ask questions in the hope of getting an answer, Kernow, with his experience, knew the ways of extracting information and would do a far better job. Joshua made up his mind.

As the three of them sat down again, Joshua went on to explain his thoughts of rationality on the prisoner and asked for their thoughts. John was first to reply by saying, ''Well, as we said before Joshua, we have already questioned him many times through the day but all he says is that his name is John Smith and knows nothing of why he is here or who the other two people are. He then remains silent as a mute.'' Joshua turned to the Security Manager, who he was becoming quite fond of, and asked for his thoughts. ''I agree with you Joshua, for now, the Mine is safe and we achieved what we wanted. But, I do think the prisoner knows more and if you want to get that information, I would bring in the experts you suggest.'' Joshua thanked both for their honesty and asked the Manager, ''Do you have riders of message?'' ''Yes, we have riders on standby twenty four hours a day, why?'' ''I would like to send a message to Kernow informing him of the situation and ask he gets here as quickly as possible. Also, can the prisoner stay here and be guarded for the night?'' Both men replied, ''Yes.'' ''Well, if you are both happy with that, then I suggest we all get some rest, it's been a heavy day for all and I will come back in the morning. We can then recap on things and if I can borrow a couple of your men John, I will take the prisoner away and have him locked him up in Bodmin jail ready for Kernow to do what he has to do, what say you both?" Both men thought it a good plan and so readily agreed. "Good, then may I say again well done to you both, I will be off to the Stags Head now and see you both tomorrow." After the three men got up and shook hands John said, "Thank you Joshua.

Chapter 39

A few hours before the expected explosion at Wheal Gof, the last of the smuggled Tin was being loaded on the ship, Celtic View on the Northern Coastline at Tye. Jose and his men had done well. The ship, as planned, had been waiting far out at sea and when the darkness fell the night before had sailed to Sally's Bottom where it would wait until the hour of ten. When that hour struck and no adverse signs of threat were seen, it weighed its anchor to sail the last few miles north to the small cove of Tye. The captain was an experienced sailor of the old Spanish fleet and knew how to steer a ship with rocks close by but not too close to give undue risk. Once in position off the cove at Tye and the white light of the lantern was seen from the cliff top the Captain gave the order to drop anchor. Once the ship was secure the loading of the Tin from the cove started.

When the loading was about two thirds done, Jose felt it time to get himself and his things ready. Once done he went over to the two security men who worked for Luisa and suggested they catch the next boat out and get on board ship. Their job was done so they could relax but Jose could not as he had to maintain leadership until the ship docked at Plymouth. Once the Tin was then safely through customs he and his men could enjoy some time off before meeting his cousin Luisa in Mayfair. When all three men were aboard the ship, the two men went to their cabins but Jose went on deck to find the Captain.

While the Captain and Jose were leaning over the side watching the final load being lifted aboard, the Captain said, "Your men have done well Jose." "So have yours,

Anton." "Thank you Jose, what say we go to my cabin and have a cognac?" "That sounds good." Once sitting comfortably in the cabin and the cognac poured Anton asked, "So, how did it all go?" "It took a while to get things sorted in line with our objectives but with careful planning here and taking out some people there, all is good." "And what of Luisa?" "She is well and most happy, especially with the future profits to be made, and of course her new Cornish Manor." "Her new Cornish Manor?" "Yes, it's called Mingoose in an ideal position just south of Wheal Coates where we collect the Tin and process it for Wheal Tye, I will tell you all about it later but first, what time are we set to sail?" "I would say in twenty minutes, I am just waiting for our ship's officer to inform us that all is ready. By the way Jose, how many men of yours are staying on board with us?" "Twenty in all, I am leaving four behind to look after the Mines until we all return in a week or so." As they chatted away it wasn't long when the cabin door was knocked and in walked the ship's officer informing them that all is ready. "Right Jose, what say we have a quick one for the sea and then us both get up on deck?"

After getting back on the top deck and looking around the Captain felt the breeze. Then waiting a few minutes to check that all was well, he put a broad smile on his face and ordered the weighing of anchor and full sails to be raised. It was nearing four in the morning and the night was clear with the moon shining and the wind direction excellent. "Standing close by but holding his hands tight on the rail Jose asked, "What time Plymouth Captain?" "It normally takes about eighteen hours with the weight we are carrying but is dependent on the wind change as we pass Lizard Point and turn eastward but I would say midnight or early next morning, either way, we will be in good time for docking as the sun rises." "Thank you Captain." "Jose, why don't you go to my cabin and get some rest, I will call you when the Lizard is in view?" Jose smiled and after lifting his head to let a fresh breeze run over his face replied, "Thank you but I would prefer to be here on deck until we leave this pagan land. The Captain nodded and took a long deep breath drawing in all the gunge from his nostrils and throat. Then turning his head to the side spat it all out over the side. He then roared with laughter and shouted, "Cornish Heathens."

With the sails now at full mast and the wind being good, the ship sailed on through the Celtic Sea on a westward bearing. It was as the hour touched near five that Lands End was seen just off the port bow and so the bearing was changed to south west. Once the ship had past Lands End, the Captain again changed course south east. Then after twenty long minutes of good sail, the Captain roared with joy as the beacon fire on Lizard Point was seen through the far night sky. The Captain grabbed Jose and while pointing to the far away light of the beacon fire said with loud joyous voice, "The Lizard Jose, we're on the home stretch." "Well done Anton, well done."

Twas then as the ship sailed close by the Lizard Point that the massive cloud of Cornish Mist drifted out from the Cove of Mullion and engulfed the ship as if it were a magnet. As the Mist hugged the whole of the ship the wind changed direction to due North but the dense Mist just would not leave the Celtic View alone. All on board could see nothing.

Chapter 40

Joshua and the two arm guards shook hands and rode away from the jail at Bodmin. As they went out through the main gate, the two men raised their hands in salute and headed off east while Joshua veered his good horse westward. The time was near four thirty in the afternoon and the sun was shining bright which it hadn't done for quite a while. It had been another long day for Joshua but was pleased that all had gone well at Wheal Gof. Although security had been lessened and the Mine was returning to normal they had agreed that more inner and outer fence patrols would be good. The prisoner had also now been safely delivered to Bodmin jail in wait for George Kernow. Joshua would probably have to return soon to meet and discuss things with his boss before he questioned the prisoner but he would sort that out when the time came. For now, the only thing in his diary apart from normal duties was the delayed meeting with the Sheriff in Truro which had now been set for tomorrow morning, Tuesday at ten o clock.

As Harry galloped freely along the highway it wasn't long before the Bolventor Inn appeared. Joshua slowed Harry down and thought about going in and having a few drinks and maybe get a room for the night but then thought better of it and pushed on. However, as the miles went by and time was nearing seven with the sun starting to drop, he came upon the village of Zelah. Knowing there was a peaceful Inn called the Half Moon decided he would ask for a room and stop over. He felt the need for some rest but in truth, he just wanted to be alone. Also, it was only an hour's ride to Truro.

With a room being free, Joshua stabled Harry and after putting his things in his room went down to the comfort of the bar. While sitting by the roaring fire and looking up through the window at the night stars, Joshua picked up his fresh tankard of cider and took a long slow gulp. Putting the tankard back down on the table, he stretched out his legs and looked deep into the fire. As he did this he felt an overwhelming sense of inner peace and even smiled at the lovely feeling. Everything had become very tense since he received the increased security status, but now just sitting on his own in a lovely cosy Inn, with the Cornish way of life all about, he started to feel that tension seep away. It was like medicine from somewhere he knew not. It was when Joshua heard the clock chime ten times that he pulled himself away and went up to his bedroom.

Waking up early and feeling refreshed after a cold wash and hearty breakfast, Joshua galloped away on Harry to Truro to meet the Sherriff. The sun was up and the fresh breeze and warmth of the morning air made him smile.

After getting to the Sherriff's office in good time and tying up Harry, Joshua dusted himself down and went in. The Sherriff was waiting in the reception area and on seeing Joshua enter smiled saying, ''Hello Joshua, good to see you, please, come in.'' Joshua followed the Sherriff into his office and once both were seated the Sherriff got straight down to business. 'Tell me Joshua, what is the situation at Wheal Gof?'' Joshua first laid the Sheriff's mind at ease by saying that the Mine is now well and operating as normal. He then went on to explain all that had happened including the prisoner being locked up in Bodmin Prison in wait for George Kernow. When Joshua had finished, the Sherriff, in his way of thanks and well done, pulled a bottle of brandy and two glasses from the draw. Joshua watched and smiled and after the Sherriff had filled the two glasses both men raised them to their mouths and drank the brandy in one.

As Joshua was just about to put his empty glass back on the table the Sherriff said, "By the way Joshua, you have heard of the ship wreck?" "No, I haven't, what wreck?" "The wreck between Mullion Cove and the Lizard Point, happened yesterday morning before sun up while you were at Wheal Gof. It is completely destroyed being split in half and now lying on the rocks laden with tons of unmarked Tin." "Who owns it? The Sherriff glanced down at the piece of paper on the table and replied, "We are checking all that out now as we found its registration document with clearance number PL001660 in the name of Celtic View." "Any survivors?" "No, all hands lost, no survivors."

While Joshua and the Sherriff were in discussion, Luisa, still lying alone and very poorly in her bed at Mingoose Manor started to move. She had not done this since she lost all consciousness three days ago. It was when she had not come down for her cream tea that the butler and maids went up to her room and found her lying on the floor. After trying their best to wake her up but getting no response they put her quickly to bed. The Butler had then sent message and paid for the best doctor in Truro to come and see her. However, after examination, the doctor told them there was nothing he could do as she had caught the infectious Smallpox in its most severe form and her life would be minimal. The doctor then advised them all to only enter her bedroom should it be absolutely necessary. If this were the case and they had to go in then they must wear full masks and gloves to reduce risk. Since the doctor had said this the Butler and the maids had not once been to see her. They had their own lives to think about. Also to protect themselves further they made the decision to leave the Manor and set up lodgings in the small cottage at the far end of the estate. They would visit when they could but had still not yet made their minds up when.

With the pain of her ulcer ridden body being too much, Luisa stopped moving and lay still but slowly opened her eyes. Gently moving her head to the side she saw two beautiful young girls with a radiance of love and warmth standing by her bedside. "Hello Luisa, my name is Deborah and this is my sister, Christine." "Am I in Heaven?" "No you are not in Heaven nor will you ever unless you change your ways of life." Without a flicker of her eyes or movement of body, Luisa asked, "Tell me what I must do." "First, we must tell you that as you did with Cuthbert Troon to obtain this beautiful Manor, he did the same to a young Cornish family called Selina and Edward Killigrew and their little daughter, Grace. Their parents and grandparents owned the little cottage on the edge of this estate where your maids and butler are now living. This little family were thrown onto the streets as beggars and are still this day living in poverty at the workhouse in Helston. If you promise to find and restore to them full ownership of this cottage and change your ways of evil to helping and being kind to others, we promise you will live long and have a good life here in Mingoose." Luisa listened quietly to what Deborah had said and sadly knew deep inside she had lived a life of total greed and gluttony without thought to anybody but herself. But that life was now to change forever and so with heartfelt honesty replied, "I promise you and your sister I will do as you ask."

The End

I would like to thank Barbara and Stephen for all their help and send my love to my Mum & Dad.

David Lenderyou (Author)

Printed in Great Britain
by Amazon